"YOU WANTED TO SEE ME?"

Reese rolled the cigarette between his fingers, the movement slow, soothing, seductive. Mary couldn't take her eyes from those nimble fingers. "Miss McKendrick?"

"Hmm?"

"Was there something you wanted from me?"

She forced her gaze from those hands to his face, and the lines about his mouth reminded her of why she'd run from the schoolroom without finishing out the day. "What's the matter with you?"

"Me? Nothing."

He placed the cigarette in the pocket of his black vest, too polite even to ask if he could smoke in her house. How had a Southern gentleman become whatever he was? Outlaw? Mercenary? Leader of a gang with guns to hire?

He presented her with his back and stared out at the fading light. A storm was coming, and from the way the sky had darkened, it was coming fast.

"I think you're lying, Reese. Something about the children bothered you. You want to tell me what it was?"

"No."

He didn't sound angry or sad or frightened. He sounded as if he'd refused a second glass of punch at the Autumn Harvest Ball. Drawn closer against her will, close enough that her skirt brushed his leg and she could see that he was still trembling, Mary wanted to touch him, but she didn't know how.

Thunder crashed, still in the distance, but not for long. He started, shook his head, and gave a chuckle of self-derision.

"You don't like storms?" she asked.

"The noise." His voice was so low that she had to lean closer to hear, and her breasts brushed his back.

He spun around, and she stumbled away. Her hands came up to brace herself against his chest, but he grabbed her wrists before she could touch him and held them away from him.

"I told you not to touch me." The eyes that had been cold went hotter than the approaching lightning.

She licked dry lips. "I'm not touching you; you're touching me."

"Well," he drawled in the voice that had haunted her nights since the first time she'd seen him, half-naked in Dallas. "That's different, then."

Dear Romance Reader,

In July last year, we launched the Ballad line with four new series, and each month we'll present both new and continuing stories set everywhere from medieval England to the American West—the kind of passionate, romantic stories you love best, written by the most gifted authors. At the back of each book, we'll tell you when you can find subsequent books in the series that have captured your heart.

Debuting this month with a fabulous new series called *The Rock Creek Six,* Lori Handeland offers **Reese.** The first hero in a series of six written alternatively by Lori and Linda Devlin, Reese is haunted by the war—and more than a bit skeptical that a spirited schoolteacher can heal his wounded heart. If you liked the movie *The Magnificent Seven,* this is the series for you! Next, critical favorite Corinne Everett continues the *Daughters of Liberty* series with **Fair Rose,** as a British beauty bent on independence in America discovers that partnership is tempting—especially with the right man.

Alice Duncan whisks us back to turn-of-the-century California, and the early days of silent films, with the next *Dream Maker* title, **The Miner's Daughter.** A stubborn young woman hanging onto her father's copper mine by the skin of her teeth has no place in a movie—or so she believes, until one of the film investor's decides she's the right woman for the role, and for him. Finally, the fourth book in the *Hope Chest* series, Laura Hayden's **Stolen Hearts,** joins a modern-day cat burglar with an innocent nineteenth-century beauty who holds the key to his family's lost legacy—and to his heart.

Kate Duffy
Editorial Director

The Rock Creek Six

REESE

Lori Handeland

ZEBRA BOOKS

Kensington Publishing Corp.

http://www.zebrabooks.com

ZEBRA BOOKS are published by

Kensington Publishing Corp.
850 Third Avenue
New York, NY 10022

All Kensington titles, imprints and distributed lines are available at special quantity discounts for bulk purchases for sales promotion, premiums, fund-raising, educational or institutional use.

Special book excerpts or customized printings can also be created to fit specific needs. For details, write or phone the office of the Kensington Special Sales Manager: Kensington Publishing Corp., 850 Third Avenue, New York, NY 10022. Attn. Special Sales Department. Phone: 1-800-221-2647.

Zebra and the Z logo Reg. U.S. Pat. & TM Off.
Ballad is a trademark of Kensington Publishing Corp.

First Printing: September 2001
10 9 8 7 6 5 4 3 2 1

Printed in the United States of America

For Linda Jones
Who, with grace and tact,
made writing a series easier
than writing alone.

One

Mary McKendrick had reached the end of her tether, which did not happen often. She prided herself on managing everything, even the unmanageable. But after days spent on a lurching stage to Dallas, then hours slogging through the mud of what was supposed to be a dusty town and still not finding the den of iniquity she searched for, her much-admired patience had gone the way of the annoying, whistling Texas wind.

In Rock Creek, Texas, Mary was the schoolteacher. Before she'd come to Rock Creek, she'd first been a schoolteacher outside of Richmond, Virginia, until the damned Yankees burned the place down. Then she'd gone on to teach in Bittersweet, Missouri. Bloody Jayhawkers burned that place, too. She was in Dallas today because she did not plan to be run off another job in this lifetime.

"Any Time. Any Time," she muttered as she stomped down another boardwalk. "You'd think I could find one saloon named *Any Time.*"

Suddenly, as if in answer to an unspoken prayer, there it was—a saloon named Any Time. Did the name mean the place was open day and night?

Surely there were rules about such things, even in Dallas. What did it matter? As long as the saloon was open now—and from the sounds of the music, the laughter, and the clinking of glass, it was—she needed to get in there and do what she'd come here to do.

Buy herself a man.

And not just any man, but Reese—gun for hire. They said he was the best. They said he always got the job done. They said . . . Well, they said a lot of things, but who were *they,* anyway, and was any of what they said true? Mary hoped so, because she needed a man like Reese, even though men like him were the one thing that frightened her. But Mary Margaret McKendrick was not a woman to let fear keep her from doing what must be done.

So she pushed through the swinging doors and stepped into her very first saloon.

The smell hit her first—smoke and whiskey and too many bodies. The next thing she noticed was a sudden silence—no talking, no clinking glasses, no music—because everyone stared at her.

Well, she supposed they didn't get too many schoolteachers in here. Her gaze flicked over the assembled crowd, mostly men with guns, women with too few clothes, and a great, big bartender, who scowled at her as if she planned to start trouble.

Trouble? Her? Not hardly.

"I'm looking for a man named Reese."

"Upstairs. Third door on the right."

Mary blinked. Could it be this easy? Nothing else ever was. "Just like that, you tell me where he is?"

The man shrugged. "You don't look like the type to shoot him in his bed." He frowned and peered at her from beneath his too long, unkempt hair. "Is that what you're planning?"

She gave him her best Miss McKendrick glare. Instead of backing down, he grinned. "Didn't think so. Third door on the right. And tell him he pays me what he owes me tonight or he's out."

Mary pondered that piece of information. Sounded as if Reese had money trouble. All the better for her.

Turning her attention to the staircase at the back of the room, Mary's unease returned. To get to the man named Reese, she would have to walk through all those people. No one spoke. No one moved. They continued to stare at her as if she were some exotic creature escaped from a traveling show.

Sweat trickled between her breasts. Though she spent most days in front of a room filled with staring eyes, those eyes belonged to children, not rough, armed men.

She straightened her spine. Rough, armed men were her problem. They were the reason she was here. To meet the lion in his den. Hire a monster to frighten away all the monsters.

The heels of her boots clipped in staccato rhythm as Mary crossed the plank floor. The hem of her dove gray traveling costume slapped wetly against her ankles. Without the crinoline she'd left at home to accommodate the horse she'd ridden to the nearest working-stage stop, her skirt had dragged through the mud all over Dallas.

Tired, wet, and dirty was not the way she wanted to meet Reese, but then again, she didn't care what he thought of her. She only cared that he came to Rock Creek. Would what she had to offer be enough for the mysterious and dangerous Reese?

At the top of the stairs, third door on the right, Mary knocked—three firm taps of her knuckles on the scarred wood of the door. The sounds echoed throughout the saloon.

"Come."

One word, softly uttered, yet she heard it clearly through the door. She reached for the doorknob, and her fingers shook. Yanking back her hand, Mary made a fist. This would not do.

"Come, come, come," the voice ordered, impatient now.

Before she could think any further, Mary opened the door and stepped inside. As soon as she shut it, the noise started up downstairs, making her jump, but the buzz of sound from below soothed her more than the waiting, listening silence had.

Just enough sun seeped around the curtains to throw the room into shadow. Despite the ghostly gray light, she could still see the man lounging on the bed, wearing black pants and nothing else.

Well, there was the gun in his hand, but Mary hardly counted a gun as clothing. He studied her for a moment, then uncocked the weapon and laid it next to his leg. They stared at each other.

He was the most interesting man she'd ever seen. That might have had something to do with his naked chest, something else she'd never seen, but she didn't think so. This man was striking. Once you saw him, you would not forget him. Mary doubted she ever would.

His hair was gold, several shades lighter than his skin, and tousled, probably from sleep. He could use a shave. The beard on his jaw looked at least two days gone. The hair on his chest was darker than the hair on his head, more the shade of his beard. The chest captured her attention, lean and firm; a flat belly was framed by black pants. The top button hung open, revealing that the curling hair, which looked so soft, trailed below his stomach, down, down, down to—

"Seen enough?"

Mary yanked her gaze back to his face, embarrassed to have been caught ogling him. This was business. Even if he chose to meet a strange woman in his room without a shirt or shoes, that did not mean she had to stare. Though it was hard not to.

She cleared her throat. "You're Reese?" Best not to even mention his state of undress or ask if he could open the window, since the room had gone hot and stuffy.

"Who wants to know?"

His voice flowed over her, reminding Mary of things best forgotten. Magnolia trees in springtime, Virginia in the rain, a place that was long gone and never coming back.

"Mary McKendrick," she blurted to stop her eyes from burning. She should offer her hand, but there was no way she was going to approach that bed or let him touch her while he lay half-naked.

"What do you want?"

He wasn't one for small talk. Well, that suited her just fine. "You."

His eyebrows shot up, and then his gaze wandered down her body, making her hotter than before. She found she didn't like being stared at by a man. She wasn't beautiful, wasn't even passably pretty. She was too tall and too thin to be fashionable, although she did have a few curves in appropriate places.

Oh, her skin was fair enough, except for the freckles on her nose, and her eyes were blue, sometimes. Most times they were just dull gray. And her hair, which was some undefined color between brown and blond, curled with wild abandon whenever she did not bind it closely to her head. Her hair was bound now, tightly enough to give her a headache, which meant her long, thin nose and high cheekbones only looked more pronounced.

She looked exactly like what she was—a twenty-four-year-old spinster schoolteacher. She was smart, dependable, and sturdy. What she was *not* was flighty, flirty, or petite. Thank God.

Still, the way he looked at her . . . For one tiny moment she wanted to be everything she was not.

Then his gaze flicked up to hers. Mary's eyes had adjusted to the dim light well enough to determine that his eyes were green. Captivating, if they hadn't been so cold.

"You want me for what?" That voice again, this time a low growl—Southern, sinful, suggestive. Those words, combined with his tousled hair, na-

REESE   13

ked chest, and long, slim, bare feet had Mary stut-
tering. Mary never stuttered.

"F-for a-a job."

He sat up in one fluid motion, all smooth skin
and honed muscle. "Where?"

"Rock Creek."

"What?"

"Th-there's a group of bandits. They ride out of
the hills, take whatever they can carry, shoot the
place up a bit, and disappear. They robbed the stage
so many times, we've been left off the route. Now
people are leaving. My town—I mean *the* town—will
die."

"No law?" She shook her head. "No soldiers?"

"I sent word to the fort, but they refused to
come. Said all the trouble with the Comanche
means they can't spare any men for us. Stealing
and breaking windows isn't much of a crime in
Texas."

"I suspect not. Tell me, Miss McKendrick, why
are you here? What makes Rock Creek so special
that you'd come all the way to Dallas for me?"

Mary wasn't going to explain about her past and
her dreams to a man she barely knew. "I'm the
schoolteacher." His eyes narrowed, and his lips
tightened. For some reason, he didn't care for her
profession, but what Reese cared for was not her
problem. "I have no family. I could be spared to
come." She didn't add that this whole thing had
been her idea.

"What about your men?"

"The war." She shrugged and spread her hands.

"We've got a preacher, old men, young boys, cripples."

And Baxter Sutton, the shopkeeper, but since he could hide faster than any woman in town, Mary didn't think he was up to leading them against the enemy.

"That's all?" Reese asked.

She nodded, not trusting her voice anymore. The way Reese spat out questions made her more nervous than being alone in a room with a strange, half-naked man. When he stood up and walked toward her, she lost her power of speech altogether.

He moved like a wild animal, with a combination of barely suppressed violence, boundless energy, and a loose-hipped grace that made her mouth go dry. She'd seen cougars in the hills, and they stalked tiny live things just as this man stalked her.

He came too close. Mary's back bumped the door.

"How much?" he whispered, and his breath brushed her hair.

Despite the heat of the room, the heat of him, she shivered. Why had she thought she could meet a wild animal in his den and come out unscathed?

She stared straight ahead, not wanting him to see that his nearness rattled her, but her eyes were level with the pulse that thudded calm and sure at his neck. Her own heart pounded entirely too fast, in perfect disharmony with the rasp of her breath in the still of the shadowed room. Mary yanked her gaze from the hollow of his throat and met his eyes.

"How much?" he repeated.

"Everything."

Reese smiled a predatory smile. If Mary could have retreated any farther, she would have, but her back was against the wall—literally.

He put a hand on each side of her head and leaned close. The muscles in his arms bunched. His chest rose and fell directly in front of her face as he took a deep breath.

"Well, now, I've never been offered everything before." His voice had gone south, from Virginia to Georgia, the lilt she loved deepening, trilling along her spine like a feather. "Would everything include you?"

Mary's mouth fell open; she was that surprised. She must remember he was not a gentleman despite the refinement of his voice and the culture in his words. She had come here alone, offering him everything; of course he thought she was offering herself. What surprised her the most was that he had even asked. Men simply never looked at her that way—until this one.

"You're gonna catch flies." Reese put one finger below Mary's chin and pushed her mouth closed.

The heat of his skin startled her; her response to it disturbed her more, because she wanted this man to keep touching her, and that was something spinster schoolteachers just didn't go around wanting.

"Everything most certainly does *not* include me, Mr. Reese."

He flinched and stepped back as if she'd slapped him. "Just Reese," he snapped, and turned away.

His back was as beautiful as his front, and the sight distracted Mary. All that smooth bronzed skin over supple, shifting muscles. He had an odd scar, low and large, but the single imperfection only served to emphasize the flawlessness of the rest.

Mary shook her head to clear the sudden and odd fascination with this stranger's body, breathed more deeply now that he did not tower over her, and got back to business.

"I will pay you all the money I have to come to Rock Creek and make them stop."

"I'm afraid I'll have to be so crass as to ask for an exact figure, Miss McKendrick."

"One hundred and fifty dollars."

The muscles in his back tensed, released, then started to shake. Mary was alarmed for a moment until she realized he was laughing.

"I fail to see anything humorous in that amount. From what I heard downstairs, you seem to be short on funds."

He stopped laughing. "You seem to have heard a lot about me."

"Word travels."

"Doesn't it, though?" He turned around, and his face was grim. "How many of them?"

"Fifteen. Sometimes a few more, sometimes a few less."

This time, his mouth hung open. At least he wasn't laughing. Mary crossed her arms and raised her eyebrows. "You'll catch flies, Reese." She frowned. "Is Reese your first name or your last?"

"Both."

She doubted that, but his name was irrelevant as long as he did what she asked.

"You think I can take care of fifteen men alone?" He tilted his head, considering her for a moment. "Just who told you about me, anyway?"

"Man called Rourke passed through. Said you were the fellow to talk to for a job like this and that I could find you here."

"Well, wasn't that mighty nice of him?"

"I thought so."

His eyes narrowed, and he looked more like a cougar in the night than ever before. "I'm going to have to bring some men along with me."

"You'll come?" Mary could have cursed the hope that lit her voice. She did not want him to know just how desperate they were. Men like Reese preyed on desperate folk, and the folks in Rock Creek had been preyed upon enough.

He stayed silent so long that Mary thought he might yet refuse. Her fingers dug into her arms to keep herself from reaching out and begging him. Doing so would get her nowhere with Reese.

After what seemed like an eternity, he sighed. "Well, hell, everything is a damn sight more than I've got right now. I'll come, with five others."

"Six of you against fifteen of them?"

"Best odds I've had in a month of Sundays."

"These men must be good."

"Together I'd say we're downright magnificent."

"And your friends will come?"

"They'll come," he said, but he didn't look happy about it.

* * *

When the door closed behind Mary McKendrick, Reese shrugged into a shirt and started looking for his boots. He had no time to waste if he was going to find the others and get to Rock Creek within two weeks, as he'd promised.

Now Reese was a lot of things, but when he took a job, he did the job, and what he promised, he delivered. That was the only way to stay alive and keep the jobs coming.

Two minutes after she'd stepped into his room, Reese should have sent Miss McKendrick on her way. But he was a sucker for a good woman in trouble. Call it a curse. He certainly did.

He should never have gone near her, but she had drawn him like a fly to melted sugar. And like that fly, he'd been caught, because despite the mud on her skirt and the dust in her hair, she'd smelled sweet and clean and good. Just the scent of her, combined with the soft sound of surprise she'd made at the back of her throat, had aroused him in ways the women he allowed himself these days never could.

She wasn't even pretty, but Reese had learned long ago that pretty didn't mean shit in this ugly world. He'd seen women so beautiful, they made you want to weep, yet underneath they were snake mean. But Mary . . . There was something about Mary that made him ache, deep down, where it hurt the most.

So he'd touched her, just one finger on her chin, and the softness of her skin had made him remember everything he had spent years trying to forget. Because Mary was a woman straight out of his secret past—a past so far gone that not even the five men who chose to ride at his side knew of it.

Oh, they supposed, and they guessed, and they even placed bets on just who and what he had been before the war made him what he was. But they didn't know, and they never would.

So he'd go to Rock Creek, and he'd help Miss McKendrick, and he'd take everything, but he wouldn't touch the one thing he wanted to the most.

This woman who had never been touched before.

Two weeks to the day after Mary had climbed back on the blasted stage and retraced her route home, dust billowed on the eastern horizon. The church bells rang once—a Rock Creek warning to herd your innocents out of sight. Thus far the bad men had taken only things, not people, but that didn't mean times weren't going to change.

The children had gone home an hour ago, and Mary was just coming out of the schoolhouse, where she'd been contemplating her fingernails and cursing Reese. He wasn't coming, and not only had she wasted two weeks believing he was, but hiring him had been her idea. If he didn't come, she doubted she'd be allowed to go hunting another man like him, even if she knew where to find one.

Her friend, Josephine Clancy, daughter of the

Right Reverend Clancy, joined her. They stared at the dust cloud approaching town. The thunder of hooves filled the air, making the suddenly deserted streets seem even more ghostly.

"We'd better get inside." Jo tugged at Mary's arm.

"Just a minute."

Mary squinted at the cloud, which had drifted close enough to distinguish the shapes of men on horses. Six men to be exact, and the one in the middle wore black from the tip of his hat to the toe of his boot.

"Reese," she whispered, and in that one word she heard too many things.

The group pulled up as they neared town, and Mary got a good look at what she'd paid everything for. They looked rougher than the outlaws they'd come to drive away, these six men of various ages and sizes with an arsenal attached to their saddles and hips. Mary hadn't seen that many guns since she rode out of Missouri.

"That's them?" Jo asked.

"Yes."

Jo's hand slipped from Mary's arm, and she laced their fingers together. "I only have one question."

"What's that?"

"Did things just get better, or did they get worse?"

Mary didn't answer, because she just didn't know.

Two

Reese and his men had been on their horses for days when they reached Rock Creek, but they weren't tired. They'd gotten used to riding during the war. Riding and fighting, that was what they did, and in the five years since surrender, they'd honed those skills to bayonet sharpness.

Each man had a story to tell of how he'd come to follow Reese. If they knew how woefully inadequate he was as a leader, they'd probably kill him. But no matter how hard Reese tried to get someone else to lead the way, they all just laughed and told him to do his damned job.

Each man had a past life, too, though Reese chose to know as little as possible about their lives before they wore the gray. Since he didn't plan to tell them about his past, he thought it only fair he did not collect theirs.

As a result, the five were a close-knit crew, which left Reese on the outside, and that sat fine with him. He didn't deserve friends, family, or a life better than the one he had. Being alive at all was more than he deserved, an opinion most folks down home in Georgia—including the woman he should have married—would have agreed with wholeheartedly.

Reese and the others pulled their horses to a stop at the outskirts of town and contemplated Rock Creek. The place looked like a hundred other Texas towns—small, rough, with a single main street of crude buildings and a few homes straggling into the land beyond. There was a church and steeple, which was more than a lot of towns had, and a white building that looked to be the school. Beyond the town, trees and greenery hinted that a river ran just over the slope, but the land everywhere else stood dry, brown, and rugged.

"There it is."

Reese spared a glance at the large, somewhat unkempt man who rode to his right. Jedidiah Rourke had a habit of stating the obvious, usually with a large amount of profanity thrown in.

"You would know, since you're the one who got us into this."

Jed grunted. "Free room and board and a little bit of change is better than a whole lot of nothing. Which is what we were all down to when you sent for us."

Reese didn't comment. He knew as well as Jed that when one of them called, the others came. It had little to do with money and everything to do with honor and loyalty, two tenets they all clung to, even though everything else had gone as dead as the Confederate army. They might be rough, but they knew what was right.

"I was doin' fine in Fort Worth, gennlemen. My ship wuz gunna come in." Nate Lang took a sip from his ever-present flask, then slipped it back into the breast pocket of his dandified suit with an ease born of practice.

Nate rode on Reese's left side for two reasons: Reese could grab him if he drank too much and slipped off Bessie, and Nate, despite his constant state of drunkenness, was the best sniper shot of the bunch. Reese often wondered if Nate could shoot straight while sober. Since he hadn't seen Nate sober since well before Gettysburg, Reese figured that was one worry he didn't have.

"Las mujeres, who are they?" Rico Salvatore always wanted to know who the women were.

Reese turned his attention toward Rock Creek. Two women stared back at him, the winds of Texas whipping their skirts. They held hands, obviously frightened, but as he watched, one of them stepped forward and waved at him.

"Mary," he whispered before he could stop himself.

"Maria?"

"Knock off that Mex talk, kid," snarled Daniel Cash. "You're in the recently reunited United States."

Rico and Cash rode hip to hip more often than not, though the two annoyed each other to no end. Rico often spoke the language of his father, even though he'd been born right here in Texas. For some reason, this grated on Cash, which only made Rico do it more. Something Reese couldn't quite figure.

Cash was the most dangerous of them all. When he wasn't with the six, he was a gunman of some renown. What had happened in Cash's life to turn him sour, Reese didn't want to know. They all had their little problems.

"Reese!" Mary's voice carried on the spring wind. She waved again, even though the girl at her side pulled on her arm to make her stop.

The woman was dangerous. She'd actually given him all of her money before telling him where to find Rock Creek. Being the man he was, Reese had taken it. He was also trotting into Rock Creek exactly when he'd promised.

Despite being run out of his home in disgrace, it seemed he wasn't much of a thief or a cheat.

Just a murderer.

Reese let out a low growl and kicked his horse into a walk. Sinclair Sullivan, the last of the six, joined him. Reese enjoyed being with Sullivan the most because Sullivan knew how to keep his mouth shut. Reese liked that in a man.

"She the one who hired us?" Reese nodded. "Sweet on her, aren't ya?"

Reese shot a narrow glare at the half-breed scout. "Keep your private thoughts private."

"That's what I thought." Sullivan snorted and dropped back to join the others, muttering, "A hundred and fifty dollars plus room and board."

Reese ignored him. Sometimes Sullivan's ability to see what wasn't visible saved their lives, and sometimes it just made Reese angry.

Mary ran out to meet them, her face one big smile. He would really have to talk with her. The woman was asking for trouble the way she trusted the untrustworthy and wore everything she felt on her face. But for a moment he let himself bask in the warm welcome of her eyes. No one had looked at him like that in far too long.

Reese stopped his horse, murmuring gentle assurances as he slipped from the saddle. He didn't want the animal spooked by Mary's flapping skirt, nor did he want Mary slashed by Atlanta's razor-sharp hooves. Nothing would have spooked Ares, the horse he'd ridden into battle. But Ares was gone, along with so many other things.

Her scent invoked memories of rainwater and cloudy nights. Reese went light-headed with hunger and leaned against his horse for strength.

"You came!" Surprise colored her voice.

Ruthlessly, he pushed aside longings for a past that was dead and gone, then turned with narrowed eyes. "You thought I wouldn't?"

Mary flinched, and her smile froze. Reese hadn't meant to sound so vicious. Sometimes the anger crept up and bubbled over when he wasn't expecting it.

Her dark-haired little friend stepped up next to her and laid a hand on Mary's arm. "*I* thought you'd be in the next state by now, with Mary's money."

"Then you're much smarter than Mary."

Mary tilted her chin. "You're here, aren't you?"

Someone behind him laughed. Reese turned and glared, but no one's face held even the glimmer of a smile—except for Nate, who looked sloshed enough to be happy the rest of the century.

"I'm here," he agreed as he returned his atten-

tion to the ladies. A movement behind them made
Reese stiffen and glance that way. "Looks like the
rest of your town is, too, Miss McKendrick."

She spun about, and her skirt touched his leg.
How was it he could feel the brush of blue cotton
even through the wool of his pants?

"Humph," she muttered. "Nosy busybodies.
Left the hiring to me, but now they want to know
every little thing."

"That's always the way of it," Reese observed. "I
suspect if you introduce us, they'll go away."

"Introduce?" Jed snorted. "I'll be damned if I'll
stand still for introductions. Just show me where
the hell I can put my horse and get me a frigging
drink."

"Here, here!" Nate agreed.

Mary's friend frowned.

Reese sighed and rubbed his forehead. "Excuse
Jed, miss . . ." He dropped his hand and glanced
at the girl.

"Clancy," she answered. "Josephine Clancy."
She refused to meet his eyes, instead, she continued to stare at the men.

"Well, Jed lives alone, Miss Clancy, and you can
see why."

"Jed would be the man of the colorful vocabu-
lary who visited Rock Creek a few months back?"

"So I hear."

"I was more concerned with the man hanging
by one stirrup."

Reese cursed. Miss Clancy smirked. He spun
about to discover that Nate had slipped free of his
saddle, but no one had put him back.

"Dammit, Cash, can't you do something about Nate?"

"I could shoot him, but you'd be mad."

"I'll take care of it." Miss Clancy walked over to Nate and set about freeing him from his horse.

Reese rubbed at his temple. Sometimes these men were worse than children, although they fought a hell of a lot better. A flash of agony shot through his head, and Reese gritted his teeth to stifle a moan. Best not remember what he kept trying to forget.

"Reese?"

Mary's soft voice, closer than before, brought his head up. He nearly bumped noses with her and took a quick step back, where he bumped into Atlanta's big behind and bounced forward. Whoever had snickered before did so again.

"What?" Reese snarled.

"These are the men I paid everything for?" Her voice but a whisper, she looked skeptical, and Reese couldn't blame her. They always made a lousy first impression. Still, he knew his men, and they were worth a lot more than everything.

"They don't look like much, but you should see them in action."

"Hmm, if you say so." She contemplated the others, then smiled brightly at one of them. *Rico*. Reese didn't even have to look. The kid had a way with women, though Mary should be able to see through a sly fox like Salvatore with ease. How did she manage little children if she believed every lie they spouted?

Well, that wasn't his business, but he would have

a talk with Rico. No seduction of Mary or Reese would kick the kid's ass all the way home to San Antone.

"If you would all follow me, I'll take you to the hotel. It's not much, but it's all we've got."

Mary walked off toward town, where the crowd awaited. Reese studied the people who studied him. She hadn't been lying when she'd told him Rock Creek had only old men, boys, and cripples. Besides women and a man dressed in black who must be the preacher, that was all Reese saw. Rock Creek did need them, no doubt about it.

Still, Reese hesitated, admiring the sway of Mary's skirt and the curve of her rump. She must have sensed they weren't following, because she stopped and turned with a raised brow, then caught him admiring her backside and blushed like a virgin.

Like? Hell, she was, and off limits to him as well as the rest.

"Coming?" she asked.

Another snort from the jokers behind him had Reese coloring, too. Not trusting his voice, he merely nodded and took a step after her, committing himself and the others to saving Rock Creek.

Mary's heart felt ready to burst from her chest. What had she done by bringing such men to her home? And Rock Creek was home, or would be soon enough, the one she'd been dreaming of all her life.

Would these men do more harm than good? She

could only hope and pray that she'd done the right thing for everyone.

Reese caught up and walked at her side. The breath she'd been holding brushed past her lips on a sigh. The man was something special to look at, and the way he looked at her . . .

She faltered a step. No one else had ever looked at her like that. Mary wasn't sure the omission was a bad thing, either, if it made her mind go mushy. She had neither the time nor the patience for nonsense.

Reverend Clancy, Jo's father and the closest thing Rock Creek had to a mayor these days, stepped out of the crowd. Personally, Mary thought he was a pompous ass, but he was all they had for a preacher, too. The way he treated Jo, his only child, sometimes made Mary want to kick the man in the shins. She was no doubt courting hell with such thoughts, but sometimes she couldn't stop them.

"Reverend," she began.

"Present!" shouted the drunk. Nate, Reese had called him.

Mary glanced over her shoulder. Jo was riding the man's horse astride, holding him in the saddle with her arms around him. With her skirt hiked up, her ankles were clearly visible, and as Mary watched, Nate laid his hand on her thigh.

"Josephine Clancy!" The reverend's impressive belly heaved with the force of his outrage, and his shock of gray hair shook like a tiny tree in a big wind.

"Hell," Mary muttered. "We're all going there."

Jo glanced over at her father's bellow, but she
did not blanch or shirk or even remove Nate's
hand from her leg. Instead, she merely nodded to
her father as if he'd been greeting her politely.
"I'm taking Nate to his room. He should lie
down." Then she turned the horse toward the
Rock Creek Hotel.

Reverend Clancy looked as if he were about to
have heart failure. Despite his constant harangues
over her behavior, Jo pretty much did as she saw
fit. Her creed was "do unto others," and a more
Christian soul you'd never want to meet. If her
father could see past his ideas of proper, ladylike
behavior, he might even be proud of the daughter
he'd raised in spite of himself.

"Reverend . . ." Mary stepped forward as
Clancy stepped in the direction of the hotel.
"These are the men I hired to help us."

Obviously torn between going after his daughter
and meeting the hired guns Mary had hunted
down, Clancy wavered. The reverend hadn't
wanted Mary to go to Dallas. But since he wasn't
willing to *do* anything, when she'd managed to get
the rest of the town to agree, he'd had no choice
but to go along with her plan. As a result, he wasn't
too happy with Mary, but then he never had been.

Reese stepped forward and held out his hand.
"Name's Reese, Reverend."

Clancy looked at Reese's hand as if he expected
to see a snake there. Instead of shaking the prof-
fered hand, he nodded once and put his own behind his back, out of reach of the rabble.

Reese's eyes narrowed, but he said nothing,

merely turned and introduced the rest of the men. "You all met Jed Rourke, I assume. Or at least one of you did." He raised a brow at Mary. "Sullivan, Rico, Cash, and Miss Clancy's new friend, Nate."

He turned back to the reverend with a smirk. Mary saw where the meeting was headed and stepped between the two men. "Thank you. Now I'll just take y'all to the hotel and you can get settled."

Clancy and Reese glared at each other like two dogs over a bone, though what the bone was, in this case, Mary couldn't quite fathom.

She didn't want to touch Reese, but she needed to get his attention. If he came along with her, the rest would follow; she'd seen that right off. An interesting pattern, considering these men. What was it about Reese that made him their leader?

Well, that was neither here nor there as long as he could keep them in line. Because if these men got out of control in Rock Creek, they'd be worse than the men she'd hired them to chase off.

Mary shivered and thought again, *What have I done?*

Before she could go down the same road, a second time, toward answers she didn't have, Mary reached out and clasped Reese's forearm. He tensed and yanked away, hand going to his gun in one fluid movement that would have been beautiful if it weren't so deadly.

"Stop! Right now!" she ordered, surprising herself.

Clancy skittered back, out of harm's way. *Coward.* Reese turned his head just a bit, and his eyes met hers. Whereas he'd been completely civilized up until now, introducing his men as if they'd come to dance at a ball, the civility was gone, eaten, no doubt, by the animal in his eyes.

"I'm not one of your students, Miss McKendrick. Don't tell me what to do."

"I'm your employer." Mary swallowed the fear she knew better than to show. "I'll tell you whatever I wish. What's the matter with you?"

"The world I live in is a bit different from yours. Don't grab me when I'm not looking. The same goes for the rest of my men. You won't like what happens if you startle them."

"I suspect not. Now take your hand off that gun."

He raised an eyebrow but did as she said. "Let's get one thing straight; I'm in charge here. You can try to tell them what to do"—he jerked his head at the four behind him—"but I don't think they'd be of a mind to listen."

Mary glanced at the others. Their gazes were dark, cold, nearly uncivilized. "Fine. You deal with them. I'll deal with you."

"Agreed. Lead on, Miss McKendrick."

Mary cast a look at the people of Rock Creek. As always, everyone waited for her to take charge and do what had to be done. Reverend Clancy had disappeared, no doubt running all the way back to the rectory.

If she'd left things to Clancy, they'd have turned the other cheek until the bandits destroyed Rock Creek, and not out of Christian charity but cowardice.

Mary had always been an organizer and a leader. She couldn't help herself. When something needed doing, everyone turned to Mary, and she accepted the challenge. She should be the mayor—except she was a woman.

Turning her back on the uneasy gazes of the townsfolk, Mary walked down Main Street in the direction of the Rock Creek Hotel. No one had used the place in a long time. As she'd told Reese in Dallas, Rock Creek was dying. The thought made her sigh.

"Something wrong?" Reese walked at her side again, leading his horse behind.

"Besides everything?"

"That bad?"

"If it wasn't, do you think I'd have gone looking for you?"

"No one ever does."

Disappointment laced his voice, and for a moment Mary felt bad. But truth was truth. She didn't think Reese was a man who needed or wanted platitudes.

"I suppose not," she agreed.

He glanced behind them, then lowered his voice as if to keep the others from hearing. "I apologize for my behavior before. You shouldn't touch me unaware."

Her brow creased. The man was a puzzlement. One moment, all animal-like grace and growls, the next, gentlemanly apologies. She nodded, accepting his words, letting them go without comment. She had as little idea how to deal with a gentleman as an outlaw.

"Here's the hotel." Mary looked up at the gray-ing plank structure. The sign hung by a single nail. The windows were broken, and there were bullet holes in the plank, both courtesy of El Diablo and crew. "There's a stable out back. It's clean, with bedding and feed for the horses."

"Is there bedding and feed for the men?"

"Of course. I know it doesn't look like much, but the roof doesn't leak—"

"Yet."

"Yet," she agreed. "It's big, so you can all be together but still have separate rooms."

"And we won't be sleeping beneath the roofs of decent folk."

Their eyes met. Understanding passed between them. "There is that," she agreed.

Reese turned and instructed his men to put away their horses and go inside to choose rooms. They moved off.

Dusk descended in the west, spreading cool shadows across them both. The street, which had been filled with people only moments ago, had gone deserted. Mary shivered.

"Cold?" He didn't wait for an answer. "Let's step inside. You can tell me what you know about the men we've come to fight."

He threw his reins over the hitching post and stepped through the doors of the hotel. Though Mary would have preferred to go home and get away from the man who made her feel as if her skin hummed during every minute spent in his presence, she had little choice but to follow him inside.

In the dim light the lobby looked worse than she remembered, and Mary fought the urge to apologize again. This was the best Rock Creek had to offer these days, and there was nothing she could do about that.

Reese lit the lamp that sat on the front desk. Although dusty with disuse, the wood of the desk was fine and, once polished, would gleam again. The guest ledger still occupied the same position it had been in when the last owner, an old man named Grady, hightailed it out of town. How was she going to get this hotel going again if everyone kept running *out* of town instead of *in*? Mary didn't know, but she'd do it. Her days of running were over.

Turning away from the lamp, Reese removed his hat and tossed it on the desk. The yellow flame flickered gold across his already golden head. Without even trying, Mary remembered what he'd looked like half-naked and looming over her. She swallowed the scalding lump at the back of her throat and prayed that her red face did not show in the dim light.

"Sit?" he asked, flicking a finger at the dusty couch parked crookedly in front of the window.

Mary looked at the small piece of furniture, imagined how close she'd be to him if they both sat on the thing, and shook her head. He shrugged, then crossed the room, passing close enough for Mary to catch his scent—horse and man and something else.

Danger? Temptation? Probably both.

He looked ridiculous perched on the tiny, ever-green-shaded couch. His legs were too long, his body too big to be comfortable there, but he leaned back, spread his arms along the top, perched one long foot atop his other knee, and stared at her. "Well?"

"Yes?" She pulled her gaze from his black boot, traveled up his black pants, lit on his black shirt, and met his green eyes.

"The bandits. Who are they? Where are they? And what do they want?"

He was back to shooting sharp questions, and that sat just fine with her. "We don't know where they go, and they want whatever they can get for the least amount of effort. Their leader is an old Indian named El Diablo."

"The Devil?" He rolled his eyes. "Spare me."

Her lips twitched. "That's what I thought. But that's what they call him. He's collected a bunch of nasty followers. Men no one else wants, they all gravitate to El Diablo. Indians, Mexicans, Texans, too. I even saw some gray uniforms the last time they came through."

"Confederates?"

"Former, obviously. Is that going to be a problem for you?" He hesitated, rubbing his chin with his thumb. "Reese?"

He glanced up, dropping his hand. "No. This isn't about my past; it's about your future. True soldiers of the South wouldn't prey on the innocent."

"Where have you been living?"

He blinked at her sarcastic tone. "Excuse me?"

"Soldiers of any type prey on anything they can."

"Why would you say that?"

"I'm in Texas today because of soldiers, and both sides are to blame. I don't trust government outlaws any more than I trust El Diablo's."

"You don't have to worry about my men."

"I'd better not. I'm trusting you to keep them in line. I brought you here to help. Don't make me regret it."

Though he continued to sit on the couch, looking relaxed, his eyes sparked green fire in the glow of the lantern flames. "And what if we decided to go rogue like wild animals? What would you do about that, Miss McKendrick?"

She could not show weakness with this man, so she moved closer, until her skirt brushed the tip of his boot, and looked down her long nose at him. "I'd shoot you, Reese, like a wild animal, and bury you where no one would ever find you."

He stood in one supple movement, now looking down at her. Even though her heart fluttered with fear, she refused to retreat, since that was what he wanted. Mary was often afraid, but that never stopped her from getting the job done.

"I'd like to see you try," he whispered.

"Cross me and you will." *Big words,* her mind taunted, words she couldn't back up or she wouldn't have hired Reese and his men in the first place. But words like that, once said, could not be taken back or you'd lose whatever ground you'd gained by saying them. A deep chuckle behind her made Mary gasp. She spun about, stumbled against Reese, then went still when his hands cupped her shoulders and held her against him. The heat that flooded the length of her body made her mind mush again, and for a moment she just stared at the man who seemed to have appeared by magic in the room. Mary had not even heard the door open.

The youngest of the six lounged in the doorway between the foyer and the dining room. His face was that of Lucifer's finest—dark, haunted, and beautiful.

"Quit sneaking up on people, kid. One of these days you're going to get shot."

"Sounds like you are the one who will be shot, *mi capitán. La mujer,* she has courage."

"Mind your own business."

"But *you* are my business. If you are shot by an irate woman, what will we do?" His tone was amused, but the dark eyes, focused on Reese, were filled with concern. "Without you we are merely five separate lost souls. With you, however, we are six that become one."

"Go away, Rico. She won't shoot me."

"No?" Rico looked Mary up, then all the way down. "I am not so certain."

But he left, sliding on silent feet toward the rear of the hotel. While she couldn't hear Rico's boots, the tromp of several others' filled the room as the men went upstairs.

"You can let me go now," she said.

"Can I? Why, thank you, ma'am."

His breath brushed her cheek, and she shivered, as much from that as from the cool air that whooshed down her back when he moved away. The man gave off heat like a stovepipe.

When she turned, he stood by the window. "You were all soldiers, weren't you?"

"Why would you say that?"

"I don't know, *Captain*. Why?"

"What difference does it make what we were, it's what we are that should concern you."

"And don't think it doesn't. So they follow you because you were their captain?"

"I wasn't their captain." He turned, and she could tell by the set of his face that the subject was closed. For now. "It's dark. I'll walk you home."

The thought of Reese walking her home like a beau sent a shred of panic through Mary. She had no idea how to behave with a man who made her feel as he did. So she talked too fast and too much. "That isn't necessary. I live behind the school. In a little cabin. I used to board with each student for a week, but when people started leaving, I was able to take the cabin for my own. It's quite adorable, really. I just have to walk a few buildings down and turn."

"How convenient," he drawled.

Mary blushed. What did that mean? Since she didn't know, she kept on talking. "Tomorrow you can come by the school and we'll talk more about El Diablo."

"I can't wait."

A single set of footsteps skittered down the stairs. Seconds later, Jo burst into the foyer. "Oh! I didn't realize you were still here, Mary. We can walk home together."

"Wonderful." She glanced at Reese. "See? We'll be fine. Truly."

He merely raised an eyebrow at Mary. "How's Nate?" he asked Jo.

"Sleeping. Can't you make him stop drinking?"

"No."

"Just like that? No? Have you even tried?"

"Yes."

"I'm sure if you tried harder you could help him."

"Some things even I can't fix." He was looking at Mary when he said it. She hoped he was wrong.

"What's wrong with Nate that you can't fix?" Jo was like a dog with a bone most days.

Reese turned his gaze back to Jo. "I have no idea."

Jo scowled, grabbed Mary's hand, and marched them both out of the hotel. "Men," she sneered as soon as her feet hit the street.

Mary had to agree.

Three

Reese stepped onto the porch, rolled a cigarette with practiced fingers, and watched the two women walk home. They progressed past a few abandoned buildings and turned at the schoolhouse, only a stone's throw from the hotel.

Before she disappeared from sight, Mary looked back. When she saw him standing there, she hesitated, as if she'd wave or say goodbye, but her little friend just kept barreling around the corner and dragged Mary along with her.

Reese had seen women like Jo Clancy before. They thought they could save the world and every man in it. She'd have her hands full with Nate. The guy had been on a slow suicide mission since Reese had met him.

He put the cigarette in his mouth, cupping his hands to light it. Atlanta snorted in protest. He didn't like smoke. The horse would have been worthless in battle. Maybe that's why Reese liked him so damned much.

Taking a deep drag of the cigarette, Reese let the familiar gesture calm and soothe him as he thought back on his conversation with Mary.

Might any of his men have heard of, or met, El

Diablo? Maybe Rico? Nah. The kid had left southern Texas when he was fourteen, and before that Reese had a feeling he'd been a pampered mama's boy, a Tejano whose father had been *criollo*—the Spanish aristocracy of Mexico. Therefore, Rico would have no cause to be acquainted with a low-down bandit. But if Rico came from the cream of Texas society, why had he gone to war when he was little more than a child?

Reese cursed beneath his breath. Why would he care? He'd learned not to get too close to his men. Because if you did and you lost them, madness wasn't far behind.

He tossed the cigarette to the ground; Atlanta pawed at it. Reese crushed the scarlet glow into dust with his boot and led the horse to the stable.

A short while later, he entered the rear door of the hotel. Clinking glass and the rumble of male voices drew him toward the remnants of the hotel's dining room. He'd planned to go in and discuss plans for the job, but when he heard his name, he hesitated just long enough to make entering at that moment impossible.

"I say Reese is his last name," Jed insisted.

"And I say it's his first." That was Cash.

"So noted, *hombres*. We have gone over his name countless times. Right now we are discussing, once again, what he was before he became a *capitán*."

The five kept up a running wager on Reese's name and previous occupation. It was a harmless bit of fun and sometimes got downright amusing. Like now.

"He was a damned Georgia tobacco planter with

a big house and a hundred servants. That's why he calls his horse Atlanta. He's still pissed at Sherman for burning the place down, and he doesn't want to forget to kill the bastard general the next time he sees him." *Not quite,* Reese thought with a smirk for Jed's ingenuity.

"He had a horse farm where he raised the finest animals south of the Mason-Dixon," Cash said. "That's why he babies that horse of his enough to make me sick."

"I believe he was a preacherman," Rico said. "Where else would he have gotten all those black clothes?"

"Nate's the preacher, kid. Haven't you been listening to him when he's in his cups?" Cash asked.

"How could I not, since he always is? But just because Nate was a preacher does not mean *el capitán* could not be one, too."

"Have you ever heard him mention God?" Jed pointed out.

"What does God have to do with it?"

As usual, Sullivan stayed silent until he had something worthwhile to say. "Could be he was a teacher."

Everyone started laughing.

"Can you see Reese wiping snotty noses?" Jed managed between guffaws.

"Yeah," Sullivan said. "I've seen him wipe up after each and every one of us."

The laughing stopped. Reese made a movement toward the door, planning to put an end to any further speculation, but Rico's next words made him freeze. "He certainly likes the teacher lady of Rock Creek."

"Never seen him look twice at a female before today," Cash muttered. "I always liked that about the man."

"Perhaps his being a preacher is why he looks at the teacher."

"Whadya mean?"

"Wouldn't you say she's a Virgin Mary?"

"That's enough." Reese stepped into the room. All eyes turned to him. "We've got more important things to talk about than my past."

"If you'd tell us the truth, then we could solve the mystery, *Capitán.*"

"Go to hell, Rico."

"But of course. I'm sure you'll be waiting there for us all."

Reese narrowed his eyes and took a step toward the slick-mouthed kid, but Sullivan stepped between them. "Forget it, Reese. He likes to push till we snap. It's his favorite game."

"Don't talk about me as if I'm not here, *amigo.*"

Sullivan gave Rico a shove with his shoulder. "Then quit acting like you're sixteen and rebelling against your daddy."

"When I was sixteen, I was already at war."

"Join the club, kid."

"But I thought I had." Rico went to sit with the others at the table, where they shared a dusty bottle. As he sipped his whiskey, Rico's dark gaze stayed on Reese. "Isn't that what we are? The six of us? A club of misfits led by *el capitán?*"

"One of these days you're going to push me too far, and then I'll tan your hide," Reese said.

Rico pulled his knife from the scabbard at his waist and turned the huge blade over and over in one hand with nimble fingers. Sometimes Reese cursed Jim Bowie for inventing such a weapon, but Rico could do amazing things with his knife—with any knife, for that matter. But he couldn't shoot for shit.

"Tan my hide, hmmm? That is something I would like to see you try."

"Keep it up and you will."

"Gentlemen, gentlemen, must you always squabble?"

Nate stood in the doorway, looking almost sober but decidedly rumpled. The dark stubble on his chin was only marginally shorter than the stubble on his head, because Nate liked to shave his head whenever his hands were steady enough. He said the less need for a comb and soap, the better, and Reese, who had cleaned him up enough times, had to agree.

"Wasn't it St. Paul who said, 'A man's friend is his castle. Do not tear him down brick by brick.' "

"I don't recall that section in the Bible, Nate. You're certain you were a preacher?" Sullivan moved to intercept the bottle before Nate could get his hands on it.

Nate shrugged and pulled a flask from his pocket. "As certain as you are that your daddy was a Comanche."

Sullivan's eyes narrowed, and it was Reese's turn to step between two men. "Boys, do you think we could quit picking at each other long enough to save this little town?"

"The quicker the better," Jed put in. "They don't seem too happy to see us."

"If you didn't like it here, then why did you tell Miss McKendrick where to find me?"

Jed shrugged. "She asked for help. I couldn't tell a face like that 'no' any more than you could, obviously. And she does have a way about her."

"What kind of way?"

"A bullheaded kind of way. Once she's got an idea in her head, she ain't going to give it up. I figured better us than anyone else."

"And when did you become an expert on women?"

"Not all women, just women like that. I've got a sister exactly like her back home in Georgia."

Reese contemplated Jed. "You've never mentioned a sister before."

"You never asked."

"And I didn't ask now."

Cash downed the last of his drink and smacked the glass on the table. "Could we just kill us a few bandidos and get the hell out of town?"

"Here, here." Nate sipped his flask.

Jed looked somewhat embarrassed to have brought up a sister no one seemed to know about. He went to stand on the other side of the room, and Reese let the subject drop. The more he knew about Miss Rourke, the worse he'd feel if Jed wound up dead. So Reese poured himself a drink and outlined his plans for Rock Creek. The bickering stopped, as it always did, once they got into the spirit of their task. When they were bored, they argued, just like brothers. And like brothers, if one was threatened, the others stood right behind him.

The single thing the six did best was fight—together. Once upon a time it had been all they had.

Before the sun rose, Mary rolled from her bed. School started early in Rock Creek so that the children could be released just as early and help with the family businesses. Though there were ranches about the town, those folks taught their own children or brought in a tutor to do so. Rock Creek was a commerce center—or it had been until El Diablo rerouted the stage line.

Scrubbing her face rosy with cool water and a cloth, Mary wondered when Reese would come to the school. This morning, while she taught spelling? Or perhaps this afternoon, when it was time for arithmetic?

Glancing in the mirror to braid her hair, Mary paused. Her cheeks were flushed, her eyes more blue than gray, and with her hair curling wildly about her face, she barely recognized herself. Was this the woman Reese saw when he looked at her?

No. He saw Miss McKendrick—of the stiff spine, straight hair, and pale, thin face. That's who she was, not this stranger in the mirror.

But if that were so, then why did he look at her, more often than not, as if he wanted to devour her whole? And why had she dreamed all night long of his hands on her body and his mouth against hers?

She tossed the cloth into the basin with a curse that would have earned her a good ear boxing as a child. Old maid, she was, and old maid she'd stay. Even if, by some miracle, Reese wanted to kiss her, she wouldn't let him.

Rock Creek was her home—the one she'd always hoped to have. If she wasn't going to let El Diablo run her off, she certainly wasn't going to allow herself to be dismissed for something as simple as a kiss from a borderline outlaw. No matter how sinful he looked, no matter how delicious he might taste.

Nevertheless, Mary dressed in her favorite green gown, which matched Reese's eyes and made her own shine bright blue. The shade also made her hair appear more blond than brown, and the cut nipped her waist to the span of a man's hands. Silly vanity, she told herself, but excused it with her need to control everything she could when faced with a man she knew she could not.

The children behaved horridly all day. Mary wasn't sure if that was because of their excitement over the men who had come to town or their teacher's distraction with one of those men. Her gaze flicked to the door at every shift of the weathered boards that composed the schoolhouse. From her window she had a clear view of Main Street, and she saw each of the hired guns pass by several times—except for Reese.

Where was he?

She finally forgot about him during a particularly harrowing moment with two of the older boys. Jackson and Franklin Sutton, twin terrors of eight, informed her that arithmetic was for anyone but them.

"Boys, what will you do when you take over your father's store? How will you know what to charge your customers if you don't know how to add, subtract, multiply, and divide?"

"We aren't taking over Papa's store," Jack informed her with all the arrogance of eight going on thirty. "He says there won't be a store to take over soon enough. Even with you hiring those bad men, Rock Creek is done for."

"Bad men?" Mary frowned. "They aren't bad men. They've come to help us."

"Papa says they've come to rob us, most like," said Frank, taking up the tale. "And he says it's all your fault for bringing them here. You're no better than a harlot, going off on your own and paying those men to come to town. He says you're asking for it. *What* are you asking for, Miss McKendrick?"

Mary studied the two boys. They were only repeating what they'd heard at home, despicable as it was. In years past, any child who spoke like that to a teacher would have been thrashed. Mary had never seen the necessity for physical violence in her classroom, and she wasn't going to start now, even with the Sutton twins.

Instead, she resorted to the stern voice that had served her well over the eight years she'd been teaching, "Do your sums, boys. Immediately."

"No. If you're no better than a harlot, then we don't have to listen to you. And neither does anyone else."

They stood. So did the rest of the class, but as

they filed toward the center aisle, they bumped into each other when the Sutton twins stopped dead.

Reese lounged in the doorway—tall, dark, and deadly. Dressed in black once again, his Colts gleamed in the afternoon sun. How had he entered without her hearing a thing?

His green gaze flicked to Mary, and the fury she saw there revealed he'd heard at least the last part of the exchange. When he pushed away from the door and stalked into the room, the nervous shuffling of the children warred with the thunder of Mary's own wildly beating heart.

"Sit," he murmured.

No one moved.

"Sit, sit, sit!"

The children scattered.

"Is there a problem, Miss McKendrick?" He kept moving toward the front of the room, his boot heels tapping slowly, like the ticks of a clock in the depths of the night.

She glanced at the children. All eyes had gone wide and were trained upon Reese. "Nothing I can't handle."

He reached the head of the room, turned, and leaned against her desk. How was it he seemed to fill the building? Neither she nor the children could look anywhere but at Reese.

"Really? Seemed to me your charges were having a bit of a problem with today's lesson." He fixed his eyes on Jack. "Is that so?"

"No, sir."

Reese switched his gaze to Frank. "And you?"

"Not me, sir."

"Hmm. I must have been mistaken, then. I thought I heard the word harlot." The children gasped. "But that couldn't be correct, because no gentleman would use a word like that in front of a lady, now, would they?"

No one answered. "Would they?" He didn't raise his voice, but the repetition of the question rolled like thunder through the stillness in the room.

Ten heads shook frantically. Reese's smile was thin. "I didn't think so." He flicked a hand at the door. "Go."

They all ran for the door. "Stop!" Mary shouted. She did not have the ability to make everyone listen with a murmur and a glare, but her shout got through, and they did stop. "We have a reading lesson to complete before day's end."

A collective groan swept the class. They all glanced at Reese. He shrugged. "Sit."

They sat. Mary moved to the front of the room. Reese kept lounging against her desk like a great black cat. When he didn't move, she went about her business, listening to each child read the lesson. The teaching of reading was a challenge in a room with five different grade levels, but she managed. Mary always managed.

As she passed Reese on her way to the other side of the room, a harsh, wavering sigh made her glance at him sharply. At first, he seemed completely relaxed, until she looked closer and observed the white lines about his mouth, then heard the tap-tap of his boot. When he raised a hand to pull his hat lower, Mary could have sworn his fingers trembled. She tilted her head so she could see his face beneath the shadow of the black brim and discovered him staring at the children as if they were trolls come out of a dark forest.

"Reese?"

His gaze flicked to hers, and for a minute he looked like a trapped beast. "I'll wait on your porch," he said, and then he fled.

What was the matter with him?

Reese reached the safety of Mary's porch and sat on the bench against the wall. He'd broken out in a cold sweat at the first word from the mouth of a boy who looked too much like—

A pain shot through his belly; Reese doubled over with a moan. The murmur of voices from the street in front of the school forced him to straighten, clamping his lips to keep the agony from spilling out. Two Rock Creek matrons stared at him as if he'd done something obscene. He nodded at them, thumbed his hat, and they hurried on their way.

Reese stood, then moved toward the door of Mary's cabin. He could not sit out here on the porch, for all the world to see, and lose what was left of his mind. He needed privacy, and he needed it now.

He tried the door, swearing when it swung open with ease. Didn't the woman know about locks? But if she did and she'd used one, he'd be on his knees on her porch. Reese kicked the door shut behind him and fell to his knees in Mary's front hall.

"Just a minute," he assured himself, pressing his hot, damp forehead to the cooler plank floor. "In a minute it will go away and I'll be fine."

Memories whirled through his mind—faces, names, the agony of the innocent, and the voices of the dead.

"Shit!" This hadn't happened in so long, he'd hoped it wouldn't happen again. The others had never seen him like this, and they never would if he could help it. The men he'd collected would have no tolerance for weakness—even less than Reese did.

How long he remained there on his knees, Reese wasn't sure, but the voices of the children calling goodbye to Mary brought him back to himself, to the small house, to little old Rock Creek. A shudder racked his body. The shivering increased, causing every muscle and bone to ache.

With a willpower born of his past and dredged from the depths of his self-control, Reese focused his mind on the here and now—the rough plank beneath his cheek, the scent of linseed oil on wood, clean, quiet air that held not a hint of smoke or a trace of screams.

After Reese practically ran from the room, Mary rushed the children through the rest of their lesson, dismissing them early, even though she should have made them stay late. But she couldn't keep her mind on their primers, and from the amount of pronunciation mistakes, neither could they.

Most days, after the children went home, Mary swept the floor and planned the next day's lessons. Today was not most days. The floor could stay dirty, and she could teach tomorrow without a plan if she had to. What good were eight years of teaching if she couldn't?

She left everything where it sat and stepped outside. Reese wasn't on the porch as he'd promised, and for a moment her heart seemed to stop. Whatever had made him go pale as a pillowcase might have made him bolt, too. She'd still have five men, but she was afraid those five without Reese would be worse than El Diablo in the end.

Mary ran across the small bit of brown grass and dirt separating the school from her cabin and burst through the front door. The place was as silent today as it was every day when she came home after school. But regardless of how lonely she felt here, this was *her* place. She'd never had one before.

"Reese?" she called, mortified when her voice shook.

"Here."

If she hadn't been listening with all her heart and soul, Mary wouldn't have heard the single, soft word from the parlor. Her shoulders sagged in relief. She took her time shutting the door, then drew a few deep breaths before she joined him.

He looked as ridiculous in her parlor as he'd looked sitting on the green couch at the hotel. Standing at the front window, he peered through a small crack in the drapes. He'd rolled a cigarette and held it in his fingers as if to smoke. But no flame reddened the tip, and the thin white band only served to emphasize how dark, how sizable, his hands were—those hands that she'd imagined all over her, all night long.

Mary cleared her throat, and Reese started as if he hadn't known she was there, which was absurd, since he'd called her in here. She wished she could see his face, discover what was the matter, so she moved closer. But when he glanced at her, she could see nothing past the shadow of his hat.

"Would you remove your hat in the house?"

Her voice sounded prim, even a mite snippy, but Reese yanked his hat from his head and, with a single flick of his wrist, sailed it onto a chair. "Better?"

"Thank you."

She could see his eyes now, but despite her agreement to his question, she didn't feel better. Those eyes were still as green as her favorite dress, but they'd gone as cool as moss and as hard as stone.

The two of them stared at each other, and the house that had always seemed too big for one old maid suddenly seemed too small for the same old maid and the man in black. Perhaps because Mary had never been alone with a man in her life. What did one do?

"You wanted to see me?" He rolled the cigarette between his fingers, the movement slow, soothing, seductive. Mary couldn't take her eyes from those nimble fingers that smoothed around and around the nub of his cigarette. "Miss McKendrick?"

"Hmm?"

"Was there something you wanted from me?"

She forced her gaze from those hands to his face, and the lines about his mouth reminded her of why she'd run from the schoolroom without finishing out the day. "What's the matter with you?"

"Me? Nothing."

He placed the cigarette in the pocket of his black vest, too polite even to ask if he could smoke in her house. How had a Southern gentleman become whatever he was? Outlaw? Mercenary? Leader of a gang with guns to hire?

He presented her with his back and stared out at the fading light. A storm was coming, and from the way the sky had darkened, it was coming fast.

"I think you're lying, Reese. Something about the children bothered you. You want to tell me what it was?"

"No."

He didn't sound angry or sad or frightened. He sounded as if he'd refused a second glass of punch at the Autumn Harvest Ball. Drawn closer against her will, close enough that her skirt brushed his leg and she could see that he was still trembling, Mary wanted to touch him, but she didn't know how.

Thunder crashed, still in the distance, but not for long. He started, shook his head, and gave a chuckle of self-derision.

"You don't like storms?" she asked.

He lifted one shoulder, then slowly lowered it,

raised his hand, shoved his hair from his eyes, then rubbed his palm along the back of his neck as if it ached.

"The noise." His voice was so low that she had to lean closer to hear, and her breasts brushed his back.

He spun around, and she stumbled. Her hands came up to brace herself against his chest, but he grabbed her wrists before she could touch him and held them away from him.

"I told you not to touch me." The eyes that had been cold went hotter than the approaching lightning.

She licked dry lips. "I'm not touching you; you're touching me."

"Well," he drawled in the voice that had haunted her nights since the first time she'd seen him, half-naked in Dallas. "That's different, then."

He yanked her into his arms, and as the thunder drifted closer, grew louder, he kissed her. Heat in her belly, fire in her breast, the man was a danger to all she'd been taught was right and true.

First kisses should be gentle, sweet embraces between couples yet children. If there had ever been gentleness in Reese, it was gone, and Mary couldn't say she was sorry. She wasn't a child, and neither was he.

He was a hard man. Harder still were his hands on her shoulders, his mouth on hers. At first, she just let him kiss her, not knowing what else to do. If this was not just her first kiss but her *only* kiss, she did not want it to end too soon. Then his tongue ran along the seam of her lips, and the sensation made her gasp, a sound both of shock and desire awakening.

He tasted of desperation, a flavor she knew well—the salt of tears, the tang of fright. Her hands, which he'd released, hung at her sides, clenching, unclenching, wanting something but afraid to grasp anything.

The line she walked between need and dread was a fine one. A single step to either side and she would be lost. So she kissed him back as best she could, but she touched him not at all.

The nimble fingers that had rolled the cigarette unrolled her hair from its pins before she knew what he was about. Then he filled his hands with the curling mass and held her tight as thunder rolled into town, at war with the toll of the church bell.

Four

Reese was lost—in her, in himself, in them. He'd made the memories go away by sheer force of will, but the thunder had brought them back, and when she came near enough to touch, he'd lost his leash on the demon inside.

Instead of howling and screaming and telling her everything, he'd kissed her. Stupid fool. From the clumsy way she kissed, he could tell she'd never been kissed before. Now he would always be her first. Women didn't forget things like that.

As she got into the spirit of things and kissed him back, he wondered if he'd ever be able to forget this kiss, or her, either. But as suddenly as the kiss had begun, it ended when Mary tore her mouth from his.

"The bell," she gasped, and stepped back.

His fingers caught in her hair, and she winced at the pull. Disentangling them, Reese felt like a schoolboy with his first girl.

He'd heard the bell, in a distant, less lust crazed corner of his mind. He held up his hands to show her he no longer held her captive with his big, clumsy fingers. "Church on a Monday?"

She shook her head, and that hair, which she

kept pinned straight and snobbish, tumbled and curled in an unbelievably arousing mass about her face. Even the color fascinated him—changing from blond to brown with each shift of the air.

"The bell means El Diablo is coming."

Reese forgot about her hair, that body, those lips. Thunder rumbled again, and he understood the sound for what it was this time—horses and guns. "I think he's already here."

Mary's face paled, but she straightened her back and tightened her lips, swollen from his ravishing mouth. He should apologize, but he really didn't have the time.

Reese drew his Colt, grabbed his hat, and headed for the door. Mary caught his arm, and he growled at her. She snatched her fingers back, as if afraid he would bite. Sooner or later she'd understand that he might. "Where are you going?"

"To do my job."

"You can't just walk out there with a gun in your hand."

"I can't? I do it every damn day. Sometimes twice on Sundays."

She sniffed. "I don't think you're funny."

"You know what, Miss McKendrick? Neither do I."

"If you walk out there like that, they'll shoot you."

"I thought they hadn't shot anyone yet."

"None of us walk around with guns."

"Maybe you should."

Her eyes narrowed. "But that's why I have you."

"My point exactly." Reese opened the door and

stepped onto the porch. The sky had gone gray with clouds, but no storm threatened—just El Diablo.

His hands were steady, his heart just fine. Facing armed bandidos was so much easier than suffering little children. His fingers tightened on the gun. The door opened behind him. He didn't even turn around. "Get back inside before I make you."

She gave another haughty little sniff that had him aching to kiss her again, even though he'd probably get shot in the back for the distraction.

"I just thought you'd like to know that they usually go to Sutton's store first, then down to the saloon. You don't have to face them alone. You can sneak back and get your men."

"I never sneak, and I'm sure my men already heard them coming."

"I suspect so, since they weren't kissing me." She slammed the door.

He stifled a laugh. He felt better than he had in nine years—which was about how long it had been since he'd kissed a virgin—a thought that stifled his laughter better than anything else ever could.

After taking a glance behind him to make certain Mary had indeed gone back inside, Reese headed for the hotel. He did not sneak, but he did go in the back way. An idiot he wasn't.

His men stood in the front hall, armed to the teeth and waiting for him.

When Reese strolled in from the dining room, Rico pulled his knife. "Little jumpy, kid?"

Rico shrugged and sheathed his sticker. "Where were you?

"Talking to Miss McKendrick."

Sullivan raised his eyebrows but kept his mouth shut.

"Took you damned long enough to get here," Jed said from his position at the front window. "Thought we were gonna have to come lookin' for you before we went after the bandidos."

"Well, here I am, boys; you can relax now."

Cash snorted and checked the load on his six-shooters.

"Everyone know the plan?"

"Refresh my memory." Nate sipped amber liquid from a dirty glass. He held his rifle loosely in his free hand.

Reese glanced at Jed, who shrugged. "He's all right."

"*He's* right here." Nate finished his drink and stood. "Just pickled enough not to care."

"When have you ever cared?" Reese asked.

"Wouldn't you like to know?"

"Not particularly."

"Which is why I follow wherever you lead. So lead."

Reese stared at Nate for a long moment. One of these days he was going to make one of *them* be the boss. See how they liked it. One day, but not today. "Fine. You're on the roof, Nate, with Jed. Sullivan and Cash are at the windows here. Rico's coming with me to have a talk with El Diablo."

Nate made a strangled sound. "Are you crazy?"

"Not lately."

"I've got a question of my own, now that you mention it," Cash drawled.

Reese resisted the urge to groan. One question always led to another with these five. "Spit it out."

"Why do you always have to talk to them first? Why don't you just shoot them and be done with it?"

"If I wanted them shot, I'd send you."

"Fine by me." Cash pulled out his pistols with a practiced flick of the wrists. "I'll be right back."

Reese stepped between Cash and the door. "Let's try it my way first. If we can make El Diablo move on without spraying this pretty little town full of blood, isn't that a better way?"

"Not in my book," Cash grumbled, but he put his pistols back.

Reese couldn't help it; he'd seen enough blood to last all of his life. Though he made his living by the gun, once he'd made it by talking a helluva lot. Times might change, but people more often did not.

"If you don't mind, I'd like to get back to *my* question," Nate said. "Why would you take that loud-mouthed kid along to talk to the enemy? Your brain is more pickled than mine."

"I doubt that." Reese didn't want to take the time to explain his reasoning, but a look at Nate showed the man in a mood to argue. Reese would save time if he just answered the question no one else cared to ask. "If El Diablo doesn't speak English, Rico can translate. My Spanish has never been very good."

Nate scowled at Rico, who was cleaning his fingernails with his backup blade. "He'd better not be a smart-ass."

Rico's dark gaze flicked to Nate's. "I know when to behave, *Padre.*"

"I'm not a priest."

Rico shrugged. "Priest, pastor, preacherman, it is of no concern to me. I go with *el capitán;* I listen to the conversation; I keep my mouth shut unless I am asked."

"And if trouble starts," Cash put in, "he'll be close enough to hit something with his knife."

"Hell," Jed said, "he'll be close enough to hit something with his gun if he had to."

The sound of horses approaching at a walk made everyone go silent. Reese jerked his head toward the stairs. Nate and Jed departed for the roof. Sullivan and Cash moved to the windows as Rico slid the long, thin silver knife into his boot, then meandered out the front door.

Reese followed, and they watched El Diablo and his men approach. Fifteen men, Reese counted, including the Devil. He shook his head. A man less like the Devil he'd not seen in a long, long time.

Long white hair surrounded a bony face that spoke of years in the sun and wind. He was Indian—most likely Comanche, considering the territory, or even Apache, given the name—and so small in stature, the stirrups on his horse had been raised above the animal's belly. His hands were large, his body withered. He looked like a harmless, little, old, Indian man until he turned his head and saw Reese and Rico watching him.

Then he laughed, and the sound sent a shiver down Reese's spine. Madness brewed beneath that laugh and behind those dark, feral, too intelligent eyes.

No one had died yet? Only because El Diablo hadn't wanted them to, and Reese had to wonder why.

"*Infierno*," Rico muttered.

"You've got that right, kid. Hell just rode into Rock Creek."

El Diablo held up a hand, and the men stopped. At a flick of his finger, one man separated from the rest, and together they approached.

"I don't know any Injun, Reese," Rico said. "Maybe you should get Sullivan out here."

"He doesn't know any, either."

El Diablo stopped his horse and stared at Reese. The second man, who was as huge as the first was not, stared at Rico. While El Diablo was obviously Indian, the other man was just as obviously white. His gray pants revealed he'd been on the same side as Reese in the war, but Reese doubted Colonel Mosby had ever recruited El Diablo's right-hand man for an elite team of guerrilla fighters.

"What are you doing in our town?" The voice did not hold even a hint of the South but rather the flat tones of a Yankee.

"Your town?" Rico sneered. "I suppose those would be your pants, too?"

The man grinned, revealing several holes where teeth should be. "They are now."

Rico took a step forward.

"Forget it," Reese ordered, keeping his eyes on the false Confederate, knowing Rico would do as he was told—for a while, anyway. "That's not why we're here."

"Why *are* you here?" the man asked.

"To make you leave."

He laughed. "I'm going to enjoy this."

Reese switched his gaze to the old man. "Does El Diablo talk?"

"If he's of a mind."

"Does his mind understand English?"

"Better than most."

Reese addressed his next words to El Diablo. "We've been hired by Rock Creek to protect what's theirs. If you leave now and don't come back, we won't have to shed your blood."

A thin, cruel smile spread over El Diablo's face. "If *you* leave now, we will not have to kill you and let the buzzards pick your brains."

The old man not only understood English; he spoke it better than his right-hand man.

"If you're smart, you'll move on to a town with less protection. You'll only end up dead if you keep coming back here."

"Is that a threat?"

"I thought that's what we were doing—making threats."

"No, I am making a promise, *señor;* you and your friend will die today."

The sound of a rifle being cocked split the silence. "One man moves an inch and the buzzards won't have to pick for El Diablo's brains, they'll be spread nice and fine all over the street."

Reese sighed. Nate never did have a lick of patience, which was a damned odd quirk for a sniper—and a reverend.

The Yankee Confederate's face turned the shade of a beet when he realized he'd been caught in a trap. Of course, if the other men chose to open fire, Reese and Rico would be dead, but so would the Yankee and El Diablo.

El Diablo kept his dark gaze on Reese. "Just because there was not a battle today does not mean you haven't begun a war." El Diablo turned his horse. "Jefferson, we will finish this another day."

After a moment of futile glaring, first at Reese, then Rico, who must have made a face or obscene gesture, Jefferson started to shake with fury before he glanced up at Nate, scowled, and trailed after El Diablo.

"We will be back when you least expect us," El Diablo called.

"You and the rest of my nightmares," Reese murmured as the bandits left town.

Mary had been pacing her parlor, wringing her hands and praying for peace while listening for gunshots. She looked out her window a hundred times and didn't see a single person after El Diablo and his crew rode toward the saloon. Still, she didn't hear shouts, breaking glass, or the usual revelry that accompanied a visit from the Devil's own. But then she couldn't hear anything very well inside the house.

Even though she should remain in the cabin and hide, as she and everyone else always did when

the bandidos came, too much silence altered her
better judgment, and Mary stepped onto her
porch. She couldn't see a thing because the
blasted schoolhouse was in the way. She'd always
liked her little cabin, set back from the main part
of town, but right now what she wouldn't give for
a front-row view.

Reese might not sneak, but Mary wasn't proud.
She crept along the side of the school until she
could see the hotel. She looked up the street, then
down. No sign of anyone—townsfolk, hired guns,
or bandidos—anywhere. How odd.

Before she ran across the distance separating the
school from the hotel, Mary took one final glance
behind her and came face to chest with a man
blocking her path.

Mary screamed. Quite loudly. She was very
proud. Until the man clamped his hand over her
mouth.

Panic had her thrashing and fighting, kicking
and biting. Then another set of arms yanked her
from the first man's grasp, and a fist shot out,
knocking Rico along the jaw. He went down like a
sack of flour dropped off the edge of a wagon.

"What in hell do you think you're doing?" Reese
snapped.

"He-he was just there. When I turned around.
I didn't hear him, and there he was."

"Not you. Him."

Rico sat on the ground, rubbing his jaw. The
four other men came running from both the front
and the back of the hotel, weapons drawn. But

when they saw who was making the ruckus, they put their guns away.

"Did you need to hit me, *Capitán*? I will have a bruise on my beautiful face."

"You'd better talk fast and make it good or you won't have a face, kid."

Reese continued to hold Mary against him, so tightly her feet dangled above the ground. Though the gun in his hand pressed just above her breasts, hard enough to bruise, Mary didn't demand to be put down, because being held felt too good.

"I am sorry, *señorita*. I did not mean to frighten you. I only meant to make certain the bad men had not doubled around back. Then I saw you and thought I should warn you not to be outside yet. I am quiet. Sullivan says it is my gift, like his" He glanced at Reese and rubbed his face again. "Also my curse, it seems."

"I'm gonna put a cowbell around your damned neck."

"But then I would be no good for spying, *Capitán*. No good at all."

"You're good for nothing that's for sure. Get lost."

"Getting lost, *señor.*"

Rico got to his feet, winked at Mary, then spun on his boot and joined the other men. Together they tromped into the hotel.

Mary glanced up the street. People were coming out of their businesses and homes to check the damage. For the first time, there wasn't any, which made Mary feel a whole lot better about having brought these six men to Rock Creek.

"You can put me down now," Mary said. It wouldn't do for the townsfolk to see her being held by Reese. What would they think?

"Hmm? Oh, sure." He lowered her to the ground and released her.

Absently, she rubbed the sore spot from his gun. His cat eyes followed the movement, drifting over her bodice; then his lips tightened, and he spun away with an annoyed curse.

"Where are you going?" She hurried after him.

"To my room."

"But . . . but . . . I want to know what happened."

"I don't care what you want. I want to go to bed."

"Wait!"

He kept on walking. She hiked her skirts and ran past him, planting herself in his path. He moved to the right. So did she. He moved to the left. She stepped that way, too.

"Move, Miss McKendrick, or I'll make you."

She lifted her chin. "Make me." *LC0.*"Aargh!" He threw up his hands. "What is the matter with you? What kind of woman comes to Dallas alone, searches out a man like me, then welcomes him and his down-and-dirty companions into town like royalty."

"A woman like me, that's who. And your friends aren't that dirty."

He made a noise that was part choke, part cough, part laugh, but when he got himself under control, he did not seem amused. "Why would a woman like you let a man like me kiss her?"

"Let? Let?" Her voice rose. "I didn't let; you just did."

"So why aren't you crying and shrieking?"

She looked down her nose at him, which was quite a trick, since he was tall enough to give her a crick in the neck, hovering over her as he was. "I haven't cried since 1862, and I *never* shriek."

"You did a mighty fine job of it when Rico grabbed you."

"That was a scream." Mary couldn't help it; she grinned. "I did an excellent job, didn't I?"

"What are you so proud of?"

"I wasn't sure if I'd be able to scream if I ever really needed to. Now I know."

He put his hand to his forehead and rubbed it as if an ache pulsed there. "Miss McKendrick, you need a keeper. Where are your parents?"

"I don't have any parents."

Reese dropped his hand. "Everyone has parents. Even me."

"I'm sure I had some. But either they or someone else dropped me on the doorstep of St. Peter's in Richmond. The sisters raised me."

His eyes opened wide. "You're a nun?"

"Of course not. I was merely raised by them."

"Well, why aren't you?"

"Why aren't I what?"

"A nun. You'd be safer in a convent. What is a woman like you doing way out here?"

"If you continue to say 'a woman like you' in that tone, I'll have to hurt you."

She ignored his derisive snort. Mary was beginning to learn that talking big worked quite well with rough, armed men—or at least with this one. She no longer felt so afraid, and that couldn't be bad.

Mary threw a glance over her shoulder. "Perhaps I should make sure everything is in order for your men. I'll heat a meal, then you can tell me what happened with El Diablo while you eat." She took a step toward the hotel. Reese grabbed her arm and yanked her back.

"I don't want you making pets of my men. They aren't as tame as me."

"You think you're tame? Whatever gave you that idea?"

His lips tightened. "I mean it. When we do a job, we do the job; we get paid; we leave. We don't make nice with the populace. We aren't fit for decent company and haven't been for quite a while."

She removed her arm from his hand, still feeling the imprint of warm fingers along her skin despite the green material that separated her flesh from his. "Oh, posh. You make it sound as if you've brought ravening wolves to Rock Creek."

He stared at her for a long moment, sorrow in his eyes. Then he reached out slowly and gently pushed a stray curl from her cheek. She hadn't realized her hair still hung loose and wild.

"But I have," he murmured, and left her alone with the night approaching.

Five

When Reese walked into the Rock Creek Hotel, he discovered his men huddled around a single table in the kitchen, shoveling food into their mouths like the wolves he'd just distinguished them as.

Perhaps he'd been a bit harsh. They weren't quite that rabid—or at least most of them weren't. Sometimes Reese wondered what trouble Cash got into when he wasn't around to keep the man from getting bored.

After filling a bowl from the pot on the stove, Reese joined the others.

"So what did Miss Teacher have to say? Or weren't you talking?" Cash smirked.

Reese kept eating. He didn't have to answer to anyone—one of the few joys of being the leader.

"*El capitán* and the woman were just talking."

"Since you had your damned nose pressed to the glass, I guess you'd know," Jed said.

Reese raised his gaze to Rico's. "Spying?" Rico shrugged. "I catch you tailing me, kid, and I'll kick you into the next county."

Rico narrowed his eyes and caressed the knife at his waist. But what he said was "Yes, *mi capitán.*"

Reese nodded; then, when the other men returned their attention to their meals, he winked at Rico. The kid winked back, his face as solemn as a casket maker.

Rico might flirt and joke, but he was dangerous. The kid looked to Reese for guidance, and he hated that, but he also knew that if he wasn't the one, Rico might start to follow Cash around, and that would be bad.

"So what did you think about El Diablo?" Sullivan asked.

"What did you think?" Reese countered.

Everyone leaned back and looked at the half-breed scout. Sullivan always saw more than the rest of them, maybe because he shut up and looked.

"Somethin' funny's goin' on here."

"Funny how?"

"I don't know, but that old Indian lies."

Cash snorted. "Like that's a surprise. No offense."

Sullivan didn't even glance at Cash. What would be the point? Cash hated everyone and everything—except drinking, gambling, loose women, and his five friends. But there wasn't a man you'd rather have at your side if it came to a fight. That's why they all ignored whatever he said when he was in a mood, which was pretty much all of the time.

"Lying about what?" Reese pressed.

"I wish I knew."

"Me, too."

Jed lit a cigar, tilted back in his chair, and blew rings at the dirty ceiling. "What are you two thinking?"

Reese looked at Sullivan; Sullivan looked at Reese. Reese nodded for Sullivan to say what they were both thinking.

"There's no reason for all those men to keep coming here and playing around." Sullivan shrugged. "Men like that kill and run."

Reese nodded. "They're trying to get the town to die, but without murder, rape, or too much destruction. Goes against the grain for men like them. So I think they don't want any attention coming this way."

"Atencíon?"

"From the law or the soldiers," Reese explained.

"Isn't much law in these parts since the war," Jed observed. "They disbanded the Rangers, and since then, the Comanches have done as they pleased. The soldiers have their hands full enough without coming to Rock Creek just to chase bandits back to the border. The army can't go across, anyway."

"I think El Diablo knows that. But why would he want this place so badly?"

"Gold? Silver?" Rico's voice was eager. "Buried treasure?"

"Not in this two horse town," Cash sneered.

"Well, it's something," Reese said. "And I'm gonna have to find out what."

"Conveniently, the teacher lady with the voice like Virginia before she burned and breasts, no doubt, the shade of Georgia peaches is the one you'll have to ask."

"If I were you, I wouldn't be thinking about her

breasts or anything else," Reese said, low and dangerous.

Cash straightened the frilly lace on his cuffs. Only Daniel Cash could wear lace and not look like a pansy. Of course, even if he did, no one would dare to say so. "But you aren't me, Reese, so I'm sure you're thinking about her pretty, little—"

Reese stood, and the chair hit the floor with a clatter that echoed loudly in the sudden silence of the room.

Cash flicked his gaze from Reese's hand on his gun up to meet his eyes. Between the well-trimmed goatee and mustache, the gunman's mouth smiled, but those eyes were dead, as always.

"Mind," he finished. "I'm sure she has a brilliant and beautiful mind."

A collective breath hissed about the room. Reese lowered his hand to his side. "You just keep *your* mind on business, Cash, and there'll be no trouble but what we make."

"There never is, my friend. There never is."

To Mary, the next day was like any other. And how could that be with six hired guns in town? One of whom looked like Satan's fallen and kissed like paradise redeemed.

She needed to quit thinking about that kiss. It hadn't meant anything. To use Reese's vernacular, no man like him would kiss a woman like her and mean it. Something had upset him, then she'd touched him, angered him, and he'd kissed her because . . .

She had no idea. Mary had no experience with men—unless you counted priests, little boys, or the fathers of her students. Reese didn't fit into any of those familiar categories.

So she needed to quit thinking about Reese and start concentrating on the recitations of her students. Every Tuesday, each child recited a Bible verse they'd picked to memorize. Not only did the task strengthen their minds; it soothed Reverend Clancy, who hadn't wanted a woman of the Catholic persuasion teaching the children.

Unfortunately for him but fortunately for Mary, no one else had applied for the position. Since she came dutifully to church every Sunday, he'd quit grumbling, at least in her presence, about the Irish papist invasion of Texas. She often wondered how a man with so little tolerance had ended up in his profession—and with a daughter as open-minded as Jo.

"The Lord is my sheep herd I shall not want. He made me lie down in green passages. He led me into the stilted waters and restorated my soul."

Mary pursed her lips as Carrie Brown's mangling of the Twenty-third Psalm at last penetrated her distracted mind. "Carrie, I think you'd better study that one again for next week. Restorated is a wonderful word, but I find it nowhere in Psalm Twenty-three."

"What a dummy! Stilted isn't in there either, Miss McKendrick," Frank Sutton pointed out.

"Thank you, Frank. I'm aware of that."

Mary turned to Carrie, who looked ready to cry. "Never mind," she said. "When I was six, I couldn't even read Psalm Twenty-three, let alone memorize it."

"Truly?"

In truth, she'd recited the psalm in question at the age of four. It was that or have the switch laid across her palm—again. But looking into Carrie's hopeful face, Mary lied without a qualm. "Truly. You'll do fine next week."

Carrie smiled, revealing a double gap in her front teeth that was so adorable, Mary wanted to pull her close and cuddle. But she wouldn't. She was their teacher. She would never be their mother, or anyone else's, and it hurt too much to touch what she'd never have.

With a sigh, Mary turned to Frank. "Since you seem to be well acquainted with that psalm, Frank, you may recite as the rest of the class leaves for the day."

"Aw, Miss McKendrick, what did I do?"

The children filed out. Mary waited until they were gone before turning to Frank once more. "You made Carrie feel bad, and that is something we don't do in my classroom."

His lips tightened mutinously. Mary braced herself for another argument. The Sutton boys were getting to be a problem. What on earth would she do when she had bigger boys than these in her classroom? Most teachers resorted to physical violence to keep their older, rougher male charges in line. Mary just couldn't.

"Frank Sutton," she snapped before he could refuse. "Begin Psalm Twenty-three."

"Yes, Frank . . ." The new voice made Mary

glance up; she found Reese lounging in the door-way. "I haven't heard the Twenty-third Psalm in far too long."

The words tumbled out of Frank's mouth so fast, that Mary could barely understand them. But as her mind caught up to the meaning, she was surprised, and pleased, to discover that Frank had every word correct. Maybe he wouldn't be in the nearest jail cell by the age of fifteen, after all.

Mary smiled at Reese, but he did not return the expression. Instead, he stalked down the aisle toward Frank like a predatory cat. Even though the boy annoyed her to no end, still Mary hurried forward to place herself between Reese and her student. Reese raised his eyebrow, amused.

" 'In the house of the Lord forever,' " Frank finished. "May I go now, ma'am."

"Again," Reese ordered, his gaze on Mary.

"Huh?"

"Again and again and again, Mr. Sutton. Recite until I tell you to stop." He glanced at Frank. "Is that clear?"

"Yes, sir. The Lord is my shepherd . . ."

Reese took Mary's arm and led her to the front of the room. "There's a slight problem."

"Problem? I didn't hear the church bell."

"Not that kind of problem. We went to the general store to get ammunition, and the man there wanted us to pay." When Mary continued to stare at him, confused, he continued. "To pay money. Which we do not have, Miss McKendrick. Are you with me yet?"

"Uh, yes, certainly. I'll take care of that."

"Excellent."

Frank stumbled over a word. Mary glanced at him, but he gamely continued. Reese turned his head to the side and froze before his gaze reached Frank, then, as if it were a great effort, he turned his face back toward Mary, pointedly ignoring the child. But the way he held his shoulders—tense and tight—one might have thought he expected Frank to shoot him in the back—or worse.

Reese inched closer to Mary, as if to move away from the child behind him, and she caught the scent of lye soap. He'd bathed—somewhere. Lye was usually an unpleasant smell, but then, she'd never smelled it mixed with the scent of a man before. On Reese it was quite appealing, sharp but clean. He'd also changed his clothes, though at a glance you'd never know it.

He wore the same cut of black shirt, black vest, and black pants he'd had on yesterday. But this close, Mary could see stitching along his collar that had not graced yesterday's choice, and this vest had two pockets, not one, while his pants were cotton instead of light wool.

"I've been waiting all day for school to let out." Her heart fluttered at the low, suggestive murmur of his voice, and she raised her gaze slowly from his pants to his face. "You have?"

He nodded. "I've got a few questions about El Diablo."

Mary's heart fell to the buttons on her boots. Silly old maid. Why would this man be waiting around just for the pleasure of her company?

The sisters who had raised Mary never minced

words. They'd believed in knowing your weak-
nesses so you could concentrate on your strengths.
The truth, in Mary's case, was that she was both
plain and poor—not marriage material at all.

She was, however, smart, dependable, and
sturdy—a perfect schoolteacher. Growing up in a
convent had taught Mary to face the truth and
never lie, at least to herself and God. And Sister
Hortensia—but never mind that little incident.

"What did you want to know about him?"

"What is there in this town that El Diablo
wants?"

"Food and whiskey."

"It's more than that. If he was just a lazy son of
a bitch—"

"Reese! Watch your language in front of Frank."

He glanced at the boy, who was on his fifteenth
recitation. "Go," he snapped, and when the child
hesitated, "Go, go, go." Reese flicked his hand at
the door. Frank went—fast.

Mary contemplated Reese as he watched Frank
run. The man dealt with children as if they were
soldiers, and they listened. But he didn't seem to
like them much at all, and she couldn't figure out
why. What wasn't there to like about children?

"There's really no need to terrorize my students."

"No? Well, I'll have to stop. Getting back to El
Diablo, if he was just lazy, then he'd also grab a few
women while he was here, shoot a few men if he
got the chance. He hasn't, and that worries me."

Mary gaped, then snapped her mouth shut before Reese mentioned flies. "Worries you? What

kind of man are you? We've got an outlaw who doesn't rape and murder at will and that's a bad thing?"

"It means he's trying to keep the law and the army out of Rock Creek, and I have to wonder why. Was there ever gold here?" She shook her head. "Silver?"

"No."

"Anything? Why is there a town here at all?"

"The stage. The town grew up because this was a major stage stop. There was some talk of the railroad coming through eventually. Though if we can't get the stage back, that won't happen, either."

"There has to be something else."

"If there is, I've never heard of it—" She broke off when he moved even closer and stared down at her intently. "Yes?"

"You smell like . . . like . . ." His face creased, and he leaned closer still, until the buttons on his vest nearly touched her nose. "Like rain." The wonder in his voice made her smile.

"I rinse my hair in rainwater." She ducked her head and blushed. "It's supposed to help tame the curls."

He leaned back, and his face creased more than ever. His big hand lightly touched the hair she'd wrestled into a straight, tight knot atop her head. "Why on earth would you want to do something like that?" He smoothed his palm over the crown of her head. "Mary."

When he used her first name, Mary's mouth fell open again. Hardly anyone called her that anymore—and no one said "Mary" quite like Reese. They stared at each other, the air thick with heat and heavy with the rasp of their breathing. Then thunder rumbled, once, sharp as lightning, and Reese whirled about.

"What was that?" she asked.

"A gunshot, damn it to hell."

Reese ran for the door. Mary was right on his heels.

The general store stood only a few buildings away from the schoolhouse, yet to Reese it seemed like a few miles. He could hear Mary trying to keep up, panting as her corset pressed on her ribs and made it hard for her to run and breathe at the same time. Women and their idiotic undergarments!

Though Reese should have waited for her to catch up, he didn't. Had one of his men shot one of the townsfolk, or had one of the townsfolk shot one of his men? Either way, there'd be trouble in Rock Creek. And when there was trouble, Reese was always the one who got to fix it.

He slowed on the boardwalk. Waltzing into the store without knowing what was happening inside would be an excellent way to get his head blown off. He might not have much to live for, but he really didn't care to die that way.

Reese flattened himself against the outside wall, drew his gun, scowled at Mary, and waved her back out of sight. Then he peeked into the store.

To find his men in the process of holding up

Baxter Sutton. Hands raised, the storekeeper stood with his back against the wall as the men pawed through his selection of bullets. Reese should have known better than to leave them alone and armed among real people.

"Coming in," Reese called. Sometimes Cash got jumpy, and Nate was always shaky this time of the afternoon.

He started into the store. Mary followed so close, her toes clipped the heels of his boots. Once inside, she maneuvered around him and planted her hands on her hips. "What do you think you're doing?" she demanded.

The five men looked at her, smirked, and glanced at Reese. He shrugged. They were on their own.

"I think it should be obvious," Cash drawled. "We're robbing Sutton."

"Why?"

"Seemed like the thing to do at the time."

"But there's no need."

"Perhaps not, but boys will be boys."

"Hmm." Voice calm, the only sign of her annoyance was the tap of her boot beneath the sweep of her skirt. "Mr. Sutton, it was agreed that these men would be supplied with whatever they wished for while they were here."

"That doesn't mean I have to give them whatever they want."

"That's exactly what it means."

"Who else has to give them stuff? They're living in a deserted hotel. Nobody's losing money over that."

"Everyone is taking turns feeding them. And I paid them. I don't have time to listen to any tales of poor little you, Mr. Sutton. You'll benefit from the town coming back to life more than most, so pay your part now. Give them whatever they want."

"And you!" She ignored Baxter and turned to the five men. "Put away those guns and that knife. Behave like human beings for a change."

"Or what?" Cash snapped. *Uh-oh,* Reese thought, *time to step in.* Cash had very little patience when it came to women of a certain type—good women, to be exact. His charm with saloon girls was legendary, but wave a decent lady in front of his face, and it was like waving red in front of a bull.

Reese stepped around Mary. "Miss McKendrick, what exactly do you think you're doing?"

She crossed her arms over her breasts, her stance considering rather than mulish, but that foot kept on tapping. "Managing things, of course."

"These men being one of those things?"

"It's what I do best. Manage."

Jed snorted. Rico coughed. Cash sneered. Sullivan shrugged as Nate groaned and put a hand to his head. "Lord spare us from a good woman who manages things."

Her eyes narrowed. "It's not a curse; it's a gift."

"Right." Cash flipped his pretty gun back into its holster, grabbed two boxes of bullets, and stalked toward the door. Before he left, he turned and glared at Reese. "You'd better manage her or I'm leaving."

The other four mumbled and grumbled as they

chose their ammunition and filed out of the store. Since Sutton glared at her, Mary thought it prudent to leave, too.

On the boardwalk she turned to Reese. "Can't you control your men?"

"They aren't mine."

"Of course they are. You're their leader."

"Only because"—his lips quirked in a wry half-smile—"one of the things I do best is manage. Not to mention that they're too lazy to lead."

Mary frowned. "That doesn't say much for their loyalty."

"Oh, they're loyal. It's one of the few things they have left."

"You'll have to do something about them walking around shooting off guns to get their way."

"Why? It works so well."

She rolled her eyes. Children with temper tantrums. Men with guns. "I'm sure it does, but such behavior is inappropriate."

"Tell *them* that."

"All right." She started toward the hotel but stopped when he reached for her. Even though his rough fingers only grazed her forearm, she felt his touch all over her body.

"Everyone else in town walks around us as if they're afraid we'll kill them for breathing. But you aren't afraid of us at all, are you?" His voice held the same wonder as when he'd said her hair smelled like rain.

She tried to look into his eyes, shadowed by the brim of his ever-present black hat, but she couldn't see them. "Should I be?"

"Hell, yes!" He dropped his hand from her arm, turned, and took a few steps down the boardwalk as if he couldn't stand to be near her.

"And what good would being afraid do me? I'm alone in this world. No one's going to back me up, keep me safe, make my life into what I wish for it to be but me."

A deep breath raised, then lowered those broad shoulders. Still he didn't turn around. "And what do you wish for when you wish?"

That was easy. "A safe home. A job to keep me from going hungry or being bored. Friends."

"No husband? No children?"

"Look at me, Reese." He turned around but moved no closer. "Do I look like marriage material to you?"

He looked her up, then down. When his eyes returned to hers, there was an odd glow in their depths. "For the right man."

Mary was not the kind of woman who would drive a man mad with hunger, but still, when Reese looked at her with those strange green eyes, she felt as if she could be. Silly old maid.

Straightening her already ramrod-straight spine, she sniffed. "Perhaps. But I know better than to believe in miracles and to depend on anyone else but me."

He gave a slow nod, as if he agreed with her, then sauntered back and held out his arm. "You're a very interesting woman, Mary McKendrick."

"Interesting?" She took his arm; it was only po-lite, even though touching him made parts of her she'd never known she had quiver. "That's a new one."

"And far too trusting. You shouldn't trust me."

"No?" They walked along, side by side, and Mary's skirt twisted back and forth about her ankles, then danced across the toe of his boot. "What kind of man tells a woman straight out not to trust him? A trustworthy one, I'd imagine."

"You don't know anything about men."

"True enough. I never saw a man, beyond a priest, until I was sixteen."

She felt him glance at her, but she kept looking straight ahead. "You're kidding."

"I doubt I'd kid about something like that."

He stopped in front of the church, glanced up at the steeple, then removed his arm from her grasp. "You shouldn't be allowed near me or the others."

She laughed, and his gaze dropped sharply from the steeple to her face. "Who's going to stop me?" When his eyes narrowed, she waved away his annoyance. "You came here to help us. You didn't have to. I'd say that makes you trustworthy."

"Maybe we came here to rape and pillage. You told me right out in Dallas that there was no one in Rock Creek who could stop El Diablo. That means there's no one to stop us, either—if we're of a mind."

"Men like you would hardly rape and pillage."

"Don't be so sure."

She tilted her head and considered Reese. He was such a strange, yet fascinating, combination of rough and gentle, outlaw and honest man, she wasn't sure what to do with him—as if she'd know what to do with any man.

"To be honest," she said, "when I saw you and the others riding in yesterday, I was scared. So was Jo. I wondered if I'd made a mistake."

"Smart."

"But I feel better about everything today."

"I'd think you'd feel worse after that display in Sutton's store."

"No. As Mr. Cash said, 'Boys will be boys,' especially when they're men." He gave her a narrow look that made her smile. "Tell me this, Reese. If you were planning to rape and pillage, wouldn't you have done it already? Why wait around, take a chance of getting killed by El Diablo and the rest? Strike and run would be your motto, I'm thinking."

"Maybe we've decided to take whatever it is El Diablo wants—there must be something—so we need to get rid of him before we get rid of all of you. You must realize, Miss McKendrick, we don't usually work this cheap."

He had a point, and suddenly the peace she'd felt since the six had taken up residence at the hotel frayed a bit about the edges. She had no idea what these men were like. None at all. And she shouldn't trust them—especially Reese—a man who'd kissed her the first day he'd come to town. He had to be half-crazy to do a thing like that.

Before she could get her thoughts in order for a better argument or more intelligent questions, the church bell tolled.

This time, Reese didn't bother to ask if there

was church on Tuesday. "Inside," he snapped, shoving her toward the building.

"I can make it home." She whirled to run, but before she took two steps, Reese cursed, picked her up, and hoisted her over his back. All her arguments whooshed out of her mouth when her stomach hit his rock-solid shoulder.

"Manage this," he muttered, and kicked open the door.

The world whirled, and everything came at her upside down. She heard Reverend Clancy sputter helplessly as he ran toward them. One growl from Reese and Clancy's footsteps receded.

Other, lighter footsteps approached, and when Reese dumped Mary onto her feet in the aisle, Jo caught her before she fell on her face. Mary looked up at him, swayed, and her eyes crossed.

"Stay," he ordered.

Thinking she might be ill, right there in front of God and everyone, Mary merely nodded.

A bullet hit the open front door, smattering wood chips halfway into the sanctuary.

"They're shooting at a church!" Reverend Clancy shouted. "What kind of heathens are they?"

"The bad kind," Reese muttered, and ran past them, then out the back of the building.

Six

Reese erupted from the rear door of the church, ducked low, and raced between the lean-tos and sheds that composed the butt of Main Street. Whenever his men began a battle without him, he panicked. If they were going to die, he was, too. He'd been left behind alive once before, and everything had pretty much gone to hell after that.

Luckily, the invading bandits knew the six were in the hotel, and that's where they headed. They didn't, at first, spare a glance for the man in black who sped in that direction, albeit the back way.

Three feet from the hotel garden, the dirt just ahead of his boot kicked up. The report of a pistol made Reese hit the ground, execute a quick roll, then come to his knees shooting. The straggler fell from his mount and lay still. The horse kept on going.

So did Reese, stumbling through the rear door of the hotel. Sullivan nodded from the kitchen, where he watched their backs from an open window. As Reese ran past and up to the second level, windows shattered on every floor.

"I hope they weren't planning to use this hotel for anything but target practice anymore," Reese murmured, and stepped into Nate's room. Nate threw him a quick glance from his position on the floor next to his own shattered window. He returned his attention to the street. "Sullivan and Rico are on the first floor. No one will sneak past them. Me here; Cash two doors down. Jed's on the third floor."

"Me, too," Reese said. They'd worked together so long and so well, Reese rarely had to ask any of his men what he wanted to know. They told him long before he ever got the question out of his mouth.

He'd forgotten, in dealing with Miss Mary, to grab ammunition of his own, so Reese confiscated a box from Nate's morning haul. They had the same rifles, taken off Yankees somewhere in Georgia. The best thing about Henry repeating rifles were the sixteen shots that could be fired before reloading. Reese loved that gun. Nate took a sip from his flask and sighted down the barrel.

"Do you have to drink while you shoot?"

"If you want me to hit anything I do."

A bullet came through the window and punched a hole in the wall above the bed.

"Bastard," Nate muttered. He took another drink, cracked his knuckles, and shot several times in rapid succession. "Got him." Nate calmly reloaded.

Reese left, shaking his head. Why did he bother? He knew Nate needed to drink so his hands didn't shake. He knew Nate could hit a locust at twenty yards. What he didn't know was why Nate drank, and he really didn't want to.

He stopped in his room to grab his own rifle. As he headed up the last flight of stairs to the third floor, a shotgun blast made him flinch. He sprinted up the last few steps and found Jed.

"Who the hell has a shotgun?"

Jed kept his attention on the street, firing his rifle with the ease born of a wartime sharpshooter. "The kid. Picked one up at the shopkeeper's this morning. We figured he might be able to hit something with it, which would be a step in the right direction."

"He's saved your ass with that knife a few times."

"I'm not complaining." Jed turned his head quickly to the side, and his eyes narrowed on something below. "Do you think you could pick a window and help out? These sons a bitches are moving up on us."

Reese went in search of a window of his own. Finding an empty room at the far end of the hotel, he glanced outside.

Jed was right. A man attempted to flank them from Reese's end. He loaded his rifle and took care of that little problem. Another shotgun blast from downstairs and the idiot who approached from Rico's side ended life with a fist-sized hole in his chest. Then a movement from the outskirts of town drew Reese's attention.

He turned his gaze toward the river, half-afraid he'd see enough men to make an army streaming over the bank. Instead, like a general surveying the battle out of harm's way, El Diablo sat on his horse and observed his men in retreat.

As they reached the river, short by four or more,

the old Indian seemed to look right at Reese. Logically, he knew this was impossible. El Diablo was too far away to see him in a third-story window, even if the man hadn't been the age of Old Scratch himself. Still, Reese could feel those soulless dark eyes pass over him before the Indian made an obscene gesture, which startled an unexpected laugh out of Reese.

El Diablo whirled his horse and disappeared into the gully where the river ran. Moments later, his men did, too, and silence settled over Rock Creek.

Reese picked up his gun and the ammunition, then moved out of the room and joined Jed in the hall. "Nice shot on the ugly bastard to your left."

Reese nodded. That was quite the compliment coming from Jed, who thought everyone should be able to put a bullet between the eyes of a deer at fifty yards. Since they had Jed, no one else had ever needed to bother with such trivialities as hunting while on the trail.

Together they descended to the second floor, where Nate and Cash waited at the top of the next set of stairs. "Everybody okay?" Reese asked.

"They're going to have to send a lot better shots than that to hit one of us," Cash said.

"Or at least to hit you," Nate murmured.

"Damn right."

The four of them tramped down to the ground level. Sullivan lounged in the kitchen doorway. "Should I take the kid and trail 'em?"

Reese shook his head. "They have to have a hideout near here or they wouldn't keep coming back. It'll be fortified; no use bringing the battle there. Let them try to take Rock Creek again. By then we'll be ready."

"I prefer to follow and blast them all to hell today." Cash wiped the handles of his pistols with a pristine white handkerchief.

"I'd agree," Reese said, "except one thing we learned in the war holds true in every battle: Inferior odds in a fortified position have the advantage."

Cash gave Reese a narrow look, followed by a cold smile. "I hate it when you're right all the time."

"It's tough, but someone has to be."

Rico skidded into the room like an overly excited puppy. Jed snatched the shotgun from his hand.

"Not bad, kid. Told you this was your weapon."

"I still prefer my knife."

"And so do we. But when it comes to long-range fighting, you use this from now on." Jed checked the chamber, earning a frown from Rico, nodded, then handed the shotgun back to the kid.

The six of them headed for the front of the hotel. "They're going to be pissed now," Nate said. "We took out at least three of their guys."

"No more talkin', right?" Cash glanced at Reese. "This was their answer to your little 'get out of town' discussion."

"No more talking." Reese sighed. "From now on this is a battleground. Clean up the glass. Board the windows. Get the bodies off the street. We need strategically placed cover all over town in case they catch some of us out there. Watches start tonight."

"But *Capitán*, there is a watcher at the top of the church who rings the bell."

"That's worked real well so far," Jed drawled. "By the time the bell rang, El Diablo was breathing fire down our necks."

"We'll take over the steeple watch. That way there'll be a man where they won't expect one. First sight of movement, ring the bell. Two men a night. Sullivan first, then me. And we'll alternate at the hotel, too, one man on the ground floor. Jed first, then Rico. Let's move." Everyone nodded but stood there lounging.

"Go, go, go," he said.

They laughed, but they went. Of course, no one went toward the bodies. They never did. You'd think men who had seen what these had would be less squeamish about dead bodies. Well, most likely they weren't squeamish, they just didn't care if the carcasses rotted in the street. Unfortunately, Reese did, which meant he got to take care of them.

Shrugging, he headed out the back way. He'd take care of the dead guys in the order they'd become that way. First in line was the straggler who had nearly gotten him while Reese ran from the church to the hotel.

Reese stepped onto the back porch and saw Mary. He bit off a curse. Did the woman ever listen? He distinctly remembered telling her to stay put. And he hadn't meant until she felt like leaving, either. If his men listened as well as she did, they'd all be dead, and so would he.

He stalked across the dry, brown remnants of a garden; his boots made crackling noises as he crushed what might have once been flowers—or tomatoes or sagebrush, for all he knew—into oblivion. But despite what seemed to him to be a very loud approach, Mary did not turn.

She'd probably never seen a dead body before, and Reese wished he could have kept her from seeing this one. Death wasn't pretty no matter how a person died. But violent death was worse than going to sleep forever at the ripe old age of seventy. That kind of death—one he'd never have—at least made some kind of sense.

Reese stopped at her side and looked down at the man he'd shot. He was dead, all right. "Miss McKendrick, I wish you'd stayed in the church. This is no place for you."

Mary didn't answer; she just kept staring at the dead man so intently that Reese began to worry. He'd known men in the war who saw too much death and retreated behind a wall of their own making, never to come out and talk with the rest of the world again. Could that happen to Mary at the sight of her first dead man? Reese hadn't thought her so frail. But what did he know about women? Little to nothing at all.

He cupped his palm gently about her elbow, planning to lead her back to her friend at the church. If there was a doctor in Rock Creek, he'd call the man; if not . . . Reese had no idea. Nate always doctored all their ills, mainly because he had all the whiskey.

"It's all right; no one will hurt you," Reese soothed in a voice he'd used on horses mad with pain.

She yanked her elbow from his grasp and turned

to look at him. She wasn't sad, she wasn't frightened, and she wasn't crying. She looked furious.

"Y-y-you killed him!"

"Looks that way."

"And how many more?"

"Today or in general?"

"Today."

"Personally or collectively?"

She stamped her foot. "Answer the damned question, Reese."

"Four today, not all mine."

The anger seemed to drain from her then, a confused, uncertain look taking its place. Reese would rather have the anger back, as odd as it was, because when she looked at him the other way, he felt as if he'd disappointed her somehow. He hadn't cared about disappointing anyone for a long time, and now he remembered why. He hated that feeling.

"But why kill them?"

"Maybe because they were trying to kill us?"

"But you weren't supposed to *kill* them."

Had she lost her mind? Why were they here if not to kill all the bad guys?

"What did you think we'd *do*?"

"Frighten them away somehow."

He snorted. "That'll work."

"But they never attacked before."

"That's because we weren't here before and we weren't going to let them steal again."

She groaned and put a hand to her eyes. "You mean if I'd left well enough alone, they'd have gone away?"

"No. They aren't going to go away until they get what they've wanted all along or—"

"Or what?"

"Or we kill them all."

"No! You can't do that. I didn't pay you to commit murder."

His mouth fell open, and his eyes widened. She couldn't be serious. "I wouldn't call it murder—exactly."

She raised an eyebrow and gave him a schoolteacher glare. Reese sighed. "You paid us to get rid of them, and that's gonna mean killing."

"Then I take it back. You're fired. I don't want bodies lying in my street; I don't want dead men on my conscience."

"Why would they be on your conscience? You didn't kill them."

"If I paid you to kill them, however unwittingly, I'm responsible, and their deaths will be on my conscience."

"These men aren't worth losing any sleep over."

"They're men. They had wives, children, homes."

"I doubt that."

"But you don't know. And now you never will. I want you all to leave."

"Sorry. We can't do that."

"But I fired you!"

"You can't do that."

"Of course I can."

"Nope. We take a job; we start the job; we finish the job. After this, El Diablo will be out for blood. He's got to know that if we find what he's looking for first, he's lost it. So he's going to come at us with all that he has."

"And then what will happen?"

Reese turned and stared at the descending sun. "Then a lot more people are going to die."

Mary spent the early evening alone in her parlor, watching six hired killers fortify Rock Creek for an invasion. She fought back the tears that burned her eyes at the thought of her town becoming a battleground. The men she'd hired for Rock Creek's salvation had become Rock Creek's doom. What had she done?

Managed things quite badly, it seemed.

Reese thought she was an idiot, or at least the most naive fool he'd ever come across. And he was right. She'd talked herself into believing she could manage anything and anyone. Managing was the only way to keep the lifelong fear of the unknown, which she held trapped in her heart, at bay. If Mary managed the unmanageable, bad things would not happen to her.

She had never considered there might come a day, a place, or a situation she could not manage. As a result, her hands shook, and her knees as well. She'd told Reese that fear did her no good—but tell that to her wildly beating heart. She'd been trying to for hours now, and her heart wasn't listening to her well-touted common sense.

So she'd been naive in thinking rough riders could frighten away the bandidos. Certainly that wasn't the dumbest mistake in the history of Texas.

So she'd hired men to murder other men. Someone had to.

Sighing, Mary leaned her head against the back of the couch, exhausted by the recriminations that went around and around in her mind. So far no one had knocked on her door to berate her, probably because everyone cowered inside their houses, terrified of the men she'd brought to Rock Creek.

This would never have happened if they'd known how to defend themselves, if one man had stepped forward and organized them into a community that could protect their own. Instead, the only person to step forward had been Mary.

So she'd gone after Reese. But what if she'd done things differently?

Mary sat bolt upright as an idea blazed through her mind, quivering excitement erasing every vestige of fatigue. She jumped up and left the house, then hurried to the hotel. She had to talk to Reese, and she had to do so now.

Wind, shrieking like a banshee between empty buildings, whipped her skirts. The bodies were gone, the blood in the dust obliterated. Her proper upbringing told her that no ghosts walked here, but Mary had an Irish soul and knew better, so she walked a bit faster.

By the time she reached the hotel, she was running. Without knocking—it was a hotel, wasn't it?—she burst through the back door. And found herself face-to-face with a gun.

She was getting very sick of guns.

Mary kept still, forcing her gaze from the long

black barrel of the rifle to the eyes of the man who held it. "Good evening, Mr. Rourke."

He flipped the rifle back to his shoulder, chomped on the unlit cigar in his mouth, and nodded. "Ma'am."

"I'm looking for Reese."

"What for?"

She raised her eyebrows at his effrontery and ignored the question. "Is he upstairs?"

Rourke chomped a few more times, then sighed. "I know it's none of my business, but I feel sort of responsible, seeing as I told you where to find him when you asked."

"Responsible for what?"

He shrugged, but his gaze slid from hers. "Things."

"I'm sure I don't know what you mean."

"I'm sure you don't. And I'm just as sure Reese does. He has no business with you."

"But he does have business with me. That's why you're all here. That's why I need to see him."

He looked at her as if she were daft. "Reese is a good man. I've trusted him with my life more times than I can count, but he's got secrets none of us even know about."

How odd. His five closest friends didn't know what Reese was hiding. What on earth had he done? Who had he been before he became whatever he was? And did she care? Not much.

"His past is of no concern to me."

Jed grunted. "It might be if his past shows up one day."

Mary stared at Jedidiah Rourke. He was trying

to tell her something, though she wasn't sure what.
A footfall from above made Mary glance up.

"Jed?" Reese called. "Who came in?"

That voice did funny things to Mary's insides.
She lowered her gaze and discovered that Rourke
was looking at her with resignation in his eyes.
"You're already too far gone, aren't you?"

Mary frowned. "Gone? I don't understand."

"Never mind." He turned to the stairs. "Miss
McKendrick wants to talk to you. Send her up?"

Reese didn't answer at first. Then a short, annoyed sigh, followed by "Yeah, go ahead," drifted
down the stairs.

Mary nodded her thanks to Rourke. As she
picked up her skirt and climbed the stairs, she
thought she heard him mumble, "Virgin Mary,"
but when she turned to glare, he was gone.

Reese was not at the top of the stairs or in the
hallway, but a door halfway down spilled light
across the floor.

Hesitantly, Mary stepped into the beam of light.
"Come," he murmured, and she moved inside the
room.

He lay on the bed, just as he had the first time
she'd seen him. But this time he wore a shirt, even
though the buttons hung open to mid-chest, revealing bronzed skin and golden hair. His feet
were bare again—pale, long, and soft against the
stark black of his pants. She swallowed the same
heated lump in her throat that had appeared in
another room, another town.

"Close the door, Miss McKendrick."

"I don't think that's a good idea."

"I have to agree, but do it, anyway. My men are loyal but nosy as hell."

"It's improper."

"More improper than you being here in the first place?"

She flushed. "You're right. But I had no choice."

"We so rarely do. Shut the door."

She turned, put her palm against the wood, and slid the door across the floor, inch by inch, until the click of the latch echoed in the heated, silent room. She was just starting to realize the line she'd crossed by coming here, and some of what Jed had said downstairs began to make sense.

Just being in this room could ruin her reputation, and a teacher with a ruined reputation did not teach very long. Teaching was her livelihood; Rock Creek was her home. She could lose both if she continued to barge ahead, thinking like a woman with nothing to lose and nothing to fear. Each day she discovered there was more to fear and more to lose in this life than she'd ever imagined.

The bed creaked, but Mary continued to face the closed door, for she didn't want to face him. When Reese placed his palm against the wood right next to hers, she started. He was nearly as sneaky as Rico.

"Hush," he murmured. "I won't hurt you."

"No?" She could feel his heat all along her back, and she resisted an insane urge to press against him, body to body. "Mr. Rourke seemed to think you might."

Reese snatched his hand back and moved away. Mary shivered at the sudden loss of heat, but at least she could think again. After a deep breath,

which was filled with the scent of him, she turned
to watch Reese pace the room like a caged cat. He
shot a glance her way. "What did he say to you?"

"That you have secrets."

"Doesn't everyone?"

"I don't."

He turned on his heel, and his pacing brought
him in her direction. She held her ground even
when he stopped close enough she could feel his
heat call to hers once more. "And that's what
makes you nearly impossible to resist, Miss McKendrick. A woman without secrets doesn't come
along every day."

"You need to stop teasing me."

His golden brow lifted toward his golden hair.
"Who said I was teasing?"

She wasn't even going to answer that ridiculous
question. Of course he was teasing. He might have
kissed her once; after all, she'd *let* him. The sisters
had told her what men were like. They would take
advantage—whatever that meant—if given half the
chance. But Reese would never kiss Mary because
he wanted her lips against his more than he
wanted life itself—no matter how much she might
dream such things were possible.

"I want you to tell Mr. Rourke there's nothing
but business between us," she said.

"Why would I lie?"

"Lie? That would be the truth."

When had he come closer? She had not heard
his step or felt him move, but he was so near that
his bare foot rested between her boots, and when

he spoke, low and soft, his breath brushed the top of her head.

"No. The truth would be that I can't stop thinking about you. I want to touch you every time you come near me. Even when you were spitting mad this afternoon, looking at me like I was evil come to life, I still wanted to kiss you again and again and again. Right now I want to do a whole lot more than kiss you."

"More?" The word whispered past Mary's lips, shocking her, shocking him, from the look on his face.

Then his mouth quirked in a self-derisive smile, and he shook his head. "Ah, Miss Mary, if I told you everything I'd do to you if you *let* me, I'd shock your virgin ears. I don't think you'd call that business, and neither would anyone else."

She stared into his face with wide eyes even as her body responded to his voice, his scent, his words. "You're crazy."

He shrugged, and his shirt shifted, giving Mary a hide-and-seek view of the chest she admired so much. "I've been called worse."

The way he said that made her heart ache. Slowly, she lifted her hand and reached for his stubbled jaw. He flinched away before she could touch him, then stepped out of her reach. Slowly, her hand fell back to her side, feeling emptier than it had ever felt before.

He hovered there, close but still far away, and stared at her with eyes that made her hurt and happy at the same time. "Tell me, why *did* you let me kiss you last night?"

Unreasonably annoyed at his withdrawal from her touch, she snapped at him. "I didn't let; you just did."

"All right, I took, but you gave back. You should have slapped me and thrown me from your house. Instead, you search me out at night, in my own room, and you stare at me as if you want me to kiss you again. Do you, Mary? Do you want me to kiss you again?"

"Yes."

He blinked. "You do?"

"Of course I do. What woman wouldn't?"

A shadow passed over his face. "I could name at least one."

She frowned. A woman had hurt him. Badly. But why? Another one of his secrets, she supposed.

Reese turned away, and the slump of his shoulders tugged at her heart. "You came here for something other than a kiss. Did you want to yell at me again?"

His stance cried out for comfort, and though she knew little of such things and even less about being comforted, she sensed despair as well as anyone. He had refused her touch before and no doubt would again. But before she could talk herself out of it, Mary crossed the small distance between them and put her hand on his shoulder, touching him, although she had been warned not to.

He turned and in one fluid movement wrapped her in his arms, holding her tight, as a child might, then pressing his mouth to the curve of her neck.

She had thought he would push her away, snarl at her, even kiss her hard and long. She had not expected an embrace, and the sweetness of it tore at her soul.

Hugging was not part of her life, not now or ever before, and she hadn't realized how soothing a mere embrace could be. She relaxed in his arms, slipped her own about his waist, and pressed their bodies together for warmth and comfort rather than need. His heart beat fast against her breast, the only movement in a man gone as still as a wild thing when dawn broke through the trees.

Before she was ready to let him go, he pulled away. Trapped in feelings she had never experienced, she could no longer think about what was right and sane but could only behave the way those feelings demanded. Afraid he could escape her completely, she cupped her palms about his cheeks, lifted on tiptoe, and pressed her mouth to his.

He stiffened in shock. He did not kiss her back. Panic lit inside her chest. He must not run away. Not yet. She tangled her fingers in his hair, tasted his lips with her tongue, plunged past that barrier and licked his teeth.

He jumped as if she'd stuck him with a pin and yanked his mouth from hers. "Where did you learn that?" he whispered.

She tilted her head and told him the truth. "There's been only you, Reese. Just you."

His mouth tightened. "Dammit, Mary, don't say things like that!"

"Why not?"

"This is why not."

He jerked her back into his arms, and whereas before they had shared a gentle, comforting embrace, this time they shared something else entirely. Neither gentleness nor comfort remained in him now. His hard body pressed against her softness. His mouth, which had been tender against her neck, now pressed firmly against her own in a heated kiss. His tongue plunged; his lips plundered; his teeth nibbled. Then his fingers plucked the pins from her hair, and the mass tumbled free. Whenever he came near her, it seemed, her hair ended up loose and flowing over them both.

He was a madman, his mouth everywhere. On her chin, her cheek, her eyelids. Lifting a handful of her hair, he crushed his face into the riotous curls.

Her hands tightened in his hair, needing to hold on to something as her body shuddered with unheard of sensations when his lips graced her ear, his breath brushed her neck, and his tongue lingered along her collarbone, tracing the skin above her bodice. Clever fingers tugged; her dress plunged low; his tongue dipped into the crevice between her breasts; then his lips pressed to the full swell, and her knees buckled.

How had her back come to be pressed against the door that should not be shut? When had his leg squeezed between hers? How had her fingers gone from the hair on his head to the hair on his chest? Why did the secret part of her throb for something she could not name?

Then his leg shifted, and the throb turned to a scream when he pressed into her just so. He swallowed her cry with his mouth. Her fingers clenched on his chest, nails scraping hardened nipples. He tore his mouth from hers with a curse.

"No!" she cried, not wanting him to stop.

He looked at her, horrified, and backed away, then rubbed a trembling hand over his mouth. "I'm sorry. God, Mary, I'm sorry."

"I kissed you, Reese."

"Why did you *do* that?"

He stared at her with wild eyes. Did she look as bad as he? His shirt hung open and crooked; his hair stood on end; his mouth was red and his face, pale.

Then his gaze lowered to her bodice. Glancing down, she discovered that her breasts, had almost popped free of every trapping, red scrapes from his beard laced across her white skin. She should be horrified at the evidence of what they'd done. But the sight made her body go hot and limp again.

"Why in hell did you come here?"

She raised her gaze, but he was busy buttoning his shirt and ignoring her. She adjusted her dress and smoothed her skirt, but she still couldn't seem to remember why she'd come to his room—except to kiss him. No, that hadn't been why. Then she remembered.

"You said there was no way to make El Diablo and his men stop raiding Rock Creek without killing them all."

Reese buttoned his shirt all the way up to his neck before looking at her. His eyes were cool emerald again, though when they passed over her, a flash of heat lit the green depths. "Are we back to that?"

"Yes," she said simply. "Is there any other way?"

"Maybe if you had more men than they do, men who could fight that is, they might cut their losses and run."

"What if we had more women?"

"Huh?"

"More women. If you taught the women how to shoot, then there'd be more of us than there are of them."

"I don't think El Diablo would be frightened of women."

"Why not? Why is a woman with a gun any less frightening than a man with one?"

"They just are. Hell, Mary, you couldn't even stomach the sight of a man I killed. How do you expect to kill one yourself?"

"I'm not going to kill one. I'm just going to make them think that I will."

He groaned. "That'll never work. Half of being tough is actually being that way. Once or twice, you're going to have to shoot somebody or no one will ever take you seriously."

Mary bit her lip. She'd so hoped she'd found a solution to their dilemma. But if she actually had to kill someone, that might be a problem.

Seven

A knock on Reese's door had Mary scrambling away, rechecking her bodice and rubbing at the scratches he'd made on her skin with his ravenous mouth. Reese pulled her behind him, but he needn't have worried that the intruder would walk in. A closed door was sacred between men. You never knew what you might discover behind one.

"Reese," Jed growled. "It's your watch."

Jed stamped off down the hall to his room. Reese wanted to stamp, too. How could he have forgotten his watch and have to be reminded like a child with chores?

"Can you help me find my hairpins?" Mary asked.

That's how he'd forgotten. Understandable but stupid. The woman was driving him to distraction.

Without turning to look at Mary for fear he'd grab her again and finish what she'd started, Reese went to the door, then bent and picked up the pins he'd torn from her hair.

Reese held them out to her, but she didn't take them. Finally, he had to look up and found himself trapped again in the wonder of Mary. The prim set to her lips contrasted with the full, ripe swell he'd put upon them. And that hair—curling wild and frée, scented like rain, shaded like sun— made him dream improper things in the middle of the night.

He was falling fast, and he'd better pull himself back right quick. She was not for him and never could be—no matter how much he wanted her, no matter how much she wanted him. She had no idea where this was leading—raised by nuns, for crying out loud! He might be any number of things, but he did not destroy innocence.

At least not anymore.

Reese strode over, placed the pins into her hand, and closed her fingers around them. He nodded to the washstand with the cracked mirror on the wall. "You can use that if you need to."

She didn't speak, just went and stood in front of the mirror. Reese hunted for his socks and boots, then sat on the bed to finish dressing for his watch. When he glanced at Mary, he froze with a boot in each hand.

The domesticity of the scene made a sudden longing for a past that was dead, and a future that would never be, shoot through his belly with such force that he became dizzy.

Mary's eyes shifted and met his in the mirror. Their gazes held, and temptation beckoned.

He could have her. Here. Now. On this bed. No one would blame him.

Except for himself.

Reese tore his gaze from hers and shoved his feet into his boots. "Come on," he said. "I'll walk you home on my way to the church."

She nodded, docile for a change. She hadn't said much of anything since he'd pointed out she might have to kill someone if he taught her how to use a gun.

He gave a snort of amusement and opened the door for her. Mary had guts, he'd give her that much. More courage than any man in this town. You had to admire her for that, if nothing else.

Together they descended to the kitchen, where Rico had taken over for Jed. A single glare from Reese had the kid snapping his big mouth shut before nodding politely to Mary.

Reese would no doubt be in for some teasing from Rico and Cash, lectures from Jed, silence from Sullivan, and dirty looks from Nate for his behavior tonight. No matter what he told them, they would think he'd taken the amazing Miss McKendrick to his bed.

And while he shouldn't care what they thought as long as they did their jobs, he didn't want them thinking any less of Mary because he appeared unable to keep his brain out of his pants whenever she was around.

Outside, she kept her distance, creating no opportunity for him to put his hand against her back, as a gentleman should. He couldn't say he blamed her. He hadn't acted like much of a gentleman upstairs. More like a beast. But she'd waved off his apology, and he wouldn't offer another. The best apology would be to make certain he never touched her that way again.

Maybe he *should* teach every able-bodied person in Rock Creek how to use a gun. Then he and his men might be able to leave more quickly. Reese glanced at Mary and found himself remembering the taste of her skin and the scent of her hair. As each hour passed, leaving looked better and better.

They reached her porch. Reese paused, holding his hands behind his back, out of temptation's way. Mary kept her hands behind her back, too. Temptation seemed a familiar foe to them both.

"Good night, Reese. Think about what I asked, won't you?"

He nodded. She might be on to something with her "more women" defense. He would think on it while he sat in the steeple. Better than thinking about his lips at her neck and his tongue between her breasts.

"Night," he ground out before he turned away and practically ran to the church. Reese didn't look back until he reached the room with the bell. Then he glanced down to see her still standing outside in the darkness.

The need to go to her hit him so hard that he leaned his head against the cool stone wall. When he looked again, she was gone.

"She gets to you." Sullivan lurked in the shadow of the bell.

Reese straightened from the window, pulled out a cigarette, and cupped his hands to light it against the wind, taking his time, thinking what to say.

He blew out a long stream of smoke, lifted one shoulder, then lowered it. "I've been without a woman a long time."

"She's not that kind of woman."

"They're all that kind of woman."

Sullivan snorted. "Now you sound like Cash."

"You better watch the insults."

They smiled at each other, and Reese offered Sullivan a cigarette, then a light. Sullivan was the closest thing Reese had to a friend, mainly because the man liked to chat less than Reese did.

Sullivan blew a line of smoke out the window, watched as it disappeared on the wind, then turned the glowing cigarette about in his fingers like a worry stone.

"Spit it out," Reese growled. "I know when you've got somethin' gnawin' at your gut."

Sullivan peered at him from between the long dark strands of his hair. "What you could have with her might replace what you lost."

Reese stiffened. This was a direction he did not want to take. "What do you think I lost?"

"I dunno." Sullivan held up a hand, palm outward. "And you don't want to tell me. That's fine. I've got things I'm not tellin' you, either. That's why we all get along so well. We accept each other for who we are now and to hell with what went before."

"Is there a point to this conversation?"

"Sure. Someday you're gonna have to trust someone."

Reese frowned. "I trust you."

"Not completely. You don't trust anyone because you don't want us to get too close. You lead, we follow, and that's okay with us. We're getting what we want, but are you?"

Reese disliked the path of the conversation more and more as they went further down it. "You know I've never heard you put this many sentences together in one day."

"I don't know that I have. You want to answer my question, Reese?"

"Am I getting what I want? That's a question for children. Men know that we rarely get what we want, but eventually we all get what we deserve."

"And what is it you think that you deserve?"

Reese flicked the stub of his cigarette out the window and watched it tumble, end over end, toward the ground. When the red ember winked out, he turned back to Sullivan. "Death, of course. What else is there for a man like me?"

Though Sullivan was as dark as the night around him, still Reese could see the shadow of anger cross his face. "A man like you? Honorable, intelligent, a leader. Oh, yeah, let me find my gun and end it for you now."

"Shut up, Sullivan. You don't know what I've done."

"And you know what? I don't give a shit. And I don't think any of the others do, either. I doubt the woman you kissed tonight cared about anything but the kissing."

"How do you know I kissed her?"

"I can smell her all over you."

"Hell."

Sullivan grinned. "Ain't it just?"

"You think this is funny?"

"Yep."

"I'm not going to kiss her again."

"Uh-huh."

"You don't believe me?"

"Nope."

Reese scowled. "I hope I'm around to see it when a woman makes an idiot out of you."

Sullivan's smirk disappeared. "You'll be waitin' a long time for that."

"I bet I won't."

"No woman's going to make an idiot out of me."

"What makes you special?"

"The kind of women who let me touch them aren't the kind a man makes a fool of himself over." Reese opened his mouth to protest, but Sullivan shook his head. "I know who I am. In this country a half-breed is only half a man, and in Texas, half-Comanche means all animal."

"I don't think that."

"And you wonder why I keep comin' whenever you call me? Maybe you should look at the men who follow you and wonder why they do. Maybe then you'll see that wantin' to die made you an idiot long before you ever came to Rock Creek."

With that parting shot, Sullivan lifted his rifle over his shoulder and left Reese alone with the night and his thoughts.

Reese saw a lot of things from the steeple that night. Amazing that he saw anything at all, since his gaze returned to the light in Mary's window every other minute. Either the woman didn't sleep or she left a lamp burning in the parlor all night long. Was she afraid of the dark? Or did she think he was?

Reese had heard of some men that came away

from the war unable to sleep without a light burning. He wasn't one of them. What he'd survived, both in the light of day and the dead of night, had left him afraid of precious little. The least of his worries was the darkness.

Many things moved in the night, none of them El Diablo or his men. Coyotes—or maybe Comanches—howled in the distance. Reese never could tell one from the other when they howled, which he guessed was the idea. A great cat squalled in the basin of the river. If Reese heard that again, he'd consider sending Sullivan out after it. A cougar did not belong that close to a town filled with women and children.

Within Rock Creek, shadows darted, too. Most he did not know—the people who lurked in the dark, or the places they sneaked to and from. As long as they weren't on horseback and coming from outside the town, Reese figured they could prowl about all they wished.

Some of the shadows he did know. The preacher's daughter strolled past from the direction of the hotel. Reese would be having a little talk with Nate. One man playing the fool was enough on this trip. He didn't need Nate impregnating Clancy's daughter, though from what Reese had seen of Miss Clancy, she might remove Nate's impregnating tool with a rusty spoon if he tried it. She could take care of herself. Which was lucky, since her father obviously didn't have the skills.

Just before dawn, twin shadows emerged from the shopkeeper's back window. When Reese saw the fishing poles, he cursed and hustled down from the steeple. A cougar would not hang around a human watering hole once the sun broke the horizon, but Reese wasn't going to bet the lives of two children, however horrific the little brats were, on the behavior of a wild animal.

The town awakened as Reese hurried down the street. Most people stared at him with wide eyes, ignoring his nod and the polite thumbing of his hat. Did the guns frighten them? Or just the man who owned them?

He caught up to the boys before they reached the outskirts of Rock Creek. "Hey," he said, then faltered when the two turned to look at him. Their matching straw-brown hair, wide blue eyes, and crooked teeth sent him back in time. He'd forgotten how much they reminded him of—

"No fishing today," he snapped.

Their faces scrunched into identical expressions of mutiny. "You aren't our pa."

"Thank God," Reese muttered, then took a deep breath so he could explain. He'd known boys like these two, and you needed to explain every little thing. "Heard a cougar at the river last night. You two ought to stay away till we get rid of it."

"Aw, that cat's been drinkin' out of the river as long as we've been fishin' there. He never comes round after sunup."

"Still, I'd feel better if you didn't fish today."

"Are you gonna make us go home?"

"I'd rather you went on your own. But if I have to make you . . ." He shrugged.

"You know it was a lot more fun livin' here before you showed up."

"Yeah, I hear that all the time."

The two went toward the store, dragging their feet and their fishing poles. Reese felt as if he'd just kicked a puppy. Or told them St. Nick wasn't coming at Christmas.

How come he always had to be the bad guy? Well, better that than picking up pieces of Jack and Frank all over the place. But try telling that to an eight-year-old.

Reese returned to the hotel, dragging his own feet. His mood did not improve when he walked into the kitchen to find he'd missed breakfast. Luckily, there was coffee left or he'd have to shoot somebody.

He took a deep pull of thick swill and choked. When he stopped gagging, Reese glared at the others. "Who let the kid near the coffee beans?"

"Not me!" four voices chimed.

Rico took a deep draft from his cup. "This is Texas coffee, *Capitán*. It will make a man out of you."

"I've been a man for a long, long while now and never needed to chew coffee beans to prove it." He picked up the coffeepot and hurled the remains out the back door.

As he went about making fresh coffee, Reese considered telling the men Mary's idea of arming the female populace. The more he'd mulled over her reasoning last night, the more it had made sense. But was it truly feasible? Or was he suffering from the effects of too little sleep and too much lust.

Only one way to find out.

Reese put the pot on to boil and joined the others at the table. "I had an idea last night," he ventured. If he told them the idea had been Mary's, not only would they reject it; they'd probably start sneering about his being led around by his—

"A way to protect the town with less killing."

"Since when did killing bother you?" Cash asked.

Killing had always bothered Reese, and he hoped it always would. If he ever crossed the line into not caring whom he killed or how many, he prayed his days would soon be numbered. But he kept that opinion to himself, considering whom he was talking to.

"I was just thinking—"

"You think too much, Reese." Nate looked hungover. Big surprise. "You always did. It's a bad habit to get into."

"Someone has to think in this crew."

They nodded and went silent, still too tired to question much, which was why Reese had decided to talk to them this morning. "There are quite a few people in Rock Creek."

"Quite a few women," Rico put in.

"Exactly. Widows, daughters—"

"Schoolteachers." Cash winked.

Reese ignored him. "The only two able-bodied men I've seen are Clancy and Sutton."

"A preacher and a coward," Jed observed.

Reese acknowledged the obvious with a lift of his brow before continuing. "A few old men and a few who were hurt pretty bad in the war, but not so bad that they can't wield a gun from a defensive position."

Cash gave an irritated sigh. "Get to the point, Reese."

"Well, I'm thinkin' if we show these people how to use guns, how to dig in and fight back, we'd be helping them more than if we just kill El Diablo and all his men. There's always another bandido down the road. For once wouldn't it be good to build something rather than destroy it?"

"What I'd like to know," Cash drawled, "is when you became a missionary?"

"What are you talking about?"

"When did you decide our purpose was to help people? I thought we came here to kill the bad guys, take our money, and leave."

"But wouldn't it be better—"

"Better, my butt. I'm in this for the money."

Sullivan snorted, the first noise he'd made since Reese came into the room. "You'd better not let it get around how cheap Daniel Cash hires out his gun or we'll have more jobs than we know what to do with."

Cash narrowed his eyes. "Watch your mouth, breed."

"*Hombres,* calm yourselves. We know why we came. *El capitán* called. That was what we agreed to all those years ago. We are six who become one. If one calls, the others answer. The money does not matter. What matters is the loyalty and honor."

"Speak for yourself, kid."

"I think Reese might be on to somethin' here."

Jed ignored the bickering as if it had never happened. "I'm all for not gettin' killed. And if we can convince El Diablo that he'd be wise to get out of Texas—or at least our little corner—I say we try it."

"I say givin' women guns is askin' for trouble," Cash insisted. "Although El Diablo might die laughing when he sees all those skirts flappin'."

Reese got up and poured himself some coffee. "As long as he dies, that would be fine with me. What do the rest of you think?"

No one said a word. Cash swore. "They'll do whatever you think is best, Reese. And I'll keep out of it. Just don't ask me to help. I've got better things to do than waste my time with good women."

"Drink and gamble?"

"What else is there?"

Nate poured whiskey into his coffee. "I have to agree."

Reese rubbed his forehead. He'd won the battle, but with these guys, the war just kept on raging.

Amid a lesson on the decline of the Spanish Inquisition, Mary felt as if she were being watched. Not an uncommon occurrence, considering her profession, but when she looked up to see Rico lounging in the doorway, she gasped and put a hand to her pounding heart.

The children turned around, too, and Mary berated herself for frightening them. Considering what had been going on in Rock Creek, the children had been bearing up remarkably well, but then children always did.

you, *señorita,* the sound of your laugh is like the water gurgling in springtime."

Carrie's hands dropped from her mouth, now open in an "O" of amazement. "Thank you," she whispered.

Frank and Jack rolled their eyes and groaned. Mary glared at them, and they stopped, an improvement over yesterday. She had to hide her own reaction as Rico strolled from the room and Carrie watched him go, her eyes glazed with fascination. Rico had gained an admirer.

Mary spent the rest of the day teaching with only half her attention, the other half occupied with listing the women she would have to speak to that afternoon and evening. And always, off in a tiny corner of her mind, nagged a question: Was Reese avoiding her? And if so, how would she make him stop?

Eight

Mary didn't see Reese the entire day. Since she ran from one end of town to the next, speaking with every widow, daughter, and mother she could find over the age of sixteen, she concluded he *was* avoiding her.

Come dawn, Reese would be unable to avoid her any longer. Though with over a dozen women present, as well as his men, perhaps it would be easier to elude her than ever before.

As Mary made her rounds, she was both excited and anxious. If her idea worked, Rock Creek would not be subject to the whim of every band of outlaws and cutthroats that drifted through this part of Texas.

The people could make El Diablo leave by a show of force instead of hired murder, and the people could continue to keep their homes safe. She wished she'd thought of this before hiring Reese and his friends, but there would have been no one to teach them if not for those same men.

Along with her excitement over the possibilities came anxiety over the decided lack of enthusiasm from the Rock Creek women. They nodded and smiled when Mary made her speech, then noted the place and time and wished her good day. She left every house feeling as if she'd done something slightly scandalous.

Only Jo expressed unbounded zeal when Mary came to call, yet she would have to sneak out to take part in the operation, since Reverend Clancy would preach Hellfire once he found out. And he would, sooner or later. Mary was hoping for later.

With the lukewarm response of the majority, Mary should not have been surprised to receive one vehement protest in the form of Baxter Sutton. She and Rose were talking at the front of the store when Baxter butted in.

"No wife of mine is going near those men." Rose blanched at the sound of her husband's voice and moved away as if Mary had the plague. "I never asked you to bring them here in the first place, Miss McKendrick."

"You're angry because they pulled guns on you, and you have every right to be."

"They're a disgrace—thieves and murderers you've brought amid decent folk—and they should be run out of town."

Mary had been willing to give Sutton a few inches, but as usual, he took the whole mile. "Need I remind you that if not for them we'd all be run out of town?"

He sniffed. "That remained to be seen. You never give things a chance to work themselves out. Even with the twins, you don't give them a chance."

"To set fire to the schoolhouse?" Mary murmured.

"That's just what I mean. They weren't going to burn it. They were just playing."

"With fire and whitewashed boards?"

Sutton waved away those little details. "At the first sign of trouble, you plow ahead, run roughshod over everyone. It's little wonder you've never married. At first I thought it was because you're so plain, but in the dark that doesn't matter."

"Baxter!" Rose gasped, but when he scowled at her, she grew quiet; then her face flushed red, and she stopped looking at Mary altogether.

"You can overlook a plain face, but a woman who can't shut up, who won't stop tellin' a man what to do, that's another matter entirely. That doesn't go away when the lights go out. So like I said, I can see why you're a spinster."

Mary tightened her lips to keep hateful words from tumbling forth. As Sister Hortensia always said, "Two wrongs do not make a right." Being mean to Baxter would not turn him miraculously into a decent human being, otherwise she'd have done it a long time ago.

Mary took a deep, calming breath, then another and another until the desire to kick Baxter Sutton in his skinny shins went away. "My state of matrimony, or lack of it, is not the issue. The issue is life and death. I can't understand why you wouldn't want Rose to be able to protect herself."

"She doesn't need to protect herself. She's got me."

Pointing out that Sutton was so terrified of El Diablo that he'd never once ventured outside when the bandit rode into Rock Creek was probably not the best course of action, no matter how vindicating such a reprisal might be.

"If you don't want Rose to come, then why don't you?"

"Me?" He blinked at her bug-eyed. "Me? I know how to use a gun! Do you think I don't know how to use a gun? Just because I don't walk down the street with a gun in my hands doesn't mean I don't know how to use one. You know what they say about guys with big guns, don't you?"

Mary opened her mouth, then shut it, stumped. Sutton snickered. "That's what I thought."

Sister Hortensia forgive her, but she'd had enough. "At least Reese and his men have grit."

His beady eyes narrowed. "If it takes grit to kill someone, then I'd rather be without it, thank you."

"You're without a spine, that's for sure."

He went red, started sputtering, and pointed at the door, so before he could throw her out bodily, Mary went. She really should learn to keep her mouth shut and her opinions to herself, but sometimes that was just too much to ask.

Mary didn't sleep well that night, and in the morning she awakened long before light tinted the eastern horizon. Meandering into the parlor, she leaned over and blew out the lamp in the window, then opened the curtains and stared up at the steeple.

Since the first night she'd watched Reese go into the church and appear in the bell tower, she'd kept a lamp burning. The thought of being up there all alone, all night long, with the whistling Texas wind in her face had made her shiver. She hadn't wanted Reese, or any of the others, to feel that alone, so she'd started leaving the lamp in the window. Whether they even saw the light or cared, she didn't know, but it made her feel better.

After dressing for the day, Mary unearthed the gun that had come with the cabin. No house in Texas seemed to be without one, but that didn't mean every owner could hit the broad side of a barn if they pulled the trigger.

Hurrying toward the hotel, Mary observed a deserted Main Street. Where was everyone? The scent of smoke reached her seconds before she sighted the man who stood at the top of the steps, leaning against the porch post. Why was Reese the only one of the six outside?

As she approached, he blew smoke, slowly and deliberately, from between those lips she'd kissed, then tilted his head to peer at her from beneath the wide black brim of his hat. "Where is everyone, Miss McKendrick?"

They were back to "Miss" again. There would be no mention of their passionate embrace, and that was probably for the best. Still, it irked her that the man could look her in the eye and pretend he'd never had that mouth on her neck—and various other places.

She straightened her spine. "I could ask you the same question."

"I'm here."

"But where are the rest of your men?"

He took his time answering, drawing in a mouthful of smoke, then allowing the gray whirl to drift away on the stillness. "The two that were on watch last night are sleeping. Two more will be on watch while we work. I think I'll be enough for this morning. It doesn't look like we're drawing a crowd."

"I'd hoped for more than me." She turned to look down the street, then sighed when she saw it remained deserted. "I don't understand this."

"How many said they would come?"

She looked at her feet. "One."

"Just you?"

"One besides me."

"Let me guess, your little friend Miss Clancy?" Mary nodded. "I wouldn't depend on her. From the reverend's manner, he doesn't like us much. No one does."

Mary looked up. "I do."

Their eyes met, and sparks ignited. He cursed and pinched the tiny butt of his cigarette between his thumb and forefinger before holding it to his lips for one final drag. Then he flicked the remains to the dirt, descended the steps, and ground the embers into nothing.

"How did you get this town to agree to hiring us? I know you manage things awfully well, Miss Mary, but the way folks are behaving, they didn't want us here at all."

"No one else had a plan—or any money."

He laughed. "Money does talk."

"They'll come around; you'll see."

"It doesn't matter if they do or they don't. I won't be here long enough to care."

"Then why do you care if they don't want you here?"

"I just don't want a bullet in the back."

It was her turn to laugh. "If they couldn't shoot El Diablo, I doubt they'll be able to shoot you."

"True enough."

Mary tightened her fingers around the barrel of the rifle. "Show me how to use this thing."

The words came out sounding like an order, and when Reese raised a brow, Mary colored. Why did she always manage everything? Because someone had to.

"Sorry," she said. "Would you *please* show me how to use this thing?"

"What about the others? This isn't going to work if there's only you standing with us against El Diablo. The idea was to make a show of force."

"We will. Let's just continue. Once everyone sees what I'm doing, once they think on things awhile, I'm sure they'll join in. If not today or tomorrow, eventually."

"We don't have until eventually."

"Please, Reese. I can't quit before I even try."

"Why can't you just let me and the others take care of this. A few weeks . . ." He shrugged. "They'll all be buzzard bait."

Mary winced. "Thank you for that image."

"You hired us to kill them. Let us do what we do best."

"I did *not* hire you to kill them. I don't want their deaths on my conscience for the rest of my life."

"You're crazy, lady."

"I've been called worse."

She heard the echo of her words and frowned.

They'd had this conversation before, but the other way around.

Were they so alike they were starting to speak each other's thoughts? How could she, a plain spinster schoolteacher, raised by nuns, have anything in common with a handsome captain of mercenaries? But she did. More than she had in common with any of the people in this town—even Jo. Mary felt as if she knew Reese, deep down inside, which was silly, since she knew nothing about him—not even his true name.

"I was raised to respect life," she said quietly.

"Those men respect nothing but their own desires. You can't fight men like that with Christian platitudes."

"Why not?" *LCO.*"Aargh!" He threw up his hands. "There's no arguing with you."

"I'm glad you finally agree. Now, where shall we have our lesson?"

At first, Reese looked as if he wanted to shake her; then he started to laugh, a rusty sound, rarely used. When Mary thought back on the days she'd known him, she could think of few times when he'd laughed, and never like this. She smiled shyly, uncertain of what she'd done that was funny, but if it made him laugh, then she wanted to do it again.

Reese walked over and put his hand on her rifle as if to take it. Mary held on.

"I just wanted to carry your gun, Miss McKendrick. Kind of like carrying your books home from school."

Bewildered, she let him take the weapon. He

checked the chamber, then put the barrel over his shoulder. "I made a place yesterday afternoon, out past the end of town, away from the livery and the animals. Got some hay bales from the barn and some burlap flour sacks from old Baxter. That man is one cranky son of a bitch."

Mary opened her mouth to correct his French, then closed it again. Baxter was exactly what he'd said. She wasn't going to waste breath arguing about that.

"Let's go shoot some flour sacks, Miss Mary." He held out his arm. "Just you and me."

As stupid choices went, agreeing to teach Mary how to shoot—just the two of them—was one of Reese's stupidest.

She wasn't *trying* to drive him mad with lust. Mary wouldn't know how, which was the reason Reese remained in a constant state of arousal for the entire lesson.

Her innocence stirred him. She might be a spinster lady, all on her own in the wilds of Texas, managing a town of cowards, fools, and women as if she were Stonewall Jackson himself, but she had no idea of her own appeal, which only made her more appealing.

He'd shown her how to load the rifle. That had been the easy part. Showing her how to hold the weapon meant he had to touch her. Mary's skin was the softest thing Reese had ever known. Just skimming her pale hands with his palms made them hum to touch her everywhere.

Showing her how to fire the gun meant he had to move up close behind and put his arms around her. She kept bumping her backside against his groin. The first time, he'd hissed in pain; after that, he'd started to like it.

She had no idea what she was doing. If she turned around and saw his state, she'd probably think she'd bruised him so badly he was swollen. Then she'd want to bandage it and kiss it better.

Reese cursed.

Mary's shot went wide of every hay bale in line. "I'm sorry! I'll keep trying."

He grunted. If she kept trying, she wouldn't be looking at him, which was a good thing. But if anyone else happened to wander by their class, they would know exactly what was the matter with him, especially his men.

Reese tugged his shirt out of his pants so that the material hung to his thighs. He did not need the men teasing him in front of Mary. They'd ruin her radiant innocence with their big mouths alone.

Of course, if he kept letting her bump her backside against him, he'd ruin her innocence for real. And that could not happen. She might be innocent, but he was far from it. He knew what would occur if he took what he wanted. She'd never be the same again, and neither would he. He needed to stop torturing himself with promises of something that could never, ever, be.

"How long did it take you to learn how to shoot a gun?"

Reese glanced at Mary with narrowed eyes, but

she was still sighting down the barrel, attempting to hit something other than nothing.

She pulled the trigger. "Oh!" she exclaimed when the bullet plunged into a corner of a burlap sack. "I hit something!"

"Was that what you were aiming at?"

She put the rifle down and glanced over her shoulder sheepishly. "I was shooting at the one two bales over."

He couldn't help it; he grinned. She was absolutely hopeless with a gun. Probably because she didn't want to hurt the damned hay.

She smiled back. "So how long did it take you to learn?"

He didn't want to share his past with anyone, but a few selected memories might cool him off quicker than jumping in the river. What harm could there be in answering a question? "My father taught me to hunt when I was a boy."

"Your father? Is he still alive?"

Pain flooded him; recriminations, too. Here was the harm. You couldn't select memories. God knows he'd tried. Memories came unbidden.

"Yes," Reese said, shortly. "He's still alive."

"And your mother?"

"Yes."

"Where do they live?"

"At home."

"In Georgia?"

He brought his gaze, which had focused on the distant hills, back to her. Well, one thing for certain, he no longer had to worry about Mary, or anyone else, wondering what he had hidden in his pants. Speaking of home had taken care of any lingering, lustful thoughts.

"How did you know I was from Georgia?" he demanded, ready to kick someone's rear into the next county. The men knew better than to talk about him to anyone else.

"I didn't for certain. Your horse—Atlanta. And your accent." She sighed. "Your voice reminds me of a long time ago."

"I thought you were from Virginia."

"I am. Your voice sounds like Virginia, only more. When I close my eyes and listen to you speak"—she closed her eyes and took a deep breath—"I can smell the trees. I can almost hear the rain. You know, sometimes it would snow, just a bit, on the magnolia blossoms. They looked like sugar-coated candy flowers. I've never seen anything so beautiful—not before or since."

Reese had seen something more beautiful. As good memories trickled over her face, he found himself trapped into watching her. She had the most amazing skin—pale and perfect but not white like a ghost, a tint of color, peach, perhaps, definitely not rose—and those freckles across her nose; he wanted to taste them with his tongue.

"I love Rock Creek." He started and yanked his gaze back to her eyes. Thankfully, she still had them closed. "But sometimes I miss green grass, cool winds, a real spring. The smells and sounds of Virginia are so much different than here."

Her chest rose and fell as if she were trying to capture a scent of grass and wind rather than tumbleweeds and dust; then his gaze slid from her closed eyes. For a thin woman she had an ample breast. He could probably span her waist with his hands, yet still run his thumbs along the ripe swell of—

Well, hell, he was having problems with his pants again.

"That's enough for today," he said.

Her eyes snapped open, and her cheeks flushed. Definitely peach. What had she been thinking of besides rain and magnolia trees?

Reese turned away and adjusted his shirt. He didn't want to know.

Rico had the day free. Big deal. Nothing to do in Rock Creek but watch the dust fly and listen to Miss McKendrick shoot. From the amount of shots being fired, she was *muy mala* with a gun.

The day began to look up when someone started to follow him long about midday. That someone was pretty good, too, but not good enough to be Sullivan. Sinclair Sullivan had seen Rico's gift the moment they'd met.

Rico had been fifteen, and Sullivan—Who knew how old Sullivan was. Sometimes when Rico looked into his friend's eyes, he saw an ancient soul very like his own. Sullivan had taken Rico under his wing and taught him everything he knew about quiet and deadly. As a result, only Sullivan ever sneaked up on Rico, which made for very few surprises in his life. That suited Rico just fine. He did not enjoy surprises. That's why he always made sure he was the one doing the surprising.

The footfalls behind him were so light as to be nearly indistinguishable, and if he leaned against a building as if to light a cigarette, by the time he turned just so, the follower was always gone.

If he'd been a superstitious man, he might think ghosts haunted him—and after all these years. But Rico was not a man who believed in ghosts—or anything much at all beyond the power of steel and the loyalty of five men. So he kept walking, waiting for his stalker to make a mistake. They always did.

There wasn't a helluva lot of town to wander through and no dark alleyways, since there was only a street and a half to Rock Creek. But an hour after he'd first heard the shuffle behind him, another came, much closer, and Rico spun about, then grabbed a swatch of pale yellow before it disappeared around the corner of the last building on Main Street.

He yanked on the yellow material, and the little girl from Miss McKendrick's class popped out, surprising him—a man who was never surprised.

"Why aren't you in school?" he demanded. She shrugged and tugged her dress from his fingers. "Won't you get in trouble with your teacher?"

She shook her head, making her brown braids fly. She had big brown eyes, too, and right now they were focused on Rico with utter adoration. No one had looked at him like that since . . .

A chill ran over him. Ghosts were *not* real. Just because this child looked very much like his little sister meant nothing. Anna had become an angel when she was this child's age, but that had been over ten years ago. Or at least he thought Anna was an angel; he had left before he had to watch her die.

This child, however, was very much alive. For the moment. She needed to stop following desperate, knife-wielding men.

Rico went down on one knee so he could talk to her face-to-face. She smiled, climbed upon his other knee, and put her arms around his neck. Rico froze.

She smelled just like Anna—a combination of soap and sweetness that only little girls possessed.

"Wh-what are you doing?"

She kissed him on the cheek. Rico swallowed the heated lump that had suddenly appeared in his throat, put her off his knee, and stood. She latched onto his leg. He sighed. "What's your name?"

"Carrie."

"That's right—"

"Of course it's right." She sniffed with all the outrage of six going on twenty. "I know my name."

"You shouldn't follow people. That's spying."

She let go of his leg, but not before giving him a quick squeeze, reminiscent of a hug, if he wasn't mistaken. "But I'm very good at it. Everyone says so. I heard you were, too, so I thought I'd see just how good I was. And I was good, wasn't I?"

"You shouldn't follow men like me. You'll get into trouble."

"No I won't. No one cares what I do. Except Miss McKendrick. She won't notice if I'm gone a day, but I'll have to go to school tomorrow or she'll show up at my house. She did last time, and Grand-dad was mad."

"You live with your granddad?"

"Uh-huh. On account of Daddy died at Fredericks-burg and Mama ran off with a damned tinker."

Rico blinked at the profanity coming out of that sweet bowed mouth. "You should not swear."

"No one cares except—"

"Miss McKendrick," Rico finished. "Well, if your granddad was mad that you weren't in school, then he cares about you."

"Nah, he was just mad 'cause it looked bad for the teacher to come. He gets upset when things look bad. Like Mama runnin' off. That looked real bad."

Rico could understand that. "You need to go back to school. Someone's going to notice you're wandering about town."

"Probably not. I sneak almost as good as you."

"Almost," he agreed. "Shall I take you back to school?"

Her eyes went wide. "You'd do that?"

"Certainly, *señorita.*"

She grabbed his hand and held on tight. Rico looked down, and Carrie grinned wide enough for him to see her missing front teeth. Anna had been missing the same two teeth the last time he'd seen her.

Rico's heart did a funny flip-flop and became lost to the angel in pigtails.

Nine

The next morning, and the next, Mary and Reese met at dawn and walked to the hay bales. No one else came despite repeated attempts on Mary's part to entice them. She'd even gone to Jo, but for the first time, her dear friend had been no help. Jo had the misbegotten idea that Nate Lang needed a friend, and Jo was going to be one. Nate needed Jo more than Mary did, or at least that's how Jo saw it, and therefore she could not anger her father any further by defying him on the matter of guns as well as Nate.

Jo did inform Mary why the rest of the women did not seek out lessons. It seemed Baxter Sutton had convinced everyone that the six men Mary had hired were killers and thieves. No decent woman would go near them.

Mary knew where that put her in Baxter's opinion; not that she cared so much what he thought. The town was another matter. No doubt she'd hear about the entire incident in a thinly veiled attack during Sunday's sermon. But neither Clancy nor Sutton would stop her from doing what must be done. Mary believed in finishing what she began.

Things would work out. The women would come around—somehow.

Since that first morning, when they'd shared a conversation, Reese had barely spoken to her beyond grunts and sharply worded orders. She'd managed to hit a few things she aimed at, but she could tell that Reese was disgusted with her. To Mary, being unable to hit what she aimed at was not exactly a bad thing, but she kept that opinion to herself.

Reese no longer touched her, either, and that *was* a bad thing. But she couldn't very well ask him to touch her with his rough, albeit gentle, fingers or encircle her body with his strong arms or let his breath brush her hair, then her brow, then her cheek, now, could she? Even though she wanted to.

Mary didn't blame Reese for keeping his distance. Every time he came near her, she acted like an idiot. Staring at him, questioning him, kissing him. No doubt he didn't want to hurt her feelings by saying he did not want to kiss again someone as plain and naive and old as she.

So Mary kept her distance, too, and she did what Reese told her, and she tried not to stare at him too much while he gazed at the distant hills. But sometimes the silence between them spoke too loudly to be ignored.

"When do you think El Diablo will come back?" Mary asked, loading her gun for one final round of practice.

She felt him glance at her, then away. "Hard to say. He lost three men last time. He may try and replace them, wait and see if we leave, or come at us harder any minute now."

"Wonderful," Mary muttered, and fired at her favorite hay bale.

The bullet hit the dirt several feet behind the target, and Reese gave a long-suffering sigh.

Mary bit her lip and narrowed her eyes on that blasted bale. She managed everything else, why couldn't she manage this? Just once she wanted Reese to praise her.

Tucking the rifle more tightly against her shoulder, she fired one shot after another without thinking or aiming. When the echoes died away, Mary stared at the holes in the target.

Reese appeared at her side. "Not bad. What did you do differently?"

"I got mad."

"Maybe you should get mad more often."

He took the gun from her hand, and the butt slid across Mary's shoulder. Her hiss of pain echoed loudly in the stillness that had followed her shots.

Reese went still. "Why did you do that?"

"It's nothing. I'm not used to having a gun kick my shoulder twenty times a day. I'll get used to it."

She leaned down to pick up her ammunition, and her dress, loose at the bodice because Reese had made her stop wearing a corset the third day in an effort to improve her aim, slid free of her shoulder.

"What in hell is that?" The rifle clattered to the ground as he stepped closer and peered at the riot of colors decorating the hollow of her shoulder.

"I told you—nothing. It'll go away." Mary tugged her dress back where it belonged and turned away from his view, irrationally embarrassed to have him see the bruise.

His fingers closed around her good shoulder. Gently, he tugged her back to face him. "You've been banging that rifle against a bruised shoulder day after day?"

Mary shrugged, then winced at the pain caused by that simple movement. Reese cursed, and his hand shifted, fingers moving her dress aside so he could stare at the purple, yellow, and green oblong mark on her skin.

His gaze flicked from the bruise to her eyes, and she saw a question there that she did not comprehend. Then his gaze went back to her shoulder, and his fingers drifted gently across the injury.

She sighed at his touch, arched against his hand before she could stop herself. When Reese touched her, all the pain went away. Silly old maid.

He stepped closer; her skirt brushed his thigh. "My mama always said . . ."

Her eyes widened as his golden head dipped. "What?" she breathed.

"A kiss will make it better."

Her mouth opened, to protest or beg, she wasn't sure which, but when his lips feathered over her aching flesh, she clamped her mouth shut so she wouldn't moan aloud.

A wet tickle slid across her skin. Had he licked her? No, why would he do that? But the thought of it made her wet, lower and deeper. Her body felt on fire, pins and needles here, there, everywhere.

She raised her hands to his shoulders—to push him away or draw him closer? Confusion flooded her. How could a kiss to make it better make things worse?

"Reese?" Her voice sounded hoarse, the voice of a woman she did not recognize. Although this man touched her in the deepest part of her mind, body, and soul, she didn't even know his real name.

When she touched him, he stiffened, then sighed. His breath brushed her flesh, and she shivered at the combination of hot breath along wet skin. He *had* put his tongue on her, and she wanted him to do it again. Instead, he kissed her pain once more, gently, as a parent might soothe an injured child, then he straightened. Without so much as a glance at her face, he returned her dress to her shoulder and walked away.

The next morning, at dawn, Rico awaited her on the front porch of the hotel.

Mary felt as if she'd been slapped. Even Rico's cheery disposition and outrageously flirtatious behavior could not help her today.

"*El capitán* says you must learn to use a knife, *señorita.*"

"He does, does he? Who died and made him God?"

"Quite a lot of people, actually. Now come, we will use the targets, but we will stand a bit closer. A knife is nothing like a gun, but I enjoy them."

Rico put his hand at the small of her back as if they were going for a stroll on a Sunday afternoon. Reese always stalked off, expecting her to keep up or be left behind. So why did she find the man so appealing when in comparison with most others he was a rude lout? She had no idea.

Rico opened a case of matched, lethal-looking silver knives. He traced the handles with dark fingers, his sooty, long lashes shadowing his cheekbones. His skin was copper and as smooth as a child's, though she had seen stubble grace his chin long about sundown. The man was so beautiful it was a disgrace, but Mary didn't feel a thing for him beyond amused fondness.

"Those look expensive," she said.

He glanced up, and for a moment his eyes were unfocused, as if he'd been looking into the past. He blinked, centered his gaze on Mary, then shrugged. "They get the job done."

Rico gathered the weapons and in one swift, fluid motion turned and threw them one after the other at a burlap sack. When he finished, a semicircle of knives stuck from the middle.

"Tell me you were shooting those at a hay bale two bales down," Mary muttered.

He turned around and grinned, white teeth flashing between full auburn lips. "I do not think so, *señorita*. What I aim for I hit. Otherwise I would be no good at my job."

"Which is?"

His smile died. "You know my job."

"Spying?"

He walked over to the bale and pulled out the knives. "Among other things. I see very well in the dark."

Spying, knives, darkness? Assassin? No, Reese

would not send this boy out to slit throats in the dark of night. Would he?

"What things?" she demanded.

"Things I would not tell a lady."

"I wouldn't mind."

He turned and approached. "I'm sure you would not. Unlike many ladies I know, you are strong."

"I'm sorry."

"Do not apologize for who you are. You are unique. And you will survive here. Texas eats ladies for lunch. But you, I think, will eat Texas." He winked and handed her one of the knives.

She held the weapon gingerly.

"Tsk, tsk," Rico scolded. "The knife handle will not cut you. Throw it."

She tried to throw the knife exactly as Rico had. The blade stuck in the dirt halfway between Mary and the hay.

Her gaze went to Rico. At least he wasn't laughing.

"Here." He positioned himself behind her, just as Reese had done, but she did not enjoy it half as much. He put his hand over hers and pulled them both back. "Like so. We will move our arms forward, and when I say 'release,' do so."

Rico pulled her arm back, and Mary's body aligned to his. He had a very nice body, but all she could think about was that Reese had sent this child in his place, and her anger returned.

"Release!" Rico murmured in her ear.

She jumped, let the knife go, and the weapon fell to the ground with a thud, narrowly missing her foot.

Rico sighed. "Perhaps we should forget knife throwing. It is, after all, a special skill. I am not much of a teacher, and I did not think this through. We should work on the hiding and retrieving of knives first."

"Hiding?"

"Upon your person."

Mary gave him her Miss McKendrick glare, and Rico laughed. "Ah, when you look at me like that, *señorita,* I feel like a child again."

"You are a child."

"At heart, perhaps. Now, tell me, how many knives do you think I am carrying?"

"Besides the bowie?"

"That is obvious, *sí?*"

Mary looked at the immense sheath filled with steel that rested on his hip. "Very obvious."

"Do you see anything else?"

She looked him over but could not find any telltale signs of weaponry. "There's probably one in your boot."

"*Sí.*" He withdrew a thin silver blade from his left boot. "Now watch closely."

With movements so graceful as to be a dance, he withdrew a matching blade from his other boot, a knife from his back pocket, one from a sheath on his forearm, and another from somewhere inside his shirt. The blades dropped at his feet with a clatter to emphasize each one.

"What about your hat?" she asked sarcastically.

He raised a black eyebrow, removed his well-worn hat, and withdrew another knife——this one short and squat——the perfect size to fit into the crown. "I'd forgotten that one. I haven't had to use it in a very long time."

"One knife is never enough?"

"Why have one when you can have seven?"

Mary's lips twitched. He was incorrigible. If he'd been in her class, she'd have had a hard time punishing him for insubordination. He did everything with such flare.

Rico bent to pick up his arsenal. "And now we will discover the best place to hide a knife on Miss McKendrick, and you will practice retrieving the knife."

"What good is a knife if you have a gun and so do they?"

"A knife never runs out of bullets and is better than nothing when it's just you and a very bad man. As long as you have one knife left, you have a chance. I cannot tell you how many times I have saved my life, and that of my friends, with one last knife. Humor me, *señorita*. *Mi capitán* said you must learn about knives."

His words brought back yesterday's lesson, the sensual interlude she and Reese had shared, all she had felt for the man and how little he must feel for her, since he'd ordered Rico to train her like a dog. Unaccustomed annoyance returned.

"Do you always do whatever Reese says?"

In the process of returning his knives to their homes, he did not look at her. "I like him to think so."

"Why? Are you afraid of him?"

"Isn't everyone?"

"No."

"They should be."

"Why?" Mary paused in her questions when she realized that Rico had told her nothing very politely. Time to get more specific. "What has Reese done that makes men like you follow him as if he were General Lee."

Rico's teasing manner evaporated, and his dark gaze rested on Mary's flushed face. "That is for *el capitán* to say. If he wishes for you to know."

She ignored the warning in his eyes and kept on asking. "You all met in the war? How?"

"I cannot say."

"It's a secret?"

He shrugged. "Perhaps I do not wish to talk about those days any more than *el capitán* does. The times were bad."

"What's his real name?"

"How would I know?"

"You followed the man to hell and back and you don't know his name?"

"Reese."

"First name or last?"

"I do not know."

"Fine, then why do you call him captain? He said he wasn't your captain."

Rico shot her a quick, dark, unreadable glance. "He said that?"

"Yes."

"He lied."

Mary frowned. "Why would he lie?"

"Ask him. Now . . ." He flipped a small, thin knife end over end, then caught it lithely by the handle. "Would this work better in a garter on your thigh or perhaps in a sheath beneath your chemise?"

Mary blushed. "Rico Salvatore, watch your mouth!"

His head tilted as if he were listening to something far away. Then he grinned a devilish grin and inched closer, then closer still. Too close for Mary, so she stepped back and promptly stepped on her skirt.

Rico grabbed her around the waist. "I'd much rather watch *your* mouth, Miss McKendrick." His gaze lowered to her lips.

She could have made him stop, but the devil inside whispered—perhaps it wasn't Reese who fascinated her so but merely the act of kissing.

So she said nothing when Rico kissed her. The man was no doubt quite skilled from extensive practice, but Mary felt nothing when his mouth touched hers. No sparkle, no warmth, no lightning or thunder. In fact, an irresistible urge to laugh came over her, and she choked.

Rico pulled back with a frown. "Were you laughing?"

Her eyes went wide. "Of course not."

"Most women would not dare."

"I'm not most women."

He smiled. "I like you, Miss McKendrick. You have *cojónes.*"

"Somehow I don't think that means I smell good."

"Well, you do."

"What in hell do you think you're doing, kid?" The growl was unmistakable. *Reese.*

* * *

The rage that rushed through Reese at the sight of Rico with his smart mouth all over Mary's surprised him. What had he thought would happen when he sent the kid in his place to teach Mary about knives? That Rico would actually teach her about knives and keep his hands to himself? Reese wasn't that stupid.

At the sound of his voice, Mary stiffened in Rico's arms and tried to pull away, but Rico held on tight, staring at Reese over her shoulder with a sparkle in his eyes that made Reese realize the truth.

No one sneaked up on the kid—except Sullivan. Rico had heard him coming, and he had kissed Mary on purpose. Though to what purpose, Reese didn't know. He'd find out later. Even if he had to beat it out of him.

"What I am doing should be obvious," Rico said.

Reese growled again, and Rico let Mary go. She spun around, eyes wide, cheeks flushed, and her hands went to her mouth, but not before Reese saw her lips. Those lips that had only been kissed by him were now wet and red from another man.

What he felt must have shown on his face because Rico stepped between Mary and Reese, earning himself life instead of death because he thought of Mary first. "Relax, *Capitán*. she thought my kiss was hysterically funny."

Reese narrowed his gaze on Mary's face, and she burst out laughing.

The sparkle in Rico's eyes died. He might have

kissed Mary for reasons other than lust, but the fact that she was laughing about it provoked him. Reese almost felt sorry for the kid, who had the idea he was God's gift to women. Obviously, Mary didn't think so. Reese coughed to cover his own desire to join in her laughter.

"I-I'm sorry, Rico. You kiss very nicely, I'm sure. But I've never been kissed until the six of you came to town, and now two handsome men are kissing me. It's just too funny."

"Two men?" Rico raised his eyebrows. "Fascinating."

"Get lost, kid."

"But I am to teach the *señorita* about knives. We were just deciding if a knife would work better in her garter or beneath her chemise."

Reese's laughter died. "Get," he spat.

Rico didn't run; he strolled, but very fast.

Reese turned to Mary. He felt like a fool. It had been nine years since he'd been near a decent woman; and he should have stayed as far away from this one as he could get. She was killing him, and he deserved it.

After spending all of yesterday berating himself for touching her, kissing her, needing her, he had spent the night dreaming of her. When dawn threatened, he had been unable to face her; so, coward that he was, he'd sent Rico, then spent the next hour wondering what the two of them were doing.

Mary had stopped laughing and now stared at Reese as if she expected him to say something. He stared back, wondering if her bruise was any better and if he'd get to see the untouched flesh of her shoulder or kiss the soft skin above her breast ever again.

Why did she fascinate him more than any woman ever had, even the woman he would be married to right now if things had gone differently?

Because Mary looked at him as if he were still the man he had been once upon a time. But he would never be that man again, and Reese needed to remember that. The man he was now did not deserve to touch the hem of Mary McKendrick's dress, let alone put his mouth where he dreamed of putting it.

"Shouldn't you get off to school?" he asked.

"That's it?" She stepped toward him. "Go to school, Mary." Another step. "Be a good girl, Mary."

She kept coming until they stood toe to toe and he could smell the scent that was hers alone. His body responded in a predictable manner, and he gritted his teeth to keep from grabbing her and erasing any taste of Rico from her mouth and any memory of the kid's pretty face from her mind.

"Don't mention yesterday, Mary." She kicked dust over his boots.

"What are you mad about?"

"What do you think?" She put her nose in the air, spun on her heel, and walked back to town.

Reese watched her go and fought not to laugh. If he didn't lust after her so damned much, he'd like her even more.

Ten

"The days are becoming dull, Reese." Cash tossed another card onto the table.

He and Nate had found the saloon, which wasn't hard, for the building faced the hotel. But it was a mess. Broken bottles, broken windows, broken tables. Cash and Nate had taken one look at the place and nearly wept.

They'd decided to spend their free time restoring the saloon to some semblance of order so they could play cards and drink. As if being without a decent saloon had ever stopped either one of them from partaking of their favorite pastimes.

At any rate, Reese found the two of them, and Jed as well, ensconced in the saloon before ten A.M. that morning. Sullivan was in the tower, and Rico had disappeared. He'd been doing that a lot lately.

"Heard you nearly took the kid's head off this morning," Cash observed, eyes still on his cards.

"If I'd have wanted his head off, his head would be rolling in the street."

"Big talk." Jed tossed his cards in the center. "I fold."

"What the hell does that mean?"

"You treat that kid like he's your own. So you can be the one to kick his butt."

"What did he do now?"

"I don't know. But he's up to something. He keeps disappearing. Maybe he's got a *señorita* stashed somewhere. And that's gonna get us into trouble in this town. Every *señorita* here is someone's little girl or wife."

Reese cursed. "I *am* gonna kick his butt."

"Except for the woman who hired you, of course." Cash gathered his winnings. Nate still stared at his cards, though the hand was done. "She has no daddy in these parts."

"She's got no daddy at all," Reese said before he could stop himself.

"Oh, really?" Cash smiled thinly. "How convenient."

"What are you trying to say?"

"Just a little advice on women, Reese."

"I can handle women."

"Now that's something we're not certain of. You haven't touched a woman since Fort Sumter."

"Just because I don't let women hang all over me in every saloon between here and Abilene doesn't mean I haven't had a woman since 1861."

"Glad to hear it. Abstinence like that can rot a man's mind quicker than whiskey."

"Here, here." Nate threw his cards in the middle of the table and poured himself another drink.

"Myself, I like fallen women. They're far less trouble than the upright ones who expect more than money from a man. Those kind of women want your soul, too."

Since Reese's soul had been lost on a battlefield in Georgia, he had nothing to worry about.

"Lost my soul long time ago," Nate murmured to the bottom of his glass. "But not to a woman."

"Did you sell your soul to Satan?" Jed clapped a hand on Nate's back.

"Maybe." Nate drained his glass. "Maybe I did at that."

"As you can see"—Cash dealt the cards, leaving Nate out of the loop—"melancholy is setting in. The boys are bored, Reese. You promised us trouble, and there's no trouble to be had. I was lookin' forward to shootin' that Indian and his Yankee sidekick, but they seemed to have turned tail and run."

"That's what El Diablo wants us to think. The longer he waits to come back, the more bored we get, the sloppier we become. He lost the last battle, but if he waits long enough, he can win the war while we aren't paying attention."

"How do you know he hasn't run off to Mexico for good?"

"Because Sullivan has seen him watching us."

All three men sat up straight and frowned. Jed picked up his cards. "I didn't see anything when I was in the tower."

"Me, either," Cash and Nate agreed.

"Which means?"

Jed sighed. "Sullivan always sees what nobody else does."

"Exactly. So stay on your toes. There'll be trouble soon enough."

Reese left them to stew on that. The rest of the

Introducing Ballad,
A NEW LINE OF HISTORICAL ROMANCES

*A*s a lover of historical romance, you'll adore Ballad Romances. Written by today's most popular romance authors, every book in the Ballad line is not only an individual story, but part of a two to six book series as well. You can look forward to 4 new titles each month – each taking place at a different time and place in history.

But don't take our word for how wonderful these stories are! Accept our introductory shipment of 4 Ballad Romance novels – a $23.96 value – ABSOLUTELY FREE – and see for yourself!

*O*nce you've experienced your first 4 Ballad Romances, we're sure you'll want to continue receiving these wonderful historical romance novels each month – without ever having to leave your home – using our convenient and inexpensive home subscription service. Here's what you get for joining:

- *4 BRAND NEW Ballad Romances delivered to your door each month*
- *30% off the cover price of $5.99 with your home subscription.*
- *A FREE monthly newsletter filled with author interviews, book previews, special offers, and more!*
- *No risk or obligation…you're free to cancel whenever you wish… no questions asked.*

*T*o start your membership, simply complete and return the card provided. You'll receive your Introductory Shipment of 4 FREE Ballad Romances. Then, each month, as long as your account is in good standing, you will receive the 4 newest Ballad Romances. Each shipment will be yours to examine for 10 days. If you decide to keep the books, you'll pay the preferred home subscriber's price of $16.50 – a savings of 30% off the cover price! (plus $1.50 shipping & handling) If you want us to stop sending books, just say the word…it's that simple.

Passion-
Adventure-
Excitement-
Romance-
Ballad!

A $23.96 value – **FREE** No obligation to buy anything – ever.
4 FREE BOOKS are waiting for you! Just mail in the certificate below!

Get 4
Ballad
Historical
Romance
Novels
FREE!

BOOK CERTIFICATE

Yes! Please send me 4 Ballad Romances ABSOLUTELY FREE! After my introductory shipment, I will receive 4 new Ballad Romances each month to preview FREE for 10 days (as long as my account is in good standing). If I decide to keep the books, I will pay the money-saving preferred publisher's price of $16.50 plus $1.50 shipping and handling. That's 30% off the cover price. I may return the shipment within 10 days and owe nothing, and I may cancel my subscription at any time. The 4 FREE books will be mine to keep in any case.

Name_____

Address_____ Apt._____

City_____ State_____ Zip_____

Telephone (____)_____

Signature_____

(If under 18, parent or guardian must sign)

All orders subject to approval by Zebra Home Subscription Service.
Terms and prices subject to change. Offer valid only in the U.S.

DN091A

Passion...
Adventure...
Excitement...
Romance...

IlluliluulllullluululululululululullllIuIluI

BALLAD ROMANCES
Zebra Home Subscription Service, Inc.
P.O. Box 5214
Clifton NJ 07015-5214

PLACE
STAMP
HERE

day passed slowly. He wandered about. There was little to do but wait for El Diablo to return and hope they could kill all the bad guys next time around. Otherwise they'd be sitting in this godforsaken near ghost town forever.

Mary's idea of arming the populace seemed to have gone bust. Which was too bad, since it had been a good suggestion. Reese was all for less bloodshed. But if that wasn't going to happen, he would stick to his original plan of blasting every one of the invaders back to hell.

So should he continue to teach Mary about guns? The lessons would be useful to a woman alone. But was he convincing himself of the advantages for Mary's sake or his own?

He'd told Cash trouble was on the way, but Reese knew in his heart that trouble was already here. He wanted Mary more than he'd ever wanted anything else. And since he couldn't take her, his mind was distracted. A good way for a man like him to get himself killed.

No wonder the others were concerned. A leader whose brain was in his pants was no leader at all. But then he'd never said he was.

Long ago they'd elected him captain. He'd declined, but they'd just kept calling him "Captain" and following him around. Like sap on the trunk of a tree, those men were stuck to him. Oh, sure, they went their separate ways, but they always came back—like bad luck.

As Reese wandered about town, people continued to scatter out of his way. Their behavior was starting to get on his nerves. Should he tell

them he hadn't shot anyone for getting in his
way in at least a year? He suspected his attempt
at sarcastic humor would be lost on the people
of Rock Creek.

Every night, a different woman showed up with
a day's worth of food for six men. They plunked
their packages down in the kitchen and hightailed
it out of there as if the hotel were infested with
smallpox. Except for Jo Clancy, who chatted up a
storm, even though no one but Rico listened, then
trounced upstairs to see Nate.

Reese had tried to talk to both Nate and Miss
Clancy about their relationship. Both had looked
at him as if he were incredibly stupid.

Nate had said, "She's an infant, Reese. What
kind of man do you think I am?" And he'd looked
so hurt when he'd said it that Reese didn't have
the heart to answer.

Miss Clancy, on the other hand, had sneered at
him. "Nate needs a friend, and since you five are
worthless, I guess it'll have to be me."

Reese had thought he was being a mighty good
friend. How many times had he put Nate back in
the saddle? How many times had he covered the
man up with a horse blanket when he was dead
drunk in the corner of a saloon? How many times
had he backed Nate up in a fight that had come
about because Nate was pretty much pissed at the
world and everyone in it?

But somehow Reese doubted Miss Clancy would
think he was any kind of hero, and since Reese
had to agree, he let Nate and Miss Clancy do what-

ever it was they did when they were together. He'd
done his best to thwart disaster.

Reese reached the schoolhouse, and as he walked
by, he cast a glance that way, but school was out for
the day. Another glance at the cabin to the rear
revealed no one sitting on the porch and no movement behind the windows.

He hunched his shoulders and tugged on his
hat. He was acting like a lovesick schoolboy walking by her house, but he couldn't really help walking by, for there was only one street in Rock Creek
to walk on.

Reaching the hotel, he sat on the porch, having
no desire to go inside and play with the boys. Just
as he lit the match for his cigarette, Reese saw Mary
headed for the creek with a basket under her arm.

Where did she think she was going? How often
did she sneak off alone? And why?

The match burnt his thumb, and Reese dropped
it to the floor with a curse, then ground out the
flame with his boot. When he looked up, Mary was
gone.

He returned his cigarette to his vest pocket and
headed across the street, through the alley, and
down into the valley where the river ran.

The warmth of the day drew Mary to the water.
Spring slid toward summer, and soon the days
would be hot, miserable, and long. Once school
was out, she would have little to do but prepare
for next session. During other summers, in other
places, she had worked in hotels as a maid, served

food in a restaurant, waited on customers at a mercantile. But the way the wind had shifted in Rock Creek, there would be no summer job for the teacher.

She dropped her basket at the side of the river and pulled out her soap and washboard. In the winter she hauled water to the cabin, heated it, and scrubbed clothes on the porch. That way took twice as long and was twice as much work as washing clothes in the river. But she couldn't bear to stick her hands in the icy water that ran past in mid-January.

Today the water was tepid, almost soothing in the languid heat. She twirled her unmentionables in the river and contemplated the sun on the water.

Mary was a champion daydreamer. Always had been, even when Sister Hortensia forbade her. Daydreaming was not something you could stop on a whim—or a prayer. Daydreaming was a part of who you were.

As a child, Mary had had little choice but to dream about a past she did not know and a future that was frightening, to say the least. She had been left on the doorstep of St. Peter's with a note naming her Mary Margaret McKendrick—Irish, to be sure—and that was all she knew. So Mary had dreamed up a father who had died too young and a mother who had loved her enough to let her go. Only in that way could Mary forgive being left alone forever.

But despite her dreams, the questions always

haunted her. Why had she been left? Would no one ever love her? Or was she, perhaps, unlovable?

A heated breeze brushed her face, and Mary lifted her head to breathe the scented wind. Dust and grass and a hint of flowers—Texas in springtime. She loved Rock Creek more than any other town she had ever been to.

The other places in which she'd lived were gone now. Even St. Peter's stood empty, the victim of a cursed war. So Rock Creek was the home she'd dreamed up all those years ago and embellished upon whenever she'd desperately needed something to look forward to.

She'd wanted a home, friends, a place of her own making, a life she'd built herself. She'd learned in those years of being alone and dependent on the mercy of others that the only way to ensure survival was to make certain you could take care of yourself no matter what happened.

Mary had seen enough women depend on a man for everything. When the man departed—through death or design, it didn't matter—the woman was left with the children and no means by which to take care of any of them. The panic on the faces of those women when they knocked on the doors of St. Peter's had impressed itself upon Mary at a very young age.

She'd been almost glad to discover she wasn't marriage material. Herself, she could depend upon. She could manage just fine alone, and if the children she taught sometimes called to the motherly soul she hid, well, she could manage that, too.

While kissing Reese had shown her what was missing in her life—excitement, passion, vibrancy—she also knew that anything other than kissing might cost her everything she'd worked so long to accomplish. Teachers with bad reputations did not teach long. And teaching was all that stood between Mary and a life many other women were forced to lead.

She was a smart woman who made intelligent choices, with her mind and not her heart. She managed herself and others with that mind, and as long as she remembered what was important, her dream would come true. She was no longer a child who longed for love. How could you long for something you'd never known? Mary had learned to settle for the best that came along, and for her, the best was Rock Creek. She was not so foolish as to throw away her home for temptation's kiss.

Sighing, Mary wrung the water from her extra chemise. Sometimes being smart was no fun at all. But then, no one ever promised that life would be fun. Life was just . . . life.

A slight shuffle from right behind her was the only warning Mary had before strong arms trapped her hands at her sides. She dropped the chemise back into the water and took a deep breath to scream. A large, rough hand clamped over her mouth; the scream went right back down her throat and into her wildly beating heart. *Idiot*, her mind ranted, even as her body struggled. She had no gun, no knife, either, and even if she had, she would be unable to get to any weapon with her hands pinned. If she'd hidden a knife in her garter, as Rico had suggested, she might be able to get to the thing later, but with the knife back in a drawer at home, later wasn't going to help her.

Mary was so annoyed with herself, she nearly forgot to be afraid. Then a voice whispered in her ear, "You shouldn't come out alone; anything could happen."

She kicked Reese in the shins, and he released her. Spinning about, she was surprised to discover that her hands were clenched into fists.

Reese rubbed his leg. He looked almost as angry as she was. "I could easily have been El Diablo or one of his men, and they wouldn't let you go because you kicked them. They'd knock you over the head with the butt of their gun and take you wherever it is they go with unconscious women, and then . . . Well, never mind. Believe me, you'll wish they would have killed you rather than kidnapped you."

Though the sisters had not been very forthcoming, Mary had an idea of what he was referring to. She had no business thinking about man-woman things, though she had thought about them a lot since Reese came to town. But he was always the man, and she was always the woman. The thought of those things and a stranger, or ten, made Mary shiver with dread.

The fight went right out of her, and she dropped her hands and hugged herself. "You scared me to death." Her voice cracked in the middle, making her sound like a terrified child.

"Good. Maybe you won't wander off by yourself again and give me heart failure."

"You? What do you have to be scared about? You're a big, tough man with guns. You're the one who goes around terrifying women who are minding their own business!"

"What kind of business do you have out here all alone?"

"What does it look like? My laundry. Haven't you ever done laundry?

"Uh, no. Can't say that I have."

"I suppose you just buy new clothes every week?"

"I . . . um . . . give things to a woman in whatever town I'm in, and she brings them back clean."

For some reason, the thought of a different woman in every town doing Reese's laundry made Mary more angry than having him scare her old before her time. Laundry was a private thing. As private as kissing, and Mary had a sneaking suspicion that the woman who did Reese's laundry was also the woman he happened to be kissing in whatever town he was in. Well, she wasn't going to be next in that particular line.

"I suspect you'll be wanting me to do *your* laundry next?"

He raised an eyebrow. "Want to?"

"I don't even want to do my own."

She looked down at her basket of wet laundry, and a swatch of white, down the river a ways, caught her attention. "Oh, no, my chemise is drifting away!"

"Let it go."

"I will not." She began to stomp off after the undergarment, but Reese yanked her back.

"I'll buy you another."

"You will not! A man is not going to buy me unmentionables."

"A man like me?"

"Any man, blast it! Now I'm going to get my chemise."

His hand tightened on her arm. "No, you're not. Where the river disappears there into the trees she gets pretty deep. I'll be damned if I'll let you drown over a bit of cotton."

"What do you care if I drown? I already gave you everything."

"Not everything," he murmured, and his thumb stroked along the inside of her arm. "I care, Mary. I care too much; that's my problem."

All the anger and fear drained away as a pulsing sense of expectation took their place. "What are you saying?"

Using the arm he still held tightly, Reese pulled her against his chest. She could have struggled, but why, when she wanted to be nowhere else but there?

"You make me crazy, Mary." He tucked her head beneath his chin. She wanted to cuddle close and stay right there forever. "When I saw you come down here, I don't know what I thought. After seeing you with Rico—" He stopped, and in the silence that followed, Mary heard the steady beat of his heart beneath her ear. "I didn't know what would be worse, the thought of you just walking around out here, alone and vulnerable, or the thought of you meeting someone by the river."

"Meeting someone? Like Jo?"

He gave a short, sarcastic snort. "No, not Jo. A man."

"A man?" She tilted her head back to look him in the face. "What for?"

"This."

He kissed her—hard and long and deep. No longer untutored in the art, she met him stroke for stroke. Maybe she *would* do his laundry if he kept kissing her like this.

She let her hands wander over the breadth of his chest. When his tongue did fancy things with hers, her fingers tightened on his shoulders so she would not sink to the damp riverbank and melt into the river.

As he coaxed her tongue into his mouth with teasing traces, she knocked his hat from his head and allowed her fingers to wallow in the softness of his golden hair.

She wanted to kiss something other than his mouth. When he'd kissed her neck, then her bruise, she'd felt so many different things. Wonderful, amazing, world-shifting things. And she wanted him to feel that way, too.

She pulled her mouth away and trailed her lips over his chin. The stubble scratched and scraped, a new sensation, not altogether unpleasant.

Next, she tasted the hollow beneath his ear—salt and man. She liked the flavor, so she tasted the hollow at the base of his throat, too.

He moaned; the sound rumbled against her lips—another new sensation to add to her rapidly expanding repertoire. What she really wanted to discover was if the bronze hair on his chest that had haunted her nights since she'd seen him half-naked in Dallas was as soft as the hair on his head.

His shirt was unbuttoned to just beneath the curve of his throat. She raised trembling fingers and unbuttoned another button. His chest heaved as if he'd run a very long distance. That, combined with her clumsy hands, made the second button much harder to release than the first. And she took too long, because his hands came up and closed over hers, stilling her explorations.

"Mary." His whisper was the wind, a gentle brush against her temple, a sigh along her cheek.

She looked into his face, and the haunted sadness there made her catch her breath and tug one of her hands free to place her palm along his cheek. "What is it?"

"I should never have kissed you, not even once. Now I can't seem to stop."

"I don't want you to stop."

"Of course not. You have no idea what comes next."

"I have an idea."

His lips tilted at the corners, not a true smile but almost one; then he covered her hand with his and turned his cheek into her palm. "You'd have a lot more of an idea if I let this continue the way it's going. You need to be stronger than both of us. Call me a bastard and slap my face."

"I never swear, and how could I slap this face?" She flexed her fingers beneath his and stroked his cheek again. "I don't want to be strong tonight. Just once I'd like to be weak."

"But you're not weak. What were you thinking when you let me kiss you again?"

They were back to that. Mary dropped her hand and narrowed her eyes on the face that haunted her nights. "I was thinking a dangerous, handsome man wanted me, if only for a moment. Silly old maid that I am." She stepped away from the temptation of his touch.

He leaned down and picked up his hat, smacking it onto his head as his lips tightened. "You aren't silly or old." He reached out and yanked her back against him, tight and true. "And as you can no doubt feel, I *do* want you, for more than a moment. But I can't be the man you need, Mary. I can't stay."

She tugged free of his hold. With his body pressed to hers, she could not think. She could not breathe. "Who asked you to stay? What do you think I need?"

He closed his eyes and released a long sigh. "I'm not for you."

"I know I'm not pretty."

His eyes snapped back open, and anger filled them. "Who told you that?"

"I can see, Reese."

"Not very well."

"You don't have to tell me I'm pretty or anything else to be able to kiss me. This may be the only chance I have in my life to be kissed by a man like you."

"You're making me mad, Mary."

"Why? Because I'm practical. Why would a man like you want to kiss a woman like me unless you like kissing. And like Mr. Sutton said, a woman's a woman in the dark."

He was rubbing his forehead, and he stopped.

The stillness of his stance made her uneasy, even before his low-voiced question. "When did Sutton say that?"

"The other day," she said warily.

"Really?" Reese dropped his hand and glanced toward town.

Something about the way he held his fingers, curved and ready, made Mary go cold, and she began to babble. "It doesn't matter. He was angry. I make people angry because I say what I think. It's a failing I'm trying to correct."

"There's not a blasted thing wrong with you, and don't let that poor excuse for a man tell you there is."

His anger on her behalf warmed Mary's heart. No one had ever defended her before. She reached for his hand, and when he started to draw away from her touch, Mary held on tight. Holding hands was another thing she'd never done but found quite enjoyable. How could the simple act of placing palm against palm feel as if you were touching another person's heart with your own

"The sun's going down," she observed. "Is it safe to stay and watch awhile?"

Reese still stared at town. "Hmm? Oh, sure. If you like, I'll stay with you."

She smiled and squeezed his hand. "I like."

He looked at her as if she were a bit touched, and she smiled wider. He really was very sweet once you got past the guns and the swearing and the growling. She had a feeling few people took the time or braved the trouble—even the men who rode at his side. But Mary wasn't like most people.

"Your friends don't seem to know much about you." She leaned against his shoulder.

He grunted and went stiff, though he continued to hold her hand, most likely because she wouldn't let his go. "You've been asking questions about me?"

"Do you have something to hide?"

"Of course."

"A wife?"

He looked horrified. "Hell, no!"

Relief washed through her. She cast him a quick sideways glance, but he watched the western sky and not her, his face like stone, no expression there at all. "You needn't worry; the others didn't tell me anything."

"That's because they don't know anything."

"Not even your real name?"

"Especially that."

"Are you on the run? Are you wanted by someone?"

"Maybe."

"Do you know as little about your friends as they know about you?"

"They aren't my friends. They're good men who ride with me."

"Sounds like a friend to me."

"We aren't friends. We work together. I don't know about their families, their dreams, their nightmares, and I don't want to." "I don't understand. How can you go through life without friends?"

"I've had friends. And when they die in front of you, or in your arms sometimes, the more you know about them, the more it hurts."

"So you know nothing? You have no friends at all?"

"That's right."

The finality in his voice and the set look about his mouth made Mary swallow the rest of her arguments. Who was she to judge or preach? She had not seen what he had seen or lost what he had lost. She wanted to keep questioning him and find out why he was so bitter, but she couldn't. She wanted to heal him, and she didn't know how. So she let the subject drop and continued to hold his hand—because he continued to let her.

After a few moments, the silence became too loud. Mary had to fill it. "The sunsets here are like none I've ever seen, even in Virginia."

At her neutral change of subject, the tension flowed from his body in a nearly audible rush. "I don't get to watch many sunsets."

"You should. They're like a gift from God—so peaceful and soothing. Bit by bit the sun slips down, and the colors change even as you're watching. One minute there's light and heat. You can feel it on your face, smell it in the air. Then, the next minute, the sun is gone, and shadows spread over the land; everything goes cool and dark. Watch."

She glanced at him and found him watching her instead of the sun. "Watch." She pointed at the bright red ball perched upon the cusp of night. "It's like magic."

"Magic," he murmured. "I think you're right."

He kept looking at her, and she couldn't stop looking at him as the sun died and the shadows eclipsed them both. Something was happening here that went beyond anything Mary had ever experienced, and it *was* magic.

As the sun slipped away completely, a cool breeze drifted over the water, washing them in the scent of river and darkness.

"Miss McKendrick," Reese said, his voice as soft as the wind and the waves, "you're trying to seduce me."

"But, Reese, I wouldn't know how."

Eleven

Reese's body was on fire, his mind a bewildered haze. Mary's innocence was seduction itself and lured the wickedness roiling in his heart. She had no idea how she made him ache for the man he had once been—a man who was gone and never coming back.

If he told her his secrets, would she still offer her untainted mouth to his?

He wasn't going to find out. He was going to kiss her while he had the chance. Just one more time, he swore. Only one last time.

When his mouth touched hers, Mary still smiled at what she thought had been a joke. Little did she know, Reese hadn't made a joke since Stonewall Jackson died.

Her lips, curved from laughter, were as cool as midnight. She tasted like rain after a desert summer day, night fallen, dreams awakened. Her touch soothed his parched soul; her sigh of surrender filled him again with desire.

How many times had they kissed? He could not recall. Enough that they already knew the rhythm and the music. He kissed her gently at first, as light as her smile, as sweet as her eyes.

"Reese," she whispered against his mouth.

For a moment, he hesitated, the need to hear his real name from her lips nearly overwhelming. But to share that forgotten part of himself would be a fatal mistake. Instead, he kissed her less gently, more deeply, and they both forgot everything but this moment.

For a woman who had never been kissed before he came to town, she caught on right quick. The thought of anyone else kissing Mary's eager mouth made Reese see red. He couldn't believe he hadn't beaten the crap out of Rico for daring. But Reese knew the kid. Kissing Mary hadn't meant a thing to him. Not what her kiss had meant to Reese.

Tongues mating, teeth scraping, lips caressing. Shared breath, shared sunset, shared dreams. What was he thinking? This was lust, nothing more. Even though Mary was a woman reminiscent of the man he had once been, she was not a woman he could call his own. Not now or ever again.

The shots, when they came, did not at first penetrate Reese's jumbled mind. His senses were filled with Mary—the scent of soap, the taste of rain, the feel of a soft woman beneath his hard, rough hands. Then Mary tore her mouth from his, blinking at him owlishly beneath the painted sky.

They didn't even bother to ask the obvious question. Gunshots from town was the answer. They ran—together, holding hands. Later, Reese would wonder if he'd grabbed her or if she'd grabbed him. But the answer to that question wasn't half as disturbing as the fact that holding Mary's hand felt like something he'd been missing all his life.

Expecting to see El Diablo and crew blasting holes in Rock Creek, Reese was surprised to find the street deserted.

Slowly, the two of them walked down the boardwalk. Reese held tightly to Mary's hand. He wouldn't put it past the woman to charge into any fray that occurred, whether between El Diablo and his men or his men alone. Reese recalled Cash's warning that they were bored and would make trouble if there was none to be had.

That was the problem when you brought six rough men to a quiet little town in Texas. Trouble kept them in business. It made them what they were. And if there wasn't enough of it with others, they'd make trouble among themselves.

As Reese and Mary neared the saloon, they heard raised voices inside. Then Rico came flying through the doors and landed on his back in the middle of the street.

Reese sighed. "They're fighting again."

"Fighting? Your men?"

"They do that sometimes."

"How . . . childish."

"I never said they weren't."

"Can't you make them stop?"

"I plan to."

"I mean completely. Forever."

"Hell, no. They're rough men. People hire us to fight. If I make them behave like humans, they won't be any good to me at all."

"So you let them behave like animals?"

"To a point. They aren't allowed to kill each other."

"Excellent rule." Mary's voice was dry.

Reese raised his eyebrows. She amused the hell out of him.

A man emerged from the saloon. Reese couldn't see his face, but he knew his men, and this wasn't one of them. The guy pulled Rico up and started shaking him.

"Aw, hell, what did he do now?" Reese muttered.

He let Mary go and stalked into the street. Just as the man drew his fist back to punch the kid in the face, Reese grabbed ahold of his arm.

Rico fell back to the dirt as the guy swung around. Reese ducked, and the punch whistled over his head. He would have laid the man flat, but a quick glance at the guy's face revealed that Rico's attacker was at least sixty.

Instead, Reese pulled the man's arm behind his back so he wouldn't try to strike out again. "Who are you?" he demanded.

The man let loose a stream of profanity, none of which sounded like his name. Somehow Reese doubted he held Jesus Christ in his hands.

"William Brown!" Mary's voice came from directly behind him, and when Reese glanced over his shoulder, he found her scowling at the man. "Your mouth should be washed with soap!"

Brown continued to curse and struggle, trying to get at Rico. A movement behind Mary revealed Jed, Cash, and Sullivan lounging against the bullet-riddled front of the saloon. All watched the exchange with varying degrees of amusement.

"What's going on here?" Reese demanded of them.

"This guy came in firin' at Rico. Firin' wide. It's no wonder they hired us if that's how they shoot in this town." Jed snorted. "He missed the kid by a mile."

"Lucky for the kid. My question is more to the why than the what."

All four shrugged. Rico managed to get up, and Reese saw that Brown had scored at least one hit. The kid's pretty brown eye was swelling shut.

Reese sighed. "Was it his wife? His sister? His daughter? Which one, Salvatore?"

Rico looked at him with his one good eye. *"No comprendo."*

"Let me help you to understand. Which one of this man's women have you been playing with all week?"

"No women. I swear."

"Brown? You want to tell me why you're trying to kill him?"

"Carrie," the man gasped.

Rico paled, a show of guilt if ever there was one.

"Dammit, Rico, I told you to keep it in your pants. I'm sick and tired of irate fathers, husbands, and brothers turning up on every job. Why can't you be like Cash?"

"Why can't everyone?" Cash drawled.

Reese ignored the gambler; sometimes that helped. Rico looked as if he'd just lost his best friend. Pale, bruised, shoulders hanging, hair in his face. When he raised his one good eye, the anguish in it made Reese shiver.

"Carrie is six years old, *mi capitán*. I am not a monster. I have been playing with her, yes. She reminds me of my little sister whom I lost long ago."

"Bullshit!" Brown exploded. "You've been teaching her how to sneak up on people and scare them half to death. The little brat prowls around like a coyote. She's driving me crazy. And she talks about *him* like he's the king of Spain. She swears a blue streak, too. I don't want that Mex bastard anywhere near her."

"Perhaps, Mr. Brown, Carrie has learned some of her curse words at home," Mary pointed out. "We've discussed this before."

"She was never this bad until he showed up. She says she loves him."

"She's six, Mr. Brown. He's handsome and young, and he pays attention to her. It's a crush, and kind of sweet, if you ask me."

"Well, I didn't ask you. You're the one who brought them here, and I'm telling you people are talking. About you and him." He yanked away from Reese, and Reese let him go. "Lessons in the morning. Do you wonder why no one but you shows up?"

Reese remained poised on the balls of his feet, ready to grab the man if he swung again at Rico or punch him in the mouth, old fool or not, if he spoke badly about Mary.

"Why would that be, Mr. Brown?"

Her voice, ice cold, impressed Reese. She had the "watch your mouth" tone down as well as anyone he'd ever seen.

"Because no one trusts them. It's not just me

who doesn't want any one of them near my family. It's everyone."

"I've been learning from Reese for a week now, and nothing untoward has happened."

"Right." Brown snorted. "Where were you coming from just now?"

Mary flushed. Even in the semidarkness, anyone could see her blush. Although they had done nothing wrong, she would be blamed, and Reese wasn't going to allow that.

He stepped in close to Brown. "I accompanied Miss McKendrick to the river so she could wash clothes. No woman should wander out of town without an escort."

"Escort? Is that what they're calling it these days?"

Reese narrowed his eyes, and his fists clenched. Mary's fingers slipped around his fist—soft over hard, peace over anger. "Never mind," she said. "He'll believe what he wants to, anyway."

"Damn right. Why don't you just kill El Diablo and get out of town." Brown stepped back and glanced at the saloon. "All of you." He turned to Rico. "Especially you. Stay away from Carrie."

Rico didn't answer; he just kept staring at the ground, which made Reese nervous. Rico had an answer to everything, and he never let anyone get the jump on him. So how had Brown managed to give the kid a black eye?

Brown stalked away, and Rico wandered back into the saloon with the others. No one spoke to each other or to Reese, though Sullivan hung back and stared at him for a long moment before following the rest. Reese felt guilty. But what had he done?

Reese let his hands relax, and Mary slipped her fingers between his. "Mr. Brown has been angry at the world since he lost his son in the war and he got stuck raising Carrie. Though stuck isn't a word I'd use for the gift of that child."

"He's right. You hired us to kill El Diablo."

"I did not!"

"Mary," he groaned. "That's what we do. Just because you're too good-hearted to believe that doesn't make it any less true. We need to kill him and get out of here before something bad happens."

"Bad? Like what?"

He pulled his hand from hers. "You know what."

"I don't think that I do."

Reese looked into her innocent face, and something shifted deep inside of him. "I want to do a lot more than kiss you."

"And that's bad?"

He shook his head and allowed himself one small brush of his lips against the soft skin where her hair met her forehead. "Didn't the sisters ever tell you just how bad a man can be?"

She sighed and leaned into him; the sound and the movement made his heart hurt. She trusted him, and he did not deserve it. "How can something so bad feel so good?"

Reese turned Mary about and led her toward her cabin, keeping a respectable distance between them. "Most bad things do," he said, then left her at the door without touching her again.

When he returned to the hotel, the place was deserted. Were the men still at the saloon? Most likely, but he didn't care to join them. Instead, he climbed the stairs to his room, stepping inside, not bothering to turn on the lamp.

He believed he was alone until a voice spoke from the darkened corner. "You must not have a sister, *Capitán.*"

Reese's hand went for his gun before his mind registered the words and the cadence of the voice. "Rico, do you want to get killed?"

The kid ignored his question. Reese sighed and lit the lamp. The wavering golden glow only served to emphasize the blackened skin around Rico's eye and the pale cast to his face.

"You look like hell," Reese said.

"Gracias."

"Any time." Reese rubbed his forehead. "What do you want?"

"When last I saw my sister she was six years old. Like Carrie."

Reese dropped his hand and stared at Rico in horror. He did not want to know this. But the way the kid looked, Reese feared if he didn't listen, something worse than hearing more than he needed to know about Rico's past might happen.

"The child is so sweet, and she looks at me as if I am her big brother who can do no wrong." He swallowed audibly. "It has been forever since anyone looked at me like that."

Rico was always cheerful and flirtatious; he had women falling into his lap from one end of the country to the other, yet he missed the adoration of a little sister. Just as Reese had suspected, this little tidbit of information made Rico almost human. *Hell.*

"*Capitán,* you do not have a little sister, so you do not know what I am talking about." Rico turned his head and stared out the window.

"True enough, but I can imagine."

Silence filled the room. The angle of the kid's face as he stared out at the night showed the sharp blade of his nose, the height of his cheekbones, the shape of the mark around his eye. Reese had never seen the kid with a bruise on his face. Mainly because Rico moved too fast for anyone to hit. So what had happened tonight?

Reese sat on his bed. "How did Brown manage to lay a hand on you?"

Rico turned away from the window, and the sadness in his eye tugged at Reese. He resisted the urge to get up and run away. "I could not hit him. He is a fool, but he is right. She should not be with me. I am no good."

Rico needed Reese to disagree. And he did. The kid was many things, but no good wasn't one of them.

"Well, teaching her how to sneak is probably not a skill she'll need as a future young lady, but you never know, it might come in handy. And there are worse things she could learn. Her granddad seems to have taught her a few choice items."

Rico's face lightened with hope. "You think I can teach her more?"

"No. I think you'd best stay away from her until

Brown cools off. Next time, he might not miss when he tries to shoot you."

"Would you care if I was dead?"

"Hell, yes," Reese growled. "I don't have time to go looking for another sneaky Tejano who can throw knives."

Rico grinned, then winced as the movement caused his sore cheek to shift. "You say the sweetest things."

Gunfire erupted below. Glass shattered. Reese and Rico leaped for the window. The street was filled with El Diablo's men, and they were shooting into the saloon.

"Didn't I say that the minute we weren't paying attention he'd attack?" Reese muttered as he loaded his rifle. "I hate being right all the time. Where's Nate? I thought he was in the tower."

As if in answer, a man cried out and fell from his horse; then another did the same.

"Must have been asleep up there," Reese said to a suddenly empty room.

Rico returned with his shotgun. "He'll make up for it now."

"If he'd been awake, we wouldn't have gotten surprised."

"You don't seem surprised. Perhaps because you are always right."

"Shut up and shoot."

It didn't take long for the combination of Reese, Rico, and Nate, in elevated positions to drive the attackers out of range. The other men might have been trapped in the saloon, but they had their guns. Within a half-hour, El Diablo's crew fled town, leaving behind two more dead men.

Mary was going to pitch a fit.

"All gone?" Rourke called.

"Yep, come on over," Reese answered.

"Me, too?" Nate's voice drifted from the tower.

"Hell, no. You stay up there until it's your time to leave. And stay awake!"

"I was awake. Mostly."

"Drunk sniper." Reese stood. "Knife-throwing kid." He unloaded his gun. "Sneaky half-breed." He put the gun away. "Cursing Irishman." He stomped out into the hall. "Slick-mouthed, gun-slinging gambler." The door opened downstairs.

"I think we're all here with the exception of the drunk sniper," Rico murmured.

Reese glanced over his shoulder. "Make that smart-aleck, knife-throwing kid."

"Thank you, *Capitán.*"

The other three were already seated around the kitchen table when Reese and Rico joined them.

"Coffee?" Rico headed for the stove.

"Sit." Reese ordered. Then: "Sit, sit, sit."

Rico sat with a smirk. At least he was feeling better.

"That, gentlemen, was an example of what happens when we get distracted."

"Big deal," Cash sneered. "I can shoot back at those guys all day and all night. If we keep picking off two or three every time, pretty soon they'll be empty. If we don't die of boredom first, we win."

"I say we go after them at dawn," Jed said. "Wipe

'em out and keep on goin'. I've had enough of Rock Creek."

"We're not going anywhere." Reese leaned against the wall next to the table. "I'm starting to think El Diablo wants us to follow him. These little shooting matches are a tease. 'Come and get me if you can.' And if he wants us to chase him, we're better off here. Like Cash said, if we get two or three every time, eventually we'll get them all. And Miss McKendrick won't think we committed mass murder."

"Aha," Cash cried. "That's the reason you've gone soft."

"Soft?" Reese repeated in his most quiet deadly voice.

Cash wasn't impressed. Probably because he was the most deadly of them all. "I knew it, but no one would believe me. That skirt's got you thinking you can talk your way out of this, and since you were halfway convinced of that already, you're listening. You're gonna get yourself killed, Reese, and you aren't taking me with you."

"I admit Miss McKendrick would prefer us not to litter the street with bodies—"

"What in hell did she think was going to happen when we came here?" Jed snapped.

"She thought we'd scare them away."

Cash snorted. "We are pretty scary, but that old Indian is worse. Spooky bastard."

"She had a good idea when she wanted to teach the people to defend themselves," Rico said.

Reese glared at him. The kid shrugged.

"*She* had a good idea?" Cash looked from Rico back to Reese.

Well, the cat was out of the bag now. No choice but to brave it out. "A good idea is a good idea. Unfortunately, it isn't working."

"Because we seem to have scared the wrong folks—the populace rather than the invaders. Shame on us."

"If y'all want to leave, I'm not stopping you."

"And what about you?"

"I'll stay. I said I would."

For a minute, Reese thought Cash might leave. If anyone was going to break a vow, it would be Cash. The two men stared into each other's eyes, and what passed between them was thicker than blood, darker than their pasts put together.

"And we said we'd come whenever one of us called and stick together when there was a job to be done. I might be a lot of things, most of them unpleasant, but when I made that vow, I meant it. I still do."

"Me, too," Jed said. *"Yo, sí."*

"Yep," Sullivan agreed.

Reese looked at his men, and he felt kind of funny. Friends, Mary had said; he needed friends. He didn't want any. He'd killed enough of them. But no matter what, these men kept following him. They would die for him, as he would for them. If that wasn't a friend, what was? He was starting to believe something he'd suspected for a long time.

Just because he refused to call them his friends didn't mean that they weren't.

Twelve

When dawn tinted the eastern sky, Mary stepped onto her porch and tripped over her laundry basket. She glanced about, but nothing moved anywhere in Rock Creek. Lying on the top was the chemise that had escaped. How had Reese captured that?

The thought of Reese touching her undergarments, even when they were in the river and not on her, made Mary's body heat up. What was it about the man that made her think all the time of things she had no business contemplating?

Mary picked up the basket and brought it inside. The clothes were still damp. They'd be wrinkled beyond redemption. But at least she didn't have to go and get them. It was almost like a present.

Last night, at the first sound of shots, she had wanted to grab her gun and run to the hotel to help. But since she couldn't hit a hay bale that was standing still, she figured she'd do more harm than good trying to hit a moving target.

Then, when the shots died away and the bandits fled, she'd barely been able to keep herself from running over there to ascertain whether Reese was unharmed. Luckily, hearing him shout to one of the men after the battle had soothed her immediate terror. Because if she'd gone to the hotel then, she'd have given in to the need to run her hands all over him and make sure he was whole and safe. Even she knew that was a bad idea, so she'd refrained.

Mr. Brown had said people were talking about her and Reese. Well, let them talk. They'd done nothing wrong. Except for the time by the river, they'd been in plain sight of everyone most of the time. Perhaps that was the problem. Still, kissing wasn't a crime. Even in Texas. They couldn't fire her for kissing, could they? Because kissing was amazing, and Mary was becoming addicted.

She left her cabin behind and walked around the schoolhouse to Main Street. The bodies were gone. She wasn't sure how many there had been this time, but there had been a few. She'd heard the men outside after dark, then the sounds of a shovel on dirt.

Reese waited on the porch, and the breath she'd been holding released on a sigh. She was coming to depend too much on starting every day with him. Even the morning he'd sent Rico instead, when Reese appeared, the day had brightened. What was she going to do when he left?

The sadness that washed over her at that thought staggered Mary. The devastation went far beyond shared conversation and stolen kisses. Mary was a schoolteacher, Reese, a gunman. They had no future, and she'd never believed that they had. But the thought of his leaving made her eyes water, and the thought of his dying—

Her mind refused to accept that image. Reese dead just might break her, and in twenty-four years of difficult living, nothing had come close to that.

He stood at her approach but said nothing. She liked that about him, too. He could be quiet and still say so many things. Unlike her, who just had to fill every silence.

"Thank you for bringing my clothes and basket."

He shrugged. "I didn't want you wandering about alone again."

"Still, it was thoughtful."

"That's me, Mr. Thoughtful."

She raised an eyebrow at his playful tone, not like Reese at all. "Everyone is all right?"

He nodded. "All of *us*, anyway. They lost two more men." He held up a hand. "Now don't yell, Mary. If they're going to come into town shooting, they'll get what they deserve."

"I wasn't going to yell. You're right. I was foolish to think a show of force would send a man like El Diablo running, and since my brilliant idea of arming the women has not gotten the response I'd hoped, we either pack up and let El Diablo have the place, or I shut up and let you do what you do best."

"Kill."

His face had gone still, the humor of a few moments ago having fled. Mary heard the echo of what she had said and wanted to kick herself. "I didn't mean that. I'm sure killing isn't your best skill."

"I guess I should take that as a compliment."

His gaze drifted to her mouth. "All things considered."

Mary blushed.

A primal scream split the dawn, so loud that it sounded right there with them—whatever it was. Mary leaped the few feet separating her from Reese, and his arms closed around her. Her heart thundered in her ears, but in his embrace she felt safer than ever before.

"Cougar," he murmured against her hair. "I'd forgotten. That's the second time I've heard the thing call from the river."

"Do cougars attack?"

"If provoked."

The big cat shrieked again, an angry call that sounded very provoked to Mary. Despite the warmth of Reese's strong arms around her, she shivered.

Then Reese stiffened and moved her gently but firmly away from him. The chill returned, and she looked into his face with a frown. He nodded down the street. "Someone's coming."

Mary turned. Baxter and Rose Sutton were running toward them. Annoyance took the place of the comforting warmth. It was too early in the morning to face Baxter Sutton.

But as the couple neared, Mary could see that something was wrong. Fear haunted their eyes; terror streaked their faces. They were both out of breath, from panic and the run.

"The twins," Rose gasped.

"Are gone," Baxter finished. "Looked everywhere. Can't find them."

"How long?" Reese asked.

Baxter shrugged and leaned his hands on his knees, breathing deeply, his head hung between his shoulders. "When I went . . . to wake them . . . to help me stock the store, their beds were empty . . . and the window was open."

"Fishing," Reese muttered. "I told them not to—"

The cougar shrieked again. Everyone's eyes widened, and they ran for the river.

"Idiot," Reese muttered. "Fool. Should have shot that cougar the first day I heard it."

He ran ahead of the others. If they couldn't keep up, so be it. Reese slid down the embankment into the belly of the river valley. His gaze searched the near side. No sign of the boys, but he did see a girl sneaking toward the trees. Must be Rico's little friend. Hell, how many kids were down here?

"Psst," he hissed, trying to get the child's attention without shouting. She glanced his way and waved, smiling sweetly.

He indicated with a sharp slash of his hand that she should come away from the trees. Her smile turned to a mulish scowl. Reese jabbed his finger toward the ground at his side and scowled right back. Thankfully, she began to creep in his direction.

Now where were those blasted twins?

A sound at the top of the embankment drew Reese's attention. Mary and the Suttons, as well as the rest of the town, had arrived. No one would come near him on any other given morning, but let there be trouble and they poured from their houses like ants from a wet anthill.

"Where are they?" Sutton shouted.

Reese flinched at the volume of the man's shout. Mary rolled her eyes and whispered something to him.

"I will *not* be quiet. I want my boys back."

"Then go get them yourself," Reese muttered, though he knew that would never happen. As usual, when trouble reared its ugly head, Reese was elected to fix things.

The cougar shrieked again, then appeared atop a boulder on the opposite side of the river. Reese narrowed his eyes. The boulder pressed up against the riverbank in such a way as to leave a small cavelike hole between the stone and the dirt. And inside that hole, movement. He'd found the twins.

The cougar's head swung back and forth, as if it smelled the boys but wasn't certain where they hid.

"Do something!" Sutton shouted.

The cougar skittered backward on the boulder and growled. The boys screamed, "Papa!"

Reese cursed as the cat's head went up, then back down between shoulders hunched into a stalking position. The animal leaped from the boulder and paced in front of the opening, its intense interest focused on the tiny cave.

Just like a barn cat with a cornered mouse, the cougar swept its paw into the hole. The boys cried out. The cat hunkered down, belly to the ground, rear in the air.

"Shoot it!" Sutton screamed.

"I can't now," Reese said from between clenched teeth. "I might hit one of the boys."

Images flashed in his mind, there and then gone again, of other boys, other dangers. Why did he have to be the one who ran to the rescue today? Why couldn't it have been any of the other men who didn't have ghosts walking through their minds at the most inopportune times?

The war had been over for five years. Reese's hope had died long before that—before he'd met the men he rode with now. Yet still he relived that past. He could do nothing about what had happened all those years ago, but he could do something now.

Without another thought, Reese jumped into the river. The splash drew the cat's head in his direction.

"Reese, no!" Mary cried.

He faltered at the sound of her voice but forced his attention to remain on the cougar, even though he wanted to reassure Mary. He didn't want to die in front of her, or anyone else for that matter. Dying was best done alone.

'Here!" he shouted, and waved his arms.

The animal swung its head between the cave and Reese, confused. Reese started walking toward it, gun drawn. As soon as the cougar charged him and moved away from the boys, he would shoot. No more fooling around.

After what seemed like a very long time but was probably only a moment, the cougar realized it was easier to come after the fool waving at him rather than play cat and mouse with the twins. Muscles bunched beneath golden shoulders, and the animal crashed into the river in front of Reese. He sighted, but just as he was about to squeeze the trigger, the cat veered in another direction.

Reese spun to the side. The little girl, Carrie, ran toward him, childishly oblivious to what was going on in any world but hers. Reese glanced at the cat that bounded toward the child a foot at a time. Reese swung his gun toward the cougar. He would have one shot.

Rico jumped from the embankment, grabbed Carrie in his arms, and turned his back to run. The cat leapt.

Sutton shouted, "Do something!"

Reese fired.

The cougar's front paws hit Rico in the back. Rico fell forward, body over the child, the cat on top of them both.

Nothing moved. Not even the cougar.

"Was that the *something* you had in mind?" Reese's voice sounded calm even as his heart thundered in his ears so loud he could barely think, and the faces flickered, then danced before his eyes.

He blinked several times, hard and fast, and the faces disappeared. He hadn't had flashes of the past for a long time. Probably because he'd avoided homey towns, children, and good women, which seemed to set him off.

When his vision cleared and his heart settled back into a near normal rhythm, Reese glanced at Sutton, who, along with the rest of the town, stood atop the riverbank with mouths agape, faces pale. Everyone stared at him as if he'd done something amazing. Reese shrugged and went to help Rico.

He removed the cougar, and the kid turned over, bringing the child with him. Though Rico's cocky grin was in place, the pale cast to his face made the bruise around his eye shine darker than before.

"Nice shot," the kid said, taking Reese's offered hand. In Rico's other arm he held Carrie, and it didn't look as if he were going to let her go anytime soon. Reese wasn't going to make him either.

"I've made worse."

"Don't tell me that. I counted on you to save my miserable life."

"You saved hers." The child clung to Rico, her face pressed against his throat. At least she seemed to understand the severity of the situation, albeit a bit late. "Looks like you're a hero, kid."

"Hmm." Rico's gaze focused behind Reese. "Perhaps you should tell that to him."

Reese turned just in time to grab Brown in his headlong rush toward Rico. "I told him to leave her be."

Reese shoved the old man back none too gently. He'd had about all he could take from Brown, Sutton, and every other so-called man in town. No wonder Mary had to manage things. These fools were worthless.

"If he *had* let her be, she'd be dead. What's she doing wandering around before dawn by herself, anyway?"

"How would I know? I can't watch her every damned minute. She's a sneak. She snuck out."

"Well, Rico just saved her life. Look around. See anything out of place?"

Brown glanced at the dead cougar, and his face creased. He peered at Rico. "You shoot that?"

"Nope."

Reese gave Rico a dirty look. Why couldn't the kid shut up? "I shot it. But Rico put himself between your granddaughter and a charging cougar." Reese looked at the animal. "The thing must have been mad to attack this close to town. Or starving, though it's not the time of year for that."

"Perhaps *loco, mi capitán*. I have seen such things before."

Reese grunted. Just what he needed—rabid wild animals surrounding a town full of cowards, kids, and women. Oh, and don't forget El Diablo, who seemed to think the town was worth taking. If it wasn't for Mary, Reese would give the old Indian Rock Creek on a platter.

Mary's rainwater scent announced her approach even before her voice drifted from just behind him. "Rico's a hero. But so are you, Reese." He shrugged. "Don't pass this off. You made that cat run at you instead of the boys."

"Big deal." He turned around. "I had the gun."

"It looked like a big deal to me. Everyone else thought so, too."

Reese glanced at the embankment, but with the exception of the Suttons, who had gathered their wayward children and were hugging them and berating them in equal measure, everyone else had returned to town.

The rest of the men—minus Cash, who must be

in the tower—stood apart from the Suttons, looking at Reese, then Rico, and shaking their heads. They must have seen everything. Reese was glad Cash hadn't been watching. He didn't feel like having his heroics dissected and sneered at. He'd rather not hear about them at all.

"I suggest, Mr. Brown, that you thank these two men. No one else did a thing."

"That's not true," Rico said. "Sutton shouted a lot."

Mary gave a delicate snort. "That's what he does best."

Brown shuffled his feet, stared at the dirt, glanced at the river and then back at the cougar. Finally, he sighed and stepped forward, holding out his arms. "Thanks. Now can I have my granddaughter?"

Reese raised an eyebrow at Mary. She shrugged. It was probably the best they were going to get from a cranky old coot like Brown.

Rico glanced at Reese. Reese nodded, and Rico kissed Carrie on the forehead and attempted to disentangle her arms from his neck.

"No!" she shouted, clinging. "I want to stay with you."

"He has that effect on every woman he meets," Reese said.

"Not on me," Mary murmured.

Which made Reese smile.

Mary had never been so frightened in her life as she'd been that morning. Yet Reese, after that

single moment when he'd looked confused and
out of place, had reacted to every move the cougar
made calmly and reasonably. If it hadn't been for
him, tragedy would have dampened the bright
spring day.

How could anyone doubt any longer that she'd
done the right thing by bringing these men to
Rock Creek?

Reese remained silent as they walked toward
town. At the outskirts, Mary turned to him. "Thank
you for what you did. No one else could have managed."

"Not even you?"

They shared a smile. "Not even me."

He glanced at the sun. "I guess our lesson is off
for this morning."

"I have to get to school."

He stared past her shoulder; first astonishment,
then confusion, washed over his features. He
looked at Mary, then back again. "What are they
doing here?"

Mary spun about, half-afraid El Diablo and his
men were lined up at her back. Instead, ten women
with rifles stood in front of the hay bales. One of
them was Jo Clancy, another was Rose Sutton, the
rest were women Mary had begged to support her
and been ignored.

She pushed past Reese. "What's going on?"

Rose looked at the ground, then at Mary, and
finally at Reese. "We decided if these men can risk
their lives for our children, the least we can do is
help fight for our town."

Mary glanced at Jo. "I thought Nate needed you

more and that you were forbidden to touch a weapon."

Jo shrugged. "I'm forbidden a lot of things. That's never stopped me before. I shouldn't have let it stop me this time, either."

The other women nodded in agreement and turned their attention to Reese. Mary did, too, and caught the stunned expression on his face before the usual mask slipped back into place.

"What's the matter?" she whispered.

"They trust me?"

"Looks like."

"Why?"

"You saved the children." He winced and clutched his belly.

Mary stepped forward and put her hand over his. Reese's fingers were ice cold.

"Are you ill?"

"No." He yanked his hand from beneath hers and stepped away from her touch. "Just a delayed reaction to the cougar, I guess. I'll be all right once I start teaching." His face contracted, as if in pain, on the last word.

Mary reached for him again, but he'd already spun on his heel and strode off to meet the women, leaving her alone.

"I say Reese was a circus performer. Having a crazed cougar out for his blood hardly made him breathe hard."

Mary glanced toward Jedidiah Rourke's voice and discovered Reese's men standing a few feet away in a semicircle, heads together. Rico held a piece of paper with a stub of pencil poised to write.

"Perhaps a marksman in a traveling show. The circus is too ordinary for *el capitán.*"

"What are you doing?" Mary demanded.

Nate took a drink before winking in her direction. "Changing our bets."

"Bets on what?"

"El capitán." Rico scribbled on the paper, his pretty face scrunched into a frown of intense concentration on his task, which reminded Mary of Carrie at work on her sums. His poor eye looked worse today than on the day it had happened.

"Explain yourselves."

The ice in her tone caused Rico to glance up. "We have a running wager on *el capitán*'s name and on what he was before he became who he is now."

"None of you know a single thing about him?"

"If we knew, what fun would it be to make wagers? Would you like to place a bet, Miss McKendrick?"

"Rico." Sullivan's voice held a warning.

"What? Perhaps she has a better guess than any of us."

"I thought you were all in the war together?"

"Not the entire war," Nate said. "We got together a year or so before Gettysburg."

Mary glanced toward Reese, who walked down the line of women, patiently explaining to them, one by one, how to load their guns. Then she returned her attention to the four men in front of her. "He could be anyone, have done anything. Why do you follow him?"

With deliberate motions, Rico put the paper and

pencil into his pocket, then straightened to his full
height and looked Mary straight in the eye. "He
is *el capitán*. He leads us. You ask why we follow
him?" He glanced at Reese, but his eyes seemed
to look much farther than that, perhaps into a
shared past. "How can we not?"

El Diablo narrowed his gaze on Rock Creek. He
was old, but he had always possessed the eyes of a
hawk. This had given him the name *Tosa nakaai*
while a child. But his name dream had whispered
Tuhkwasi taiboo? Satan. And since one's true name
held great power, he had tried to live up to that
distinction.

"What is he doing?"

El Diablo's lips tightened. Jefferson had his gifts.
Intelligence was not one of them. Which was why
El Diablo had allowed him to live this long.

"Teaching the women how to use their guns."

Jefferson snorted. "What an idiot."

"This could be a problem," El Diablo murmured.

"Huh? Women? They'll fall like split wood."

El Diablo didn't answer. From the moment he'd
looked into the green eyes of the man in black,
he'd been uneasy. He knew a leader when he saw
one. He'd seen the power in the teacher lady right
off. Unfortunately for her, she had the body of a
woman, and the white eyes were too foolish to look
past her shell. A happy mistake for El Diablo. Un-
happily, she'd had the foresight to hunt down

someone who would be troublesome, to say the least.

Some men had to be taught to lead, and some men were born with leadership in their soul. The man called Reese was the latter. No matter what he did, others would follow. Just as they followed El Diablo.

This still would not have been a problem. El Diablo could keep throwing bodies at Rock Creek for a long, long time. Men paid to fight would give up and leave eventually, once the money ran out. These six men had no stake in a dusty Texas town.

But El Diablo had been watching Rock Creek, and he didn't like what he saw. The hired guns and the town were becoming one.

At first, the townsfolk had held themselves aloof from their rescuers—at first, but no longer. This morning's incident with the cougar had put a crack in that barrier, and the people were beginning to follow Reese, just as his men did. Together, the six hired guns and the town would become a serious threat to what El Diablo had in mind.

With a leader and enough guns, Rock Creek could hold on longer than El Diablo. Because when a town became a home rather than a place to sleep, attacking only made things worse. Folks defended their homes with all that they had. El Diablo knew that better than anyone.

Look at the foolish war the white eyes had fought only five summers past. The bluecoats had invaded the land of the gray, and the war had dragged on and on and on. Because the graycoats had defended their homes until there was nothing left to defend but dust.

"The one called Reese is the key," El Diablo said. "He is the one they all respect. The one they will all follow. If we can get rid of him, the rest will break."

Jefferson smiled. "Fine by me. But how do we get to him?"

When the teacher moved off toward the schoolhouse and the man in black watched her until she disappeared inside, El Diablo smiled, too. "I'll think of something."

Thirteen

Each morning, Reese taught the women. Sometimes Rico or one of the others helped—never Cash, of course, and that was probably for the best, considering the nature of those being taught.

The women learned quickly, now that they'd decided to, and while he missed spending that hour after dawn with Mary alone, having the townsfolk accept him and the men made life in Rock Creek a whole lot less tense.

El Diablo had not returned, and Reese had hopes that by the time he did, the women would be ready. The combination of them, the older men, and injured soldiers, along with Reese's men, would convince the old Indian that continued attacks on this town would be fruitless. Reese hoped that would be the way of things, but he didn't believe it.

Reese and the others would have to kill a few more bandidos before they made their point—maybe even the two lead bandidos. One of the first rules of war was to take down the leader if you could. Often that was all it took to make the rest run. Reese knew that better than anyone.

So if things were going well on the outside, why did Reese feel so awful on the inside? He was exhausted, for the nightmares had returned. He was strung as tight as a fiddle, because as soon as school let out every day, hell followed him wherever he went.

Today he hid in the stall with Atlanta. Reese wasn't proud. If hiding kept him away from *them*, he'd hide in here all night.

Besides, he hadn't been paying nearly enough attention to his horse, evidenced by the way Atlanta kept running his big nose down Reese's back and shoving him into the far wall.

Reese smiled and rubbed between the animal's eyes. He *had* named his horse Atlanta so he would remember his past. Not Sherman's march or the burning of Reese's hometown—as if that would ever be forgotten—but what Atlanta symbolized.

Reese's mistakes, his failures, his dead dreams. If he rode a horse every day named for the place that reminded him of those things, maybe he wouldn't make the same mistakes, fail so utterly again, or bother to dream.

But here, in Rock Creek, he had not been spending enough time with the horse, and therefore he'd started to dream impossible dreams. Like having a future, a life, a family, even a wife.

The morning at the creek had reminded Reese how foolish such thoughts were. The entire town looked at him as if he were a hero because he'd saved those children. But they'd never have been in danger at all if he'd done what he should have and hunted down the cougar the first time he'd heard the animal scream. Little mistakes like that could ruin a whole eternity.

"Nice horse."

"Yeah, nice horse."

Atlanta snorted, lowered his head, and threw his nose back up, narrowly missing Reese's jaw. Reese sighed.

They'd found him. *Again.*

"Don't you two have somewhere to be?"

Reese met two identical pairs of blue eyes, framed by shaggy mops of straw-brown hair——his latest shadows, the Sutton twins. Saving their lives seemed to have made him their new best friend.

"Nah. Nowhere to be. Papa said we didn't have to help in the store today on account of we almost died."

Reese rubbed his forehead. "That was nearly a week ago, and you didn't almost die."

"That's not what everyone else says."

Stepping out of the stall, Reese gave the horse one final pat. "Well, that's what I say. Carrie was in more trouble, and Rico saved her. Why don't you follow him around for a while."

"Nah. He likes girls."

"So do I."

The twins scowled at Reese for a minute before deciding to ignore that issue and follow him anyway. Every time Reese had turned around this past week—after the hour of two o'clock—he tripped over a twin. So far he'd managed not to lose his temper—or his mind. But the cold sweat trickling beneath his hatband, and also down his back, was becoming tiresome.

"Listen." He spun about, and they bumped into his belly. "Go home. I've got things to do."

"Can't we help? We want to be like you."

Faces flashed before his eyes, taking the place of those that stared up at him in adoration. The expression might be the same, but the faces were different. And long dead.

Reese turned on his heel and stamped away. For once, the twins did not follow. But the ghosts did.

Mary sat on the porch at night just in case Reese was out walking. Perhaps if he saw her he might wander over. She'd sat here every night since the incident at the creek, but she hadn't seen Reese, except from a distance.

Silly old maid, she was. Silly old maid, she would always be. But that didn't mean she couldn't dream of a handsome, dangerous man coming to call. What could it hurt?

The sound of the women practicing each morning, long after she left for school, had been a welcome distraction. Together the people of Rock Creek and the six hired men could save this town. Mary just knew it.

Teaching this week had been a monstrous task, with the continued excitement of the children, but she'd managed. The Sutton twins came in every day with a new story about Reese. They seemed to be following him all over town—whenever they weren't in school.

That afternoon, Mary had seen Reese wave his hat at them and shout. They'd hung their heads and watched him walk off; then, moments later, they'd glanced at each other and scampered after him again.

Mary shook her head at the memory. The twins had found a hero, and that wasn't all bad. With a father like Baxter Sutton, she had worried how they might turn out. Although Baxter had been extremely nice to her of late—falling all over himself trying to help her whenever she went into his store—he still wasn't much of a manly example.

Mary did not believe cowardice was in the blood. But if all those boys saw was a father with no gumption, then how could they figure out how to become men worth their salt?

Though a hired gun wasn't exactly the best choice as a hero, the twins could do worse than emulate Reese. He was still a remarkable man. Too bad he didn't seem to care too much for children.

"Mary!"

The whisper was soft, but the desperation in the voice made her jump to her feet, eyes searching the darkness for whoever had spoken.

Reese lurched into view around the schoolhouse. Mary didn't pause to think he might be as mad as the cougar at the river; she ran to him.

His hat was gone, his hair as wild as his eyes. His shirt was half-buttoned, his chest damp with sweat. The gold of his skin had paled, the usual warmth of his flesh gone clammy. He stumbled, and she caught him in her arms. Luckily, he did not sag with all his weight. She was a strong woman, but she would fall, too, and then where would they be?

Reese clung to her like a child, and like a child,

she held him, whispering nonsense against his brow.

"What is it?" she asked when his trembling subsided a bit.

"Don't let them see me like this."

Desperation again, in his voice, in his eyes. "Who?" Her eyes swept the dark shadows surrounding Rock Creek. "Who don't you want to see?"

"The men. They've never seen me like this. And they never can."

The men? *His* men? That was a relief. When he'd staggered out of the darkness, she'd feared a secret sneak attack by El Diablo. And if the Devil had sneaked past the Rock Creek six, there would be hell to pay.

Her relief was short-lived, however, when Reese managed to gain his feet and look into her face. The tortured expression in his eyes made her gasp. "Please," he begged. "Let me come in."

She hesitated, not because she didn't want him in her home; she wanted him there very badly. But what she wanted, what she needed, what she dreamed, meant nothing in the face of his panic. She had never seen this man show fear. Yet he *was* afraid of his men seeing this weakness—as only a strong man could be.

"Come." She turned, putting her shoulder beneath his arm.

He let her lead him, which scared her more than anything else. What had happened to make Reese tremble and sweat and beg?

They gained the porch and stumbled together to the door. Mary managed the doorknob, but once inside, Reese's legs gave out, and he fell onto the rug in her hallway.

She kicked the door closed with her heel and followed Reese to the floor. He murmured words that sounded like a prayer, and she leaned close, closer still, until his breath brushed her cheek.

"Just a moment and I'll be all right. Smells like linseed oil and sunshine. Better than smoke and death. The guns are so loud. They hurt my ears. Too many faces, too young to die." *The war,* Mary thought. There were so many men who had been crippled by it, and not just by losing a limb or an eye. Some had lost their minds, their hearts, their souls.

What had Reese lost? And how was she going to give it back to him?

Mary sat on her heels. Reese clutched the carpet. She brushed his damp hair away from his forehead, and his sigh drifted toward a sob. So she kept stroking his hair, something she'd wanted to do for a very long time. As the moments passed, they inched closer and closer until his arms were about her waist, his face pressed to her belly.

If anyone saw them, she would be ruined despite the layers of clothing and the hard shell of a corset that kept her from feeling his warmth where she wanted to feel it the most. Still, his lips were pressed to a part of her where no man's lips had been before and no doubt ever would be again. But Mary could not push him away, not even to save herself.

She hummed a tune from her memory and played with his hair. The peace that washed over them both was worth whatever happened later.

Far too soon Reese shifted, then stiffened, as if

he realized where he was and what they were doing. Slowly, he sat up, and when he did, they were face-to-face, nose to nose, lip to lip.

She kissed him. She couldn't help herself. He might not love her, but he needed her. No one else ever had.

Slowly, she moved her mouth over his. With gentle touches of her tongue, with movements of her lips, she tried to make him forget everything else but her. She feared he would deny her what she craved—the chance to comfort him in the only way she knew how.

Then he sighed and met her tongue with his own. Soft strokes, tiny nibbles at the fullness of her lower lip, the glide of his fingertips along the back of her hand, then the joining of palm to palm.

"Mary," he murmured. "I shouldn't have come."

"Shh," she soothed. "Where else would you go?"

She lifted the hand he did not hold and placed it against his chest. The thud of his heart echoed the pulse in her palm. Their gazes met; his slid away.

She touched his face and tilted his chin until he looked into her eyes again. "Whatever happened, it doesn't matter. It can't be worth this agony. Tell me what hurts you so."

He yanked free of her touch, his body vibrating with tension once again. She feared he would stand up, walk out the door, and leave her holding nothing. Instead, he threw himself back into her arms and buried his face against the curve of her neck.

"Don't make me tell you. At least not right now."

Reese held her too tightly, but she couldn't pull

away. Especially when his damp face stuck to her equally damp neck and she considered that it wasn't that hot in her house.

Mary cupped his face, then pressed her lips to his wet cheeks. No tear tracks, perhaps she was wrong. What did it matter if he cried or not? Did the lack of tears make him any less upset? Would the tears make him any less a man? *No.*

She had been foolish to believe she could manage her feelings, or his. Some things were unmanageable. As she held Reese in her arms and he clung to her, Mary's lonely heart fell in love.

Silly old maid. She'd loved him long before now—maybe from that first moment in Dallas when he'd asked if everything included her and he'd looked as if he meant it.

Mary had no illusions that Reese might love her, but he wanted her. Perhaps, just once, that would be enough. If she had to spend a lifetime alone, at least she would have a single night with the man she loved.

She had wondered what she could do to give him back what he had lost. Maybe giving herself would do. Regardless, her body was all that she had to give.

"Reese." She pulled his hands from her waist and stood, not letting go of him lest he run. "Come with me."

Still disoriented from whatever he had been through in the shadows of his mind, he stood and followed her like a child, down the hall and into her room. But in the doorway he hesitated. "I should go."

"Soon." Mary reached for the cloth next to the

washbasin. After dipping it into the tepid water, she returned and wiped his hot face, then his damp neck.

Reese moaned. "Shh," she soothed. "Let me make you feel better."

It was a testament to his state of mind that he did not argue but merely leaned against the doorway and closed his eyes. She continued to wipe his heated skin, but too quickly the cloth became as hot as his flesh.

"Here." She took his hand and led him to her bed. "Sit." She pushed him, but he resisted. "Sit, sit, sit!" she said, as he always did. "You're too tall for me to reach."

Reese raised a brow at her tone but sat. Mary brought over the bowl of water and continued to wipe down his face, then across the back of his neck. As he continued to let her, she became bolder, sliding the cool cloth over his chest and surreptitiously releasing more buttons on his shirt.

Her back began to ache, hovering over him, so she placed the water on the floor and went down on her knees. As if she'd opened the door of a stove, his heat brushed her face. Mary skimmed the cloth over his belly. The muscles jumped beneath her touch, and she stared at them, fascinated.

Reese swore, grabbed her hand, and tossed the cloth into a corner. Seemingly of its own volition, her free hand reached for the muscled ridge of his belly. Her fingertips grazed through the hair that covered his golden skin. He grabbed that hand, too, and held both away from him.

"Are you crazy?"

She looked up into his face, tight and harsh but no longer in pain. Instead, his green gaze burned as it touched her mouth. She licked her lips.

He shook her. "Look at you."

She looked down but didn't see anything amiss. When she looked up, her confusion must have shown in her eyes, for he made a sound of impatience deep in his throat.

"Mary, you need a keeper. You can't ask a man like me into your bedroom, bathe my chest, touch my skin, then get down on your knees in front of me—" He cursed again and let go of her hands as if she were a leper.

"I don't understand."

"You don't. That's the problem."

"I want you to teach me." "Teach?" He covered his eyes with his long fingers and laughed, though the sound was anything but amused.

"Yes, teach me what happens between a man and woman. Show me the things I don't understand. Someone has to. I want that someone to be you, Reese. Only you."

She curled her palms around his thighs. His breath rushed through his teeth on a hiss before he grabbed her hands.

He looked angry, and for a moment Mary was afraid, not of Reese but of what she was doing to him. He'd been hurt enough, and if she was hurting him more, she would never forgive herself.

"You're making a mistake if you think I can kiss you and touch you and teach you but not take you. I'm not as tame as I look, and I'm not the man I'd hoped to be."

"You think too little of yourself."

"And you think too highly of me." He moved one of her hands from his thigh to the hard length between them. "This is what I feel for you, Mary." He pressed her palm to the ridge. "Sweet, virginal Mary, run away now and hide."

He released her and leaned back, as if expecting her to do it. But he was the one who was mistaken. Instead of running, she cupped her hand and ran a fingertip up, then down the pulsing heat beneath the black cotton.

He grabbed her wrist—none too gently. "What's the matter with you?"

"You're the one who wanted me to touch you." She tugged on her wrist. "Let me touch you some more."

He gentled his hold, though he still kept her hand away from his body. "This isn't working. I thought I could scare you away."

She snorted and raised a brow. He almost smiled. "Stupid thought, I agree. But Mary, we can't. Someday you'll get married, and then—"

"No, I won't. I know who I am, what I am." A thought occurred to her, and she glanced into his face with trepidation. "You want me, don't you?"

He hesitated, as if to deny that, and her heart fluttered; her stomach roiled. No one had ever wanted her, not even her parents. But after staring into her eyes for a long time, he sighed, and the fingertips of his free hand brushed her cheek. "Of course I do. I just don't want you hurt. I'm still leaving, Mary. Whatever happens between us isn't going to stop that."

"I never thought it would. I need you, Reese, and I think you need me. Just once, let me have this. Let me have you and you can have me. No one else need ever know."

Before he could refuse her again, she leaned forward and pressed her mouth to the fascinating ridges of his belly, brushed her cheek against the softness of his hair, let his scent flow through her and into her, then ran her tongue beneath the waistband of his pants.

He growled and shoved his hands into her hair. Hairpins scattered, pinging against the ground like frozen rain. He pulled her mouth up to his and kissed her hard, then fell back on the bed, dragging her after him.

This was what she'd wanted; this was what she'd dreamed of. Reese in her bed, his mouth on hers, his hands against her skin. Yet the force of his need frightened her.

One moment, she was atop him; the next, he gently lowered her to his side. And as he kissed her, he fumbled with the buttons along the front of her dress. He could not seem to get a single one open.

She wanted his hands on her. She wanted his mouth where no one else's had ever been. Raising her hands, she covered his, and he trembled, then went still.

"You asked if I wanted you." He leaned his forehead against hers. "I want you so bad, I haven't been able to think of anything else since you found me in Dallas. I've dreamed of touching you like this, and now I'm shaking so badly, you'd think this was my first time."

"It is your first time." He raised his head and frowned at her. "With me."

His smile was the first smile of joy she'd seen on his face. She couldn't help but reach up and touch his lips. He kissed her fingertips, and her eyes stung.

"Let me take off a few layers. Women's clothes are meant to be a prison. They hold us in."

"And keep us out."

"There is that." She stood, releasing the buttons of her dress.

"Mary?"

She glanced over her shoulder and saw him light the lamp. A golden glow filled the room, washing over Reese as he sat and reclined on her bed. Her breath caught at the beauty of the man.

"Could you let me watch?"

"Hmm?"

"Turn around?"

Her face heated. He wanted her to face him and undress. She'd led the man to her room, touched him intimately, begged him to teach her things she did not quite understand. Undress as he watched? Why not?

She turned and shrugged the garment from her shoulders. The dress slid down her body, pooling at her feet. She found she could not look at him.

So she concentrated on her task, tugging the strings of her corset loose and pulling the whale-boned device from her body, then tossing it to the floor. The thud nearly drowned out the deep breath she took. Both echoed in the silence of her room. As she bent to unlace her boots, her hair fell across her face. With an impatient huff, she straightened and blew the strands out of the way. She found Reese staring at her as if she were an exotic creature that had stepped out of a picture book.

"What?" she asked, startled at the intensity of his expression.

"You're the most beautiful thing I've ever seen."

She turned her face aside. "Don't," she murmured. "Don't tease me now."

A sudden rustle, a sharp creak, and he stood too close, once again a wild creature who stalked the night—her. His hands descended upon her shoulders, heat against her chill, yet she shivered.

He turned her about so that her back rested against his front. Where her chemise did not cover her shoulders, the hair of his chest brushed and tickled. "Look," he whispered in her ear, and his fingertip raised her face.

The mirror over her nightstand was just big enough to hold them both—Reese . . . and a woman she'd never seen before.

Untamed golden hair curled about her face, the mass giving an illusion of roundness to the usual sharp planes of her nose and cheekbones. He slid a finger down her nose. "These freckles do sinful things to my insides. I've been wanting to put my mouth on them since the moment I first saw you just to see how they might taste."

Her hated freckles, he adored, which made Mary look at them just a bit differently. And as she looked, her blue eyes shone bright against the flush of her cheeks, and the pale skin of her chest sloped to the rounded fullness of her breasts.

His hand slid over her shoulder; a single dark finger circled the fading bruise from the rifle's kick and made her remember when his mouth had traced the same path. She forgot that quickly enough when it traced the lace of her chemise and scraped the valley between her breasts. Then, as she continued to watch, transfixed, his hand dipped inside and freed one rose-tipped breast, cupping the softness in his hardened palm.

"You *are* beautiful. Not just to me but to anyone with eyes to see." His head lowered, and he pressed a kiss to her neck, then rolled her nipple between his thumb and finger. The sensation exploded throughout her body—his touch, and the sight of it, more erotic than anything she had ever imagined.

He pulled the ribbon on the chemise and slid the garment from her shoulders, baring her to the waist. His hands cupped both breasts, lifted them, held them, taunted them as she watched all the while in the mirror.

His hands, her body, her face, his mouth.

The world narrowed to this room, the mirror, her bed, the two of them as entwined as their discarded clothes on the floor.

Dark against light, ivory, bronze, gold—colors danced across them, though them, into them. She closed her eyes and saw every beautiful secret in the world.

She'd wanted a teacher, and she couldn't have asked for a better one. Patience and understanding, gentleness and care—he was everything she could have dreamed of in a secret lover. Everything she could have wanted in a man.

He worshiped every inch of her body and let her explore every inch of his. Her fascination with his muscles, his ridges and valleys, so different from her own, made him smile.

Even his scars lured her to touch, trace, taste. And after his initial stiffness, the first time he pulled her away and she refused to go, he let her do whatever she wished with every part of him— body and soul.

She knew better than to ask where this knife slash had come from, to demand why that bullet hole had been made, to let him see the tear that dripped onto the scar on his back that no weapon she'd ever seen could match.

The perfection of her skin seemed to entice him as much as the marks on his enticed her. He ran his mouth from her toes to her eyes and back again, murmuring nonsense against her belly, tracing his tongue along the back of her knee, finding places on her body she'd never thought of before and making them scream to be touched again.

He had more patience than any man she'd ever known; not that she'd known so very many. He caressed her and kissed her, whispering what he would do and how she would feel, how he would feel, until she wanted to scream for him to do those things now.

And when he shifted, just enough, to fit himself in the hollow that shrieked with emptiness, she gasped and arched against him, calling him by the only name she knew.

"Mary," he murmured, the cadence of his voice trilling along her sensitive skin like a spring breeze. "Once we go further, there's no going back. I can still stop." He kissed her damp brow, and she rubbed her forehead along his lips. "All you have to do is ask."

When she opened her eyes, his were close enough for her to see yellow flecks amid the green. His face was tense, his body the same, but his eyes were gentle. If she said no, even now, flesh to flesh, heart to heart, hill to valley, he would not touch her anymore.

Smiling, she ran her hand over the curve of his buttock, pulling him tighter against her. He started, and his eyes widened in shock before he grinned. "I guess that's as good an answer as any."

They kissed, their mouths still curved on a smile, and he moved forward again and probed gently but firmly at her entrance. On a sigh she welcomed his tongue into her mouth, his body into hers.

Deeper, harder, fuller, he stretched her, sinking into an incredible emptiness she'd never known was there until he filled it. Then he stopped.

She clutched his back, and his shoulders trembled. "Reese?"

"You know what happens now, don't you?"

"Not exactly. But don't stop!" She arched, and he slid deeper, stopping at the edge of something she couldn't quite understand. Good or bad, she did not know, but she wanted all of him.

He cursed, shifted to the side, and put a hand on her hip, holding her still even as she ached to move. "This is going to hurt, Mary, just for a minute."

"Fine." Her head thrashed on the pillow. Her body was on fire. She didn't care what happened as long as something did.

He took a deep breath and the movement rubbed their bellies together; she moaned at the sensation. The hair on his chest tickled her breasts. He plunged forward, and her eyes shot open as something broke and gave within her.

His mouth took hers, swallowing her cry, kissing her and tasting her until she thought of nothing but the kiss for a while. Then began to move. He had been right. She'd hurt only for a minute, and now the pain was gone.

She couldn't think; she could only feel. Empty, full, him, her, harder, faster. Something . . . something . . . something. . . . *What?*

His mouth left hers. His breath licked her skin; his lips nuzzled at the fullness of her breast. Her fingers tangled in his hair, holding him to her, never wanting to let go.

Then he plunged one last time, deeper than all the other times, and she felt a pulse so far inside that it touched off an answering quake within her. His lips closed over her nipple and he suckled, hard. She cried out as the world went bright and shiny behind her closed eyes, and all her questions suddenly had a single answer. *Them.*

Fourteen

Nearly as good as the act itself was what came after. Reese gathered Mary to him, tucked the blanket around them both, and held her against his chest as they drifted toward sleep. The reassuring cadence of his breath past her ear, his arm across her waist, and his palm cradling her stomach made her sleep more deeply than she ever had before.

Who would have thought sleeping in a stranger's arms could be so soothing? But then Reese was hardly a stranger anymore.

Mary awoke in the darkest hour just before dawn, and he was still there. Waking up in a man's arms was even better than going to sleep in them. She had to stop thinking this way, since she'd promised him one night only. And she needed to keep that promise—for both their sakes. The sisters had told her little of men and less of marriage. But one thing she *had* overheard was how children were made—or near enough. A woman must endure—Mary paused to giggle at the endure part—many trips to the marriage bed for the sake of giving her husband a child.

Recalling the ecstasy of her single trip—albeit not to a marriage bed—made Mary think it a good thing that many such experiences were needed to make a child.

Nevertheless, once was all she would have. No child would come from that. Only the joy of the memory, which she would cherish for the rest of her life.

Mary stole out from under Reese's arm. Mumbling, he turned away. She smiled and wished that she could keep him there forever. But he'd told her he could not stay—for whatever reason—and she'd said she understood. She would not cling and beg, adding to the burdens that haunted his heart. Mary Margaret McKendrick could take care of herself.

She kissed Reese gently on the brow, a whisper so as not to awaken him, then dressed and slipped from the room and the house. Sitting on the back porch, she stared at the midnight sky. Dawn would be breaking soon. Mary could feel the sun tremble at the edge of the earth.

The last breeze of night brushed her face and iced her tears. She rubbed them away with impatient annoyance. She'd wanted one night, and she'd had it. How could she have known that touching Reese just once would make her ache to touch him forever?

She heard nothing—not a breath, not a shuffle—to indicate she was not alone. But the world went dark, and Mary never saw dawn break the sky.

Reese kept his eyes closed until the door clicked shut behind Mary. The moment she'd awakened, he had, too. He'd been sleeping with one ear cocked for so long, even in the bed of a good woman while sleeping better than he had in years, he still listened for the telltale whisper of danger.

The danger this morning had been in the way she moved so as not to awaken him. If Mary didn't want to face him, Reese couldn't blame her. He would let her slip out; then he'd do so himself. It was the least he could do for this woman who had let him cry in her arms and had still taken him into her bed, then into her body.

He was the fool who should have stopped this, though Reese couldn't say he was sorry. Mary had soothed his raging soul, given him back a tiny part of himself he'd thought dead and buried with the others. He'd had women since then; he'd had sex. But loving Mary had been different—better than sex.

Reese had no illusions there'd be other nights. What else did sneaking out before dawn mean? So whatever had happened in this bed would be his only such experience, because there would never be another woman like Mary—at least for him.

He could not stay. She knew that. She said she'd never marry. He knew better. She thought she wasn't pretty. She couldn't see past the elegant nose on her face. She hadn't been out west long enough to know that even if she'd been hound ugly, women like her were more valuable than gold to lonely men trying to make an empire out of nothing. So, eventually, another man would give her children, and Reese could not stay around to watch. *Children.* He sat up so fast his head whirled.

Damn! Sometimes he was too stupid to live. Last night, in the aftermath of one of his embarrassing episodes, he had not had the strength to resist her allure. He'd denied himself any warmth, any friendship, any comfort, for so long that at his weakest moment he hadn't been able to deny himself any longer.

He was a selfish bastard. He'd never said he wasn't, but he would not leave here until he made sure Mary did not carry his child.

And if she did?

Reese sighed. Then he would marry her. He'd give her the best that he could—whatever she needed. Protection, money, his name, then his absence and word of his death. Because Mary deserved much better than him.

He would dress and slip from the house before the sun came up. If anyone saw him, he'd just have to kill them.

As he left Mary's bedroom, Reese gave a snort of derision. He'd never killed needlessly, and he wasn't about to start now, no matter how cranky he felt.

In the hall, he hesitated. He could not make himself leave without saying goodbye. Sneaking away was something you did when you were embarrassed over what you had done or with whom you had done it. While he might be embarrassed at his lack of control where Mary was concerned, he could think of *what* had passed between them with nothing but joy.

So Reese trolled the house, and when he could not find her, he began to worry. He peeked onto the front porch. She wasn't there. So he went to the back porch. She wasn't there, either, but she had been, and so had someone else.

Pinned to the floorboard with a knife, directly in front of the door, was a note. *We have your woman. Come and get her alone. Past the river and the trees. Go west. We'll find you.*

Reese leaned his head against the door, cursing softly, futilely. Because he had touched her, they had taken her. But how?

He pulled himself upright, placed his hat on his head, and patted the guns at his hips. No time to waste on how. There was only time to get Atlanta and ride west. Alone.

He had no illusions he would survive the day. Mary was bait in a trap set just for him. Take out the leader and the rest would run. he adage followed Reese's own philosophy.

Reese had once said he did not sneak, but he did so now. From the back of Mary's house to the stables, where he saddled Atlanta and led the animal out into the darkness, then away from the town. By the time the watch changed and his men realized he wasn't in his room, or anywhere else, Reese would have Mary safe.

Or they'd both be dead.

Mary had heard stories of soldiers who'd slept with the reins of their horses in their hands, only to awaken and discover that the Comanches had stolen every single animal. She understood now how such stories could be true.

El Diablo had come to Rock Creek alone, slipped in, knocked Mary on the head, and escaped with none of the six any the wiser. If she hadn't been the one stolen, she might never have believed it.

"Reese will rescue me." Mary tilted her chin and looked El Diablo straight in the eye. "That's what he does."

Terror might pound beneath her breast and in her sore head, but she'd be damned if she'd let El Diablo see it. She tightened her lips and hugged herself to prevent the shiver that came despite the midday sun blazing on her uncovered head.

"But, *señorita,*" he said in his annoyingly perfect English, "that is what I am waiting for."

A trap! The old man wanted Reese, and he was using her as bait. Mary cursed herself again for being taken, though how she might have avoided it, she had no idea.

El Diablo sat on his horse and stared back the way they had come. When she'd awakened, he'd allowed her to sit up on his horse, instead of slung over it like a dead body, until they'd gotten here—wherever here was. Then he'd placed a rope about her neck and shoved her to the ground. She'd also heard of Comanche captives being made to run behind their captor's horse; if they fell, they were dragged until they died.

That shiver came again. Mary filled the silence so that she wouldn't keep listening to the memories of all that she'd heard. "Where are the rest of your men?"

"Not here."

"Why not?"

"They are animals who have not been near a woman in many weeks. I need you alive and sane. If I let them near you, neither one would be true for very long."

The image his words conjured up made Mary's mouth go dry, and she had to swallow a few times before continuing. "You can't think that you can take Reese alone."

That black gaze flicked over her again, and though El Diablo's face never moved, a sneer colored his voice. "No?"

"No."

He shrugged. "I don't mean to *take* him anywhere."

Mary didn't like the sound of that. Perhaps if she kept El Diablo talking, she might distract him enough to give Reese a chance.

"Reese thinks there's something in Rock Creek that you want."

El Diablo returned his gaze to the land. "Reese is a smart man."

"So there is something?"

"I have told my men Rock Creek is golden."

"Gold?" Mary frowned. "I don't think so."

"One man's gold is another man's yellow rock."

"What does that mean?"

"Think about it, *señorita*. Perhaps you will understand before you go back where you came from."

"I'm not leaving."

He threw his poncho over his shoulder, revealing a gun slung across his chest. "We shall see about that."

The distant sound of hoofbeats made Mary spin about. The rope scraped her neck, but she didn't care. Reese was coming.

But was that good or bad?

The old Indian must be half-crazy. He just stood out in the middle of nowhere, backed by a tiny grove of trees, with Mary on a leash. Reese had seen them for miles. No doubt El Diablo had been watching him for twice that long.

Reese had figured El Diablo would take Mary back to his hiding place—in a cave or a canyon or even over the border into Mexico. He'd feared by the time he reached her, she would be dead, or worse. So he couldn't understand why the old man was waiting for him all alone. But Reese would take every gift he was given.

He pulled to a stop in front of them. A quick glance at Mary revealed her unhurt except for the welt on her neck from the rope. When their eyes met, she took an involuntary step toward him, and El Diablo yanked her back.

She winced, and her hand went to the rope. But she didn't cry, and she didn't beg. Reese gritted his teeth to keep from jumping off Atlanta and cutting her free. He returned his attention to El Diablo, who watched him intently. Reese kept his hands in plain sight. Moving too fast around a wild thing would get you killed.

"How did you manage to get her?"

"I have been watching you."

"You think I don't know that?"

El Diablo dipped his head in acknowledgment. "I know Rock Creek, the land upon which she sits, the land that surrounds her like a mother's arms surround a child. And I was not so foolish as to come when the one who is like me was watching."

"Sullivan would have seen you."

"Yes. But I know how to disappear so a white eyes would never see me at all."

Reese doubted that, but he could understand how a single old man could slip in and out in the dark, though he wasn't pleased about it. "Let her go," he said.

"That was my plan. Her for you. See how safe she has been with me?"

Her neck was raw and might carry a scar but in truth Mary was lucky. El Diablo could have done nigh onto anything to her, and Reese would have done whatever it took to get her back. From the smirk on the old man's face, he'd known that all along. *Fool!* Reese berated himself. He had put Mary in danger because he could not stay away from her; he could not stop kissing her, touching her, needing her. Was he any better than Rico, who took every woman who fell at his feet into his bed? Reese had touched Mary with love and brought her nothing but hate.

"Her for me." He nodded. "All right."

"No!" Mary lunged against the rope again, choked, coughed, then glared at him. "It isn't all right."

"Don't start to manage things now. I know what I'm doing."

"He's going to kill you."

"I figured that out all by myself." Reese just didn't plan to let him, if he could manage it. First he had to get rid of Mary, then he'd see what he could do about the old Indian. "I'd do the same thing. Take out the leader and the rest run."

"But they won't run!"

He narrowed his gaze on Mary, willing her to shut up. She was right; they wouldn't run—right away. They'd avenge him first. But if El Diablo didn't think his plan was working, he might kill Mary, too, and that Reese wasn't going to allow.

"I'm afraid they will. I'm the only thing holding them here. You didn't think it was one hundred and fifty dollars, did you?"

He turned away before she could answer. "I want Mary to take my horse and head back to Rock Creek."

"You don't trust me?" Reese snorted. "What's to keep me from riding after her once we've finished our business?"

"Whatever's kept you from killing her so far. The soldiers?"

El Diablo lowered his head. "There is only so much trouble they will ignore. Killing the schoolteacher would bring more attention than I wish."

"And you don't want attention. Why?"

"Gold," Mary blurted out. "He says there's gold."

Reese frowned. "Since when did a Comanche care about gold?"

"Since I discovered how important it is to the

white man. They will do anything if they think gold is involved. Enough." He flipped his weathered hand at Reese. "Drop your guns."

Reese hesitated. He had hoped that one-on-one he could take El Diablo. But without a gun the odds dipped significantly.

"You want the woman? Drop the gun. I am not a fool. As soon as she is gone, you will shoot me dead."

Reese shrugged, dismounted, and unbuckled his belt. "You have to admit, it was a good idea."

"Yes, but it was *my* idea. Throw them over here." Reese tossed the guns near El Diablo's horse. "Get her gone." He threw Mary's rope at Reese.

Mary ran the short distance separating them. Unable to put her arms around him because of her bound hands, she placed her cheek against his chest. Reese held her for one moment, kissed the top of her head, glanced at El Diablo, and found the man watching.

Mary looked up at him, and he kissed her again—long and good. What difference did it make now if El Diablo knew he would do anything for her? The damage was done. If he had to die today, at least he'd do so with Mary's taste on his mouth.

He broke the kiss. Staring into her panicked eyes, he cut the bindings at her wrists and the noose about her neck. "Get on Atlanta and go home."

The panic left her eyes so fast, he almost heard a snap as anger took its place. "No."

"I don't mind dying for you, Mary, but I'll be damned if I'll let you watch me do it."

Her mulish expression didn't change. Perhaps he would have to tie her to the horse. Reese turned toward El Diablo to ask for more rope and caught a hint of movement in the trees.

Hell, had the old man brought the rest of his crew? If so, Reese had no chance of getting out of this alive.

A single shot whizzed by the Comanche's head. Reese caught the expression of surprise on the old man's face before he disappeared from the saddle.

If it wasn't El Diablo's men in the trees waiting to kill Reese, then who was it? Who had the ability to sneak up on an ancient Comanche? Reese had an idea, and he was going to do some serious butt kicking—if he lived long enough.

Shoving Mary to the ground, Reese dove for his gun. As his fingers closed about the familiar grip, he saw where El Diablo had gone. Hanging beneath the horse's neck from a sling in the Comanche way, his rifle was trained on Reese. Reese rolled the other way; but the gun went off, and fire exploded in his chest.

Before the world went completely black, Reese saw El Diablo race away, pursued by the unknown assailants who had hidden in the trees.

Fifteen

Mary hit the ground hard and lay there for a moment, stunned. But gunshots had her crawling in the direction Reese had jumped. If she had to, she would throw herself on top of him and hope El Diablo was serious about not wanting to shoot the schoolteacher. If he wasn't, too bad.

Reese would die for her, would he? Who said only men could be heroes? She'd die for him, too.

Before she could crawl a foot, horses surrounded her. She dragged herself upright. She would not die crawling. Brushing her hair from her face, she looked up, prepared to see El Diablo's right-hand man, Jefferson, and the rest of his thieves and murderers staring down at her.

The sight of Cash, Nate, and Jed nearly made her fall back to the ground. "Wh-where did you come from?"

She glanced in the direction of the first shot, only to see El Diablo being pursued by two riders—Rico and Sullivan—from the looks of the missing. Then her gaze lit on the still, dark form bleeding into the dirt.

She cried out and ran to him, fell to her knees and let her hands flutter over his face, his neck.

He breathed; his heart beat. But his shirt was soaked, the black material gruesome with blood.

She tried to unbutton it, but her hands trembled so badly, she couldn't. When someone grabbed her arm and tried to pull her away, she snarled at them, fought like a mad thing, and when they released her, she ripped the shirt open. Blood seeped from a hole just below his shoulder.

Now what? She had no idea what to do with a bullet wound. Faced with the truly unmanageable for the first time, Mary panicked. She tore a strip from her petticoat and mopped at the blood, only making things worse.

"Miss McKendrick?" Nate knelt beside her. He replaced the bloody strip with a silver flask. "Try this."

A glance at the others showed Jed looking away as if embarrassed and Cash staring at her with cold, dead eyes. They would be no help.

She glanced back at Nate, who nodded encouragingly, so she poured the alcohol over the open wound, and Reese's eyes snapped open. He arched in pain, then passed out again.

"I'm sorry; I'm sorry." She leaned over him, kissing his face, touching his cheeks. When Nate pulled her back, she stared in horror at the bloodstains she'd left all over Reese's face.

"We've got to get him back to town," Nate said.

"All right."

That docile voice couldn't be coming from her. And who was that woman allowing Nate to lead her to his horse while Jed carried Reese to his? That couldn't be Mary Margaret McKendrick, could it? The woman who managed the unmanageable. She'd never realized just how unmanageable some things could be.

Mary lost track of time, her entire being focused on Jed and his burden. A few times she swayed, but Nate held her tight. She was grateful Cash rode behind them, because every time he looked at her, Mary sensed his anger, and she had no idea what she had done to deserve it.

When they reached Rock Creek, people poured from their houses, but when they saw Reese, their jubilance turned silent. Jed turned toward the hotel.

"No." Mary's voice rose above the clip-clop of the horses' hooves. "Take him to my place. I'll be responsible."

Jed glanced back and frowned. Mary felt Nate shrug. Then Cash spoke. "She *is* responsible. Take him there."

No one said a word as Jed carried Reese into Mary's house and laid him on her bed. She could not help but remember, looking at him pale and bloody on her tousled sheets, that not even a day had passed since they had joined together in that very same bed.

Nate shoved her out of his way. "I need to get the bullet out. Jed, get me hot water and clean cloths." He turned to Cash. "Fetch Rico's knives."

Mary winced. Nate rolled up his sleeves and started to remove Reese's torn shirt.

"Can you do this?" she whispered.

"I've done it so many times, I've lost count. Maybe you should wait in the kitchen, Miss McKendrick. Bullets never come out half as pretty as they go in."

She looked at Reese's face, pale beneath the tan. He looked both younger and older, if that was possible. "I can't leave him."

"Suit yourself. But if you faint, don't expect me to care. All I care about is Reese."

His words brought her back to herself. That was all she cared about, too.

Mary straightened and stepped briskly to the other side of the bed. "Mr. Lang, I never faint."

He gave her the ghost of a smile. "I'll just bet you don't."

Hours later, the bandage around Reese's chest shone as stark against his skin as the clean sheets at his back. The bullet was out. Nate had done all he could. Now they would wait and see if the lead had nicked anything vital or if infection would set in.

Night fell. Everyone was tired, for Rico, who had gone looking for Reese when he didn't show up at the morning's lessons, had rousted the men from bed far too early that morning. It hadn't taken them long to discover that both Reese and Mary were missing—and Reese's horse as well. They had followed immediately, and Sullivan—the next best thing to a bloodhound—had found them in short order.

Mary could hear the low rumble of three men's voices from her parlor. They weren't going anywhere. Rico and Sullivan hadn't returned, but no one seemed worried. Yet.

She sat in a chair next to the bed and rested her aching head next to Reese's hip. She planned to be the first face he saw when he awoke—or the last face he saw, if it came to that.

Her eyes prickled with tears she would not shed. Tears were for weaklings, and she had to be strong. For Reese.

Someone stepped into the room. Mary, looking up, found Cash staring at her with those frighteningly cold eyes. She'd known he would come. Maybe that's why she hadn't been able to fall asleep yet.

"He'd better not die."

The words sounded like a threat—no doubt they were—but Mary wasn't afraid. If Reese died, she didn't care what Cash did to her.

"He won't."

"You know that for certain?"

"I won't let him."

His mouth, framed between the neatly trimmed mustache and beard, twisted into the usual sneer. "You might manage this town of women and weaklings—and the kiddies, too. You might have even managed Reese for a while, but only because he let you—God knows why. But you can't manage this. And you sure as hell aren't going to manage me."

"I never thought I could."

"I know about women like you."

"Do you?" He was starting to make her angry. And the anger felt so much better than the fear.

"I would have thought you only knew about women who could be bought."

His eyes narrowed. "All women can be bought. With some it takes money; with others, a wedding band."

They stared at each other over Reese's still body. Why was she arguing with Cash? He loved Reese as much as she did or he wouldn't be so upset. *Love.* She sighed and rubbed at the welt on her neck, which burned fiercely, a strong reminder of what had happened and what Reese had done for her. She loved him, and it didn't matter at all. He was going to leave her—one way or another.

"You blame me for this, don't you?"

"Hell, yes. You're his weakness. Men like him, men like me, can't afford a weakness. That's where the bandidos strike first. We found a note. They told him to come alone, and the fool went alone. For you. Anyone else, he would have taken us, and to hell with the consequences. He was going to give his life for yours."

"I know," she whispered.

"That man is worth ten of you, Miss McKendrick."

She looked up into Cash's angry eyes. "I know that, too."

Near dawn Mary heard horses approach. She glanced at Reese. During the night he'd awakened a few times, taken water, then fallen asleep again. He had not called her by name or asked for any of the others.

She didn't know if all that sleep was bad or good, but so far he hadn't become delirious, and he didn't feel hot.

Mary moved to the window, but the three men who'd taken over her front parlor were already on the porch. The horses belonged to Sullivan and Rico. She relaxed and returned to Reese's side.

The five men joined her; some sat on the floor, some leaned against the wall, one sat on a chest at the foot of the bed. They filled the small room. For some reason they needed to be near Reese while they spoke. Since they didn't kick her out, Mary kept quiet and listened.

"They're holed up near the big river, in an old ranch butted up against the hills." Sullivan removed his hat; his hair hung in his face, making him look even more exhausted. "Only way in is from the front. And nothing but dirt for miles around."

"*El capitán* was right. To attack would be difficult. They would see us coming, dig in. I do not know how we would get them out."

"We could just keep shooting until we don't need to get them out," Cash growled. "Unless we want to bury them."

"Or we could continue to wait for them here," Jed said. "Like we were told."

"It's a shame we have no minds of our own." Nate sipped amber liquid from one of Mary's glasses. It was the first time she'd seen him drink since Reese had been hurt. "I suspect that's what happens when you let someone else make all the important decisions for so long."

"Speak for yourself, preacher. I know my mind. I say we go blast them back to hell."

"Perhaps we should wait a few days. I would like to be here when *el capitán* wakes up."

All eyes turned to Reese. A collective sigh brushed through the room, dispelling the tension and the anger.

"Anyone remember the last time he was flat on his back wounded?" Jed asked.

The question elicited slow, thoughtful nods. Mary huddled in her chair, still as a mouse, afraid if she breathed too loudly they would quit talking about a past they all seemed to hide. But for the moment they had forgotten she was there.

Sullivan brushed his hair back and glanced out the window. "After the Wilderness. He put himself in front of me, and that bayonet sliced him deep enough to stitch."

Mary recalled tracing with her tongue the thin scar marring his side. Her face heated, but no one paid her any mind.

"He was too sore to ride," Jed said. "So we left him sleeping at that farmhouse and chased after those Yanks."

"And when we came back, I had never seen *el capitán* so angry." All eyes turned to Reese again. "He said if we ever went out without him again, without orders, he would make us sorry to come back alive."

"I guess El Diablo can wait a day," Cash muttered.

Mary glanced at the gunfighter in surprise. He loved Reese; of that she was certain. And he respected him as a soldier. But she would never have thought Cash would be afraid of him. She didn't think Cash was afraid of anything. Except maybe a good woman.

"You were in the same company during the war?" The question was out before she could stop it. When they all looked at her, she flushed.

"Reese didn't tell you?" Jed asked.

"No. He just said he wasn't your captain."

Nate started coughing, so Cash reached over and slapped him on the back so hard, Nate nearly dropped his glass.

"He *is* the captain," Jed said. "He just didn't want to be."

"But someone had to."

"Reese is a leader. He can't help it, he just is."

Mary could understand that. "So how did y'all end up together?"

Jed glanced at Nate, who shrugged and glanced at Cash, who scowled. Rico and Sullivan remained silent. The silence built until it was broken only by the sound of seven people breathing.

"It's not a secret anymore." Jed sighed. "I guess we don't need to keep hoarding information like Alan Pinkerton."

Mary frowned. "The spy?"

"Secret service."

"The operative word being secret. And Pinkerton was on the wrong side."

"Wrong?" Jed laughed. "I like her."

Mary ignored him. "What did y'all do in the war?"

"Secret things." Nate winked.

Jed shot him an exasperated look before returning his attention to Mary. "You've heard of Colonel Mosby."

"Of course. I'm from Virginia."

"He wanted to reproduce Pinkerton's success for the Confederacy. So Old Mose put together a group of men, with varying talents, who had nothing left to lose."

"The six of you?"

Jed nodded. "Either we'd lost our companies or didn't fit in where we were, but we had a talent that got us noticed. A few years into the war, we were all ordered to Atlanta. We met Mosby and Jefferson Davis and each other. We were to capture intelligence, both papers and people, while harassing Union lines in the same way Mosby's Rangers did."

"A band of guerrilla fighters with orders to spy."

"Pretty much."

"But you stayed together even after the war."

"War makes men out of boys and lifelong friends in the process."

"There's got to be more to it than that."

"*El capitán* made us into something to be proud of. We were misfits, lost souls, but once he came into our lives and showed us the good we could do together, we did not want to go back to the way we had been."

Rico shrugged. "We each have our stories of why we came to be in the war, how we came to the notice of Mosby. Many of them are not pleasant stories. But Reese never once asked what we had done. He accepted us without question, trusted us to guard his back, and risked his life for each and every one of us at one time or another. How could we not do the same?"

"And when he asked you to do jobs after the war?"

"He did not ask; we vowed to be there for each other—always."

"Why?"

"We are family."

"You have no other families?"

"None such as this."

"You don't even know his name."

"Names mean nothing if you know a man's heart."

Mary had to agree.

Reese heard them talking from a long way off. He'd been wounded enough times to know he was wounded again, and this time it was bad.

He drifted in and out, listening to the rise and fall of the voices. Those voices gave him comfort. Those men would never let him die.

Some sense of what they were saying penetrated his hazy, heated mind. Mosby and missions, secrets and lies. So many things they had all shared, yet in reality so little.

Regardless of his attempts to remain aloof, he was as much a part of them as they were of him. And just because he did not know Jed's sister's name or why Rico had gone to war or how Sullivan could be a Comanche with an Irish name or why Nate drank or what woman had hurt Cash so badly he couldn't bear to be civil to anyone didn't mean that if he lost them, he would not be lost himself.

They were his friends, even though he didn't want them to be any more than he'd wanted to be the damned captain. He should know by now that what you wanted you rarely got. You made do with what you had.

The revelations of Reese's men about their past in the war only confused Mary more. Reese had been a hero not only to his superiors but also to the men who chose to follow him. Why, then, did he refuse to open up to them? To her? To anyone?

What secret horror lurked in the years before he'd met Mosby in Atlanta? And did she really want to know?

Time had no meaning except in relation to Reese's needs. Mary nursed him day and night. Everywhere she turned, she tripped over a man. They refused to return to the hotel, sending one man to the tower at a time just in case El Diablo was stupid enough to return here after he'd dared to shoot their leader.

Mary posted a notice adjourning school for the year. The session had only been a few days away from the end, anyway. When Clancy came by to protest, Sutton at his heels, she'd heard Cash tell them both to—Well, something obscene. That he'd stood up for her made Mary think he might be softening, if such a thing was possible. At least he'd stopped sneering whenever she came into a room.

In between practice shots, the women brought food. The older men——Brown and some of his cronies——had taken up teaching the women and helped to keep watch in the tower. According to Jo, who stopped by each day, everyone had decided that to make the town theirs, they had to protect it, which was what Mary had been saying all along.

She walked into Reese's room at midday and shrieked when she found two figures bending over Reese's bed. The Sutton twins whirled about even as Cash pounded down the hall and burst through the door. "How did you get in here?" he growled.

They nodded at the open window. "Rico and Carrie were up in the tower showing Miss Clancy how to keep watch."

Mary glanced at Cash. "Jo's learning how to keep watch?"

He shrugged. "Need more help than Brown and his friends if we have to go away awhile."

They were still considering going after El Diablo, against Reese's wishes. She couldn't say she blamed them. If Reese died, she wouldn't give a plug nickel for El Diablo's chances.

"So you were in the tower?" Cash encouraged.

"And we saw Miss McKendrick's window was open. Rico said it should be closed, for sec-sec-security. We just wanted to make sure he wasn't dead. Our pa said he was dead."

"Your pa's the one who's gonna be dead if he doesn't shut his trap."

The twins blinked at Cash, eyes wide and scared.

"Go frighten someone your own size," Mary told him.

But Cash no longer glared at the twins; he stared at the bed. "What's wrong with him?" His voice had gone as dead as his eyes, and a chill ran over Mary even before she spun about to look at Reese.

His face unnaturally flushed, he trembled so hard the bed shook, and his teeth chattered.

"What did you two little brats do to him?" Cash thundered.

"N-nothin'!" Frank wailed. "We just talked to him awhile. Told him how much we liked him. Said we wanted to ride with him, like you do. We never even touched him!"

"Cash, let them go." Mary heard the twins flee. Then she lifted the corner of the bandage on Reese's shoulder.

The room spun. Cash's hands came down on her shoulders, steadying her. Mary cast him a surprised but grateful glance. "Get Nate," she said. "This doesn't look good."

Sixteen

The men filled the parlor doorway. Mary stood in a circle of light that fell from the bedroom. Nate hovered between them.

"Infection and fever. It's what I was afraid of."

"He gonna die?" Cash asked.

"I don't know." Nate pulled out his flask, then, with a sigh, put it away again. "I just don't know. But I have to say—it doesn't look very good."

Mary's heart pounded so loudly, her chest hurt. She'd hoped Nate would come in, baptize Reese with alcohol again, pat him on the head, and pronounce him cured. Instead, he'd drained a foul-smelling liquid from the wound, shaking his head and muttering all the while.

Reese thrashed and burned and mumbled like a madman. Mary was scared to death. She wanted to scream and rant and rave at the sky. She wanted to get her hands around the throat of the man who had done this. She wanted to curl up next to Reese on the bed and hold him close forever.

"I'm through waitin' around," Cash announced. "I'm goin' after that Comanche bastard. No offense, Sullivan."

Sullivan merely turned his usual stoic expression on Cash and said nothing.

While Mary understood Cash's sentiments, she also recalled that Reese had not wanted them to go after El Diablo in his own lair. "What good will it do you to kill El Diablo and the rest now, even if you can?"

"If?" Cash sneered. "I can kill anything that walks."

"Not something I'd be very proud of."

"Spoken like a woman."

They glared at each other. Since Reese's injury and their subsequent talk, they had reached a truce of sorts. They both loved him, so they would put up with each other, but that didn't mean they wouldn't pick at each other, too, whenever the opportunity arose.

"Children." Nate raised his hands. "Bickering won't help."

"What will?" Cash asked.

"I don't know. There's nothing more I can do for him."

"Well, I'm not waiting around to watch him die when I can be out doing something. Who's in?"

No one bothered to answer. They all followed Cash out the front door.

Reese was by turns hot and cold. He ached all over, so deep in his bones that he could hardly bear the pain. The only thing that helped at all was when Mary's sweet voice penetrated the limbo where he lived and her fingers entwined with his.

The warmth of her hand in his darkness was like the flicker of the lamp she left in her window, reminding him that she was there, steady and sure as the sun, always.

Not long ago he'd heard other voices. Voices that had sent him over the edge once before. This time, weak from pain, wrung out from the fever, he did not have the strength to fight the worst pain of all.

His memories.

Reese sank into the gray mist of a past long buried. Down a long corridor lined with faces he flew, faster and faster, toward something he did not want to see because he already knew what it was.

The thunder of the cannon and the burst of the guns jerked his body, causing a shaft of agony that made him remember he was not really here—not really on this battlefield in Georgia again, even though it seemed that he was.

"Mr.—I mean, Captain."

Reese glanced at the soldier-child who stood at his elbow, a shock of brown hair tucked beneath his gray cap, his wide blue eyes focused on Reese with respectful adoration.

Robert Gow. Reese had known the boy all of his life. He'd known many of the boys in this company since the day they were born.

As the head schoolmaster at Garrison's Boys' Academy, outside Atlanta—a man whose father had attended West Point, then taught his scholarly son everything he knew—Reese had been offered a commission when the war broke out. He had not expected his fourth-year students to follow him into battle, but they had. As a result, the company Reese led consisted of the young men he'd been teaching since they were in short pants.

But he had taught them well—not only reading, writing, and the like but the importance of loyalty, honor, and devotion to friends, family, and country.

Reese was a leader, and he led well. His enthusiasm for the cause—the protection of their homes against the invader, the right to live as they chose—had kept the spirits of his men high when the morale of so many other companies flagged. Reese was proud of what they had accomplished, proud the boys admired him, proud they would follow him into hell itself—or so they said.

"Sir, shall we advance?"

Reese squinted against the damp, swirling gray mist—smoke, rain, and fog all mixed together. Somewhere out there were the Yankees. They were always out there somewhere.

Attack? Retreat? Wait? A choice he had to make every damned day. So far his choices had been good ones. Reese was confident he would continue to choose wisely. His company of soldier boys depended on him. Their families had entrusted them to him, and he would not let them down.

The scouting report he'd received that morning had said two companies waited over the ridge, but they were bedraggled from a battle not many days before. If Reese and his men could break through their line, they could join with another company to the east, flank the Yankees, and drive them back where they came from. Though the federal force was superior in number, Reese believed his soldier boys would triumph.

"Attack," Reese decided. "While the fog lingers."

"Sir." Gow saluted and moved quietly through the mist to gather the men.

Reese patted the letter in his pocket—the latest missive from the fiancée who awaited him in Atlanta. When the war was over, they would be married, and he would resume teaching young minds in the daytime, with the pleasurable bonus of enjoying his lovely wife each night.

His company having assembled, Reese joined them. Every time he saw them thus, lined up together, he was struck again by their youth.

Not a man was over twenty except for Gow and himself. But there was little Reese could do about that. The Confederacy needed every man it could find, even if some of the men had spent too little time as boys.

He nodded to Gow, who gave the silent order to advance. That was the last order Gow ever gave.

The Yankees spilled over the ridge, more than two companies, more than an army it looked like from the sea of bluecoats that poured down the hill toward them. Reinforcements must have arrived after Reese's scout had returned. He should never have attacked. He should have done what his daddy always told him to do when faced with a superior force—dig in and defend.

Reese didn't have time to curse fate. Fate crawled all over them. Gow went down first, without even a sound, falling backward into Reese's arms. His blue eyes looked surprised, and then he was gone, just like that.

Several of the boys stared at their lieutenant in horror and shuffled about as if they might run, but Reese shouted, "Stand firm, men!" and the panic did not erupt right away.

Having no time to get his horse, Reese dove in, using his sword this way, his gun that way. A bullet hit him in the thigh, and he went down on one knee. That was all it took for panic to engulf his soldier boys. A year of success in the field went the way of the west wind when they saw their lieutenant die and their captain fall.

Reese struggled upright. "Hold the line," he shouted.

But the swarm of gray rushing past him no longer heard anything but the buzz of terror.

Cursing, Reese turned to follow, hoping that if he got in front of them, if they saw he was all right, he would be able to turn the tide. But the sight that greeted him was a nightmare. Another wave of blue came over the crest. They were trapped.

He was a fool. He took one step toward his men, and the minié ball hit him in the back. He fell to the ground with the horror-stricken faces of his soldier boys imprinted on his mind forever. Not even the darkness that swallowed him made the faces go away.

Reese awoke to darkness so complete, he thought he must be dead. But the dead did not feel pain. Worse than the pain was the silence. Reese turned his head to the side and saw the trees and the sky beyond. He was all alone in the dark woods.

His feet were cold. Flexing his toes, he discovered his boots were gone; his socks, too. When he dragged himself upright, the pain in his back and his thigh made the world spin in a sickening lurch. When it stopped, Reese found that his guns were gone, along with his bullets and his best horse.

The only thing left with him in the grove of trees set between two ridges in Georgia were the bodies of every one of his soldier boys.

Mary learned more about Reese while he was unconscious than he'd ever shared with her while awake.

She spent the rest of that day and all through that long, dark, lonely night changing hot compresses on his shoulder and bathing the rest of his body with cool cloths. She dribbled water into his mouth every time he seemed semiconscious, though he babbled about boys and Georgia and a woman named Laura.

Reese had sworn he had no wife. Should she believe a man who refused to share his name, though he'd shared her bed? Did it even matter? Would she love him any less if he belonged to someone else?

Mary sighed and rubbed at her grainy eyes. She hadn't slept much—only snatches in between Reese's ravings, which invariably woke her up. When he was upset, she held his hand, and that seemed to send him back into short periods of sleep.

"Why don't you let me sit with him awhile?"

Jo stood in the doorway. Mary flipped the sheet over Reese's bare chest.

"I'm fine," she said.

"You look fine, if fine is half-dead. Go lie down."

Mary hesitated, but a glance at Reese's face made her realize the truth. "I couldn't sleep. I can't leave him."

Jo shrugged. "Figured that, but I thought I'd try."

"Who's in the tower?"

"Rose Sutton."

"You're kidding."

"No. Since Reese saved her boys, she's grown a spine. Told Baxter to shut up and get behind the counter, she was going to take her turn like any other citizen."

"Wish I could have seen that."

"I enjoyed it."

They exchanged a smile of affection. From the moment they'd met the two had shared a bond. Mary had found that some people you just liked and some you just didn't.

"And your father?" she asked. "How does he feel about your toting a gun and spending nights in the tower?"

"He doesn't like it, but since he's never liked much that I do, I'm not surprised. I've given up trying to please him. What's this I hear about El Diablo thinking there's gold in Rock Creek?"

"That's what he said. Do you know anything about it?"

"The old guy who owns the hotel mumbled about gold sometimes before he took off, but no one ever believed him. If he had any gold, why did he live here? But since this was once Comanche land, maybe El Diablo knows something we don't."

"Comanche land?"

Jo leaned against the doorway and nodded. "The people who began Rock Creek built the town on Comanche land. That's why there aren't any original settlers. Comanches killed them all or drove them off."

"When was this?"

"During the war, all the soldiers went east. The Comanches went crazy. They thought they'd won, that the bluecoats had been driven off. So they took back whatever they could."

"And then?"

"When the soldiers came back, they scuttled every Comanche they could find off to Indian Territory."

"So folks came back to Rock Creek."

"For a while, anyway."

"Hmm." Mary returned her attention to Reese. He slept peacefully, and his shoulder looked better. Perhaps he wouldn't leave her by dying, after all.

"You're in love with him, aren't you?"

Mary shifted her gaze to Jo. "It shows so much?" Jo said nothing, just continued to look at Mary with acceptance in her eyes. "I didn't want to love him. I've managed everything since I was child, but I couldn't manage this."

"You can't manage how you feel; you can't change who you love. What do *you* want, Mary?"

'It doesn't matter. Reese isn't staying, and he never said he was."

"Men change."

"Name one."

"There must be one somewhere, sometime, who's changed."

Mary laughed. Jo always knew what to say to raise her spirits.

"You could go with him," Jo said.

Mary's laughter died. "He wouldn't ask."

"But if he did?"

Mary sighed. "I'd probably go. I'm discovering that I'd do just about anything for this man."

"Then you're a bigger fool than I am."

Both Mary and Jo started at the hoarse voice from the bed. Mary spun about. Though sunken, Reese's eyes were lucid and focused on her with annoyance.

She ignored that, along with the burning in her cheeks that came upon realizing he'd heard her admit her deepest secret. She reached for his forehead, but he caught her wrist and held her hand away from him. "Don't fuss. What happened?"

"Well, he seems fine now, so I'll just trot on back to the tower," Jo said.

Neither Mary nor Reese said goodbye. They were too busy staring at each other. For her, one touch brought everything back. Mouths searching, tongues tasting, hands seeking. Him beside her, above her, within her. His body and hers, theirs, together, right here on this bed.

She tugged on her wrist, and he let her go. Quickly, before he could stop her again, she placed her palm on his forehead. He scowled at her. She smiled. "Your fever's broke."

"I knew that."

"Oh, you did? Did you know you've been lying here for three days, scaring all of us half to death?"

"Three days?"

She shot him an "I told you so" look, and he snarled at her. Oh, yes, he was going to live, all right. She wanted to skip and dance and sing.

Instead, she sank down into the chair and laid her head next to his hip. "You scared me, Reese. You really, really scared me."

Then, to her horror, she burst into tears.

Reese stared at the sobbing woman on his bed. Mary hadn't cried since 1862, but a few weeks in his company and he'd reduced her to tears. Excellent work.

Because of him she'd nearly died. The story of his life. Everyone he'd ever cared about either died or wished they had never known him. He wondered which it would be for Mary in the end.

He shouldn't touch her. Since that rainy night in Georgia, he'd learned to smell a mistake a mile away. Touching Mary reeked of a very bad idea.

So whose hand was that stroking her hair? Couldn't be his, could it? Reese cursed beneath his breath and gave up, savoring the softness of the strands through his fingers and the warmth of her head next to his thigh. If he wasn't half-dead, he might just enjoy this.

"I'm not worth crying over, Mary. Don't make me out to be some kind of hero."

"But you are. Why do you keep insisting you're bad when anyone with eyes can see that you aren't?"

He could barely understand her for the weeping. His chest felt tight. She was going to make *him* start if he didn't stop her soon.

"That's enough. You'll make yourself sick."

She raised her head. Tears shined in her eyes, on her cheeks. *Damn.* She was one of those women who looked good crying. "You saved my life, Reese. If that isn't a hero, I don't know what is."

"You wouldn't have been in danger in the first place if it hadn't been for me."

"And you wouldn't be here with another bullet wound if I hadn't come to find you in Dallas. If you want to blame me for that, go ahead. I did what I had to do. But I'm going to believe what I want to believe. You're a wonderful man."

"The last people who believed that ended up dead."

She shrugged. "I'll take my chances."

He couldn't help it. He kissed her. She was so perfectly bullheaded. So wonderfully bossy. Who'd have ever thought he'd discover a woman just like him way out here in Texas.

At first, she stiffened with surprise; then she softened on a sigh. Kissing her in this bed made him remember everything else they had done here. And everything they hadn't.

The smell of her skin brought back its taste—at the curve of her hip, along the inside of her knee. Her moan of surrender recalled another of completion. The soft glide of her lips on his brought back the alluring memory of those lips in several other places.

He pulled away. This was getting out of hand, and he really wasn't up to it. But staring down at Mary's face, watching as she opened her eyes and smiled at him with her heart and her soul, for a moment he almost believed things could change, he could change, they could have a future, here, together.

Then memories of a past she didn't even know about reared their ugly heads. Once she knew who he had been, what he had done, how he had come to be what he was, she would never let him touch her again.

He kissed her brow in his favorite spot, where the hair grew downy at the temple. He wanted to ask where the men were, but before he could, he fell asleep again. This time, there were no dreams, he slept the sleep of the exhausted, and when he awoke, he felt much stronger. From the slant of the light through the window it was still daytime, and Mary slept in a chair next to the bed.

"Mary?" Her head went up. She looked better, too. "Guess I dozed off."

Her smile was soft, sleepy, and he fought the urge to yank her into the bed with him and kiss her dreamy mouth. "An entire day isn't a doze."

Reese blinked. "A day?"

"Yes. You feel better?"

"Much." He struggled with the idea that he'd slept an entire day and it had felt like an hour. "Where are my men?"

Like a cloud passing the sun, a shadow moved across her eyes. "They went after El Diablo."

Shiny black dots danced in front of Reese's face. Thankfully, he was already lying down or he would of had to as thoughts he'd hoped never to have again sped through his mind.

Jed's sister; Rico's, too; Nate's new friend, Jo; Sullivan's family—whoever they were—and anyone who might love Cash besides Reese—the list made him sick with trepidation. He had once traveled to the houses of the dead and been shunned at every one.

He'd promised himself he would never again get so close to anyone that their deaths would send him on such a journey—both to their families and into the madness that awaited the loss of everyone you loved—while you had to keep going on.

"I told them not to," he managed.

"You were unconscious. They thought you were dying."

"That's a good reason to go and get themselves killed."

"Which is exactly what happened, I am not sorry to say."

Mary let out a squeak of alarm at the voice behind her. Reese yanked her back to his side when she would have stood between him and the two men in the doorway.

Jefferson and El Diablo.

From the guns in their hands and the looks on their faces, Reese would not have to worry about going on alone much longer. If it hadn't been for Mary, he wouldn't care.

"What are you saying?" Mary's voice shook.

"They're dead. Every last sneakin' one of 'em," Jefferson sneered. "We waited for them to come. Knew they would. And they did."

"So why are you here?" Reese asked.

"To kill you. I been waitin'."

"You can't mean to shoot a sick man in his bed?" Mary demanded, easing in front of Reese again.

Jefferson laughed and walked into the room, moving so that he was in front of the bed and Mary was out of the line of fire. Reese relaxed a bit. "He doesn't look too sick." The man eyed Mary. "Too bad I can't touch you, lady. You look like a hot one."

"I'd shoot myself before I'd let you touch me."

Jefferson's eyes narrowed, and he took a step toward her. Reese braced himself to spring. Danger to Mary made him feel a whole lot stronger.

"Enough!" El Diablo's voice cut through the tension. "We have come here for one thing. Dispose of the leader."

"Why? If all his men are gone, what possible harm can he do you?"

"He is the only man in a town full of women, children, and cowards. He will lead you as he led the others. I cannot allow that."

"Take your gold; we don't want it."

"There is no gold, foolish woman."

"What?" Jefferson demanded. "You said this town was full of gold."

"I said this town was golden. A place of the sun. Land of the People. Mine. I said what I had to say to get you to help me."

Jefferson's face darkened. "Once I tell the rest there ain't no gold, I wouldn't give a Confederate dollar for your sorry hide."

"Then I guess you will not be telling them."

The gunshot was impossibly loud in the small room. Mary threw herself on top of Reese, and for a moment he thought she'd been shot. But red blossomed across Jefferson's chest. He dropped his gun and followed the weapon to the ground.

"Y-you shot him!" Mary moved just enough to look at El Diablo while keeping herself in front of Reese. "Just like that. What kind of monster are you?"

"El Diablo," the old man said, as if that explained everything. "Now, teacher lady, move. I must take him away with me to die."

"He's not going anywhere."

"He will accompany me out of town. To make sure no one has gotten brave enough to harm me. I will kill him close enough to town so that you can come and get the body later."

"No," Mary said, her mouth turning mulish.

El Diablo sighed. "I do not wish to kill you and bring the soldiers here. But if I must, I will, and bury you with him out there somewhere."

"Mary, move."

"I will not!"

Reese struggled to push her aside, and as he did,

he whispered in her ear, "I have a plan. Now get out of the way."

She stopped struggling and stared into his face. He nodded, and she got up. Mary understood a good plan. Too bad he didn't really have one.

Reese dressed quickly and accompanied El Diablo out of the room and down the hall toward the front door. His mind groped for some way to make this entire mess come out all right. But without his guns and his men, he was helpless.

Reese opened the door, and he and El Diablo stepped onto the porch. The sound of guns being cocked made them both freeze. Reese stared in amazement at the line of Rock Creek citizens in front of Mary's house. Each one held a gun, and they looked as if they not only knew how to use them but planned to.

El Diablo jabbed his pistol into Reese's side. "I am taking him with me."

"No, you aren't," Jo Clancy said. "Put him back where he was and we'll let you live."

"I can shoot him where he stands; then what will you do?"

"Fill you so full of holes there won't be enough left to bury. Kill him, we kill you, it's that simple. Let him go"—Jo shrugged—"and we'll turn you over to the soldiers alive."

"I would rather die, here, on the land of my ancestors, than live a thousand years anywhere else."

Reese didn't like the sound of that. He tensed, ready to die. But someone hit him from behind.

He fell, smacking into the plank floor of the porch, a body on his back, just as a gun went off.

Another thump next to him had Reese turning his head to find El Diablo lying dead a few inches away. The body atop his back moved, and when he flipped over, Mary sat next to him on the porch, staring at El Diablo with a combination of anger and disgust. Reese glanced from the old Indian to William Brown, who stood at the side of the porch with his rifle.

"Comanche for a cougar," Brown said. "Your miserable life for my grandaughter's. I'd say we're even now, wouldn't you, Reese?"

Seventeen

The entire town of Rock Creek poured into Mary's house, or so it seemed. The bodies were removed, the blood wiped away. Mary sat on the bed next to Reese, still in shock at all that had happened and how fast things had changed.

In taking responsibility for defending Rock Creek, the people had solidified into townsfolk. In destroying El Diablo, they had answered a threat to their homes and won. The victory would keep them there regardless of future threats, and the town would grow because it was now a home for everyone rather than just a place to live until things got too bad.

Unfortunately, Reese was the one who had paid for the hometown Mary had always dreamed of.

With all the people in her house, fixing, cleaning, talking, she could not talk to Reese. He lay on the bed, so pale and quiet, she was terrified he would take a turn for the worse again, just when he'd started to get better.

"I didn't see them until it was too late," Jo said. "I was watching the river. They must have thought we would be unprotected without the men."

"Hey!" Brown protested. "There are men in town."

"You never would have known it before today. Anyway, I ran downstairs and over to Sutton's, then sent the twins to round everyone up. I snuck up to the window. Like Rico said, it's a security risk. I could hear everything. When I heard that gunshot, my heart nearly stopped."

"Mine, too," Mary muttered.

Jo smiled at her and continued. "I was going to run in right then, but El Diablo said he was taking Reese away. So we lined up outside, figured he couldn't take all of us. Brown insisted he had to be alongside the house just in case. I wasn't sure what we were going to do when El Diablo refused to give up, then Mary came barreling out the door. . . ." She threw up her hands. "And it was all over."

"That's usually the way these things go," Reese said, dryly.

Mary glanced at him. Those were the first words he'd spoken since El Diablo died. He still looked ill, and she couldn't blame him. If El Diablo had told the truth, his men were dead because they'd gone on a vengeance mission. And she'd let them go without saying a word because she'd wanted El Diablo dead, too. But things had turned out badly, which was perhaps why vengeance should be left to the Lord. Mary wasn't impressed with the results of earthly attempts.

"Reese has to rest now," Mary announced, suddenly needing to hold him close, to soothe him, and in doing so, soothe herself.

Everyone filed out, and Mary shut the door behind them. The silence they left behind was almost deafening after the noise they had brought.

Mary returned to her room and found Reese staring at the ceiling. She came in and sat on the bed.

"Looks like you didn't need us, after all." He kept staring at the ceiling.

"Of course we did. Until y'all came to Rock Creek, everyone minded their own business. No one cared about anyone else. No one did anything more than they had to do to get by. People left as soon as things got tough. They had no reason to stay."

"And now they do?"

"Sure. They fought for this town. They won't give up so easily the next time there's a threat because they stood together and they earned this place."

"They would have stood up for something eventually."

"I don't think so. In you and your men they saw honor and loyalty and unselfishness at work."

Reese groaned. "Because of honor, loyalty, and me, five men are dead."

"You don't know that."

"If they aren't dead, then where are they? Do you think they'd let El Diablo and Jefferson get back to me, to Rock Creek, unless they were dead?"

"I don't know."

"Well, I know. Those buzzards wouldn't have gotten within ten miles of Rock Creek if my men were alive."

"So where's the rest of El Diablo's men?"

"I'm sure he had them waiting outside of town, figuring he and Jefferson could ride in and kill me without too much trouble. Maybe no one would even notice. But once they saw it happened the other way around, those hyenas would run. Like El Diablo said, without a leader, the followers scatter. But if they find another leader, you're going to have trouble. They think there's gold in Rock Creek."

Mary snorted. "If there was gold here, do you think the town would look like this?"

"Mebe." He closed his eyes. "I'm so tired, Mary. I feel like I want to sleep away eternity. But I've got to go and find my men."

"Not tonight," she murmured. "Sleep."

"No." He struggled to open his eyes, to sit up, but she pushed him back, easily.

"You aren't going anywhere until you can make me let you."

"What if they need me?"

"They don't need you like this."

"Suppose you're right." He sighed, and his eyes slid closed. "Maybe by morning they'll show up."

The hope in his voice broke her heart. He sounded like a child who'd lost his mother but continued to hope that she might come back if he only believed strongly enough.

Mary ran her fingers through his hair, then across his brow. "Maybe so," she agreed.

"I sleep better when you're here." He gave a sigh of contentment and caught her hand. "Don't go, Mary; don't go."

"I won't," she whispered, but he was already asleep.

Mary's eyes burned, and her head bobbed with fatigue. She couldn't remember the last time she'd slept all night. When she tried to disengage her hand from his, Reese held on and made a sound of distress that broke her heart.

Did she dare lie down next to him and hold him close, just for tonight? Why not? She'd done far more than that on another night. This might be the last chance she had to lie at his side.

She was able to free herself long enough to strip down to her chemise; then she slipped beneath the sheet and curled against Reese's side. Immediately, his arm came around and held her closer. His breathing slowed, evening out into a deeper sleep. The soothing cadence lulled her, and within minutes Mary followed him into the void.

Reese awoke in the darkest hour of the night. His left side was warm, his right side cool, and a weight across his legs had him afraid for a moment that he was back in the Confederate hospital again. Wounded, alone, dying. Had he lost his legs this time?

Then the sweet scent of Mary penetrated his mind, calming him as nothing else ever had. He shifted against the weight, and one of her legs slid between both of his.

His poor battered body kicked into a familiar dance. Reese was surprised he could still manage desire after what he'd been through, but if he could want Mary with a force that was nearly over-whelming, then he could get up in the morning and go looking for his men.

She sighed in her sleep and murmured his name. The sound only served to make him hard—or rather harder. Her breasts, barely covered by her chemise, brushed up, then down, his ribs. Her foot ran down his calf, and their toes tangled.

Reese's teeth ground together. This was getting out of hand. He glanced at her face and found himself captured in the glow of her eyes.

"I thought I was dreaming." Her breath brushed his chin.

"You were."

He didn't realize he was touching her until she shuddered when his fingertips brushed the tops of her breasts—full and ripe and nearly bursting from the neckline of her chemise.

He jerked away, shocked at what he'd done with-out even knowing he planned to do it. But Mary caught his hand and drew it back against his will, pressing his palm to her heart.

"Feel that?"

Her heart thudded, fast yet sure, against the flut-ter of the pulse in his hand.

"That's what happens every time I look at you. When you touch me, sometimes I think I might die. What I feel for you is like nothing I've ever felt before."

"Mary, I—"

"Shh." She put her lips to his, perhaps to stop him from telling her something she did not want to hear.

With her mouth against his and his fingers against her, he lost any capability of speech or intelligent thought. All he could do was feel—her, him, them. The last time they would ever have.

He wanted to give her pleasure—all that he had to give. He had no name, he had no home, he had no occupation beyond his gun any longer. The voices of children that had once given him joy now only gave him nightmares in the daytime. He would never again be able to do what he had planned to do forever.

The man he'd been had died on a battlefield in Georgia. The man he had become after that would no doubt die when he buried those who had given him something to live for ever since. Then what? How many chances did one man get?

Reese had a feeling his last chance had died with the five men he'd refused for too long to call friends. But he didn't want to think of them right now. He would be thinking of them for a long time to come. Right now he planned to have one last night with Mary.

Reese deepened the kiss she had begun, parting her lips, teaching her a new rhythm with his tongue. How could she taste so good and smell so sweet? How could she feel so right when he knew this to be wrong?

He had been a fool once; he would not be again. He would make this night about giving, instead of taking, for a change.

They had kissed many times, and each time the burst of fire in his gut and the warmth in his chest were like the first time. The knowledge that she had never been kissed before him, never been touched before him, made him want to be the last man, too. That was impossible, but it didn't make him want it any less.

She met his kiss stroke for stroke. Her hands roamed over his chest, across his belly, then lower. His hands clenched on her shoulders when her fingers curled around his length and tightened. Temptation whispered, and he considered shoving her back, making them both mindless with want and need, then plunging into her one last time.

What could it hurt? He'd already taken her virginity.

With a strength of will he had thought long lost, Reese reached down and took her hand from him. He swallowed her sound of protest with another long, soul-searching kiss, and when their mouths broke apart, she lay limp in his arms.

He began to remove her last bit of clothing, and she let him, like a child being undressed for the night. When he pushed her back on the bed, she lay there smiling at him, all her trust visible in her eyes.

Reese turned away from that look. He had seen it too many times before, and every person who had ever looked at him like that was dead.

Stifling a curse, he dipped his head and let his mouth wander over every visible curve and dip. Snagging a finger in the neckline of her chemise, he tugged, and her ample breasts sprang free. They shone like the pearl handles on Nate's guns.

He pressed his lips to the curve where a breast met a rib—full and soft, blending into sharp and hard. Her skin was warm, not cool like a pearl. He let his lips follow the slide of her chemise, downward on a journey past her waist, then across her belly.

Spending a good amount of time at her navel, he tested the dip with his tongue, lips, and teeth. When her fingers pulled his hair and the muscles beneath his mouth trembled and clenched, he murmured soothing sounds against her skin and moved lower.

"Reese?"

Her voice, that blending of the South and sin, would haunt him forever. She reminded him of things best forgotten and made his heart hope even when his mind knew there was no such thing for a man like him.

"Hush," he told her, continuing on his journey. "I know what I'm doing."

He kissed her where he'd wanted to all along. Her body bowed, her mouth cried his name, he held her still, large palms against slim hips, and kissed her there some more.

Tasting Mary was heaven in the midst of his hell. He spread his hands down her thighs, let his mouth follow his fingers, to her knees, then back again to her essence. He teased the burgeoning bud with his thumb until she thrashed and moaned, watching her face as she went higher and higher.

When she cried out the beginning of her release, he replaced his fingers with his mouth and took her over the edge again and again, with relentless fervor, until she lay beneath him, damp and spent.

His body perched on an edge of his own. Just watching her, touching her, tasting her, had been the most unbelievable experience of his life. He wished he could do it again, but he didn't have the strength to touch her and not take her once more. So he shifted to lie at her side, and when she took his hand, he held her fingers in his own and willed himself to do nothing more than that.

"Why?" she whispered. "Why did you do that?"

"You didn't like it?"

"Are you blind and deaf? Of course I liked it. But what about you?"

"I'm good."

"Yes," she purred. "You are."

She sat up and stared down at him, an odd expression in her eyes. Then, before he knew what she was about, she leaned forward and licked all the way up the hard length of him.

"Mary, no." He tried to push her away, but she grabbed his wrists and held them apart.

"Let me touch you, taste you, feel you. Let me have a part of you I've never had before."

She had given him everything from the moment he'd met her, and he had done nothing but take. So how could he deny her when she put it like that. Especially when he wanted nothing more than to have her touch him as no woman like her had ever done?

His surrender must have shown in his eyes, for she smiled a siren's smile that had never been on her sweet face before, yet did not look out of place.

He had ruined her in more ways than one. Then, slowly, holding his gaze all the while, she lowered her head and took him into her mouth.

Untutored she might be, but she was a very fast learner, and bolder than he'd ever believed possible. She taught him things he'd never known about himself. That he could deny completion for a long, long time and that in denying, he changed the pleasure into exquisite pain.

Rough and gentle by turns, she took him to the edge, then kissed him back down. His frantic fingers pulled her hair loose, and the locks made a curtain about her face, hiding the sight of what she was doing, making each kiss of her lips, each touch of her tongue, each tug of her teeth, a surprise.

When he could bear no more, he yanked her up with his good arm and kissed her—tasting him, tasting her—as he pulsed against her belly.

She eased up on one elbow and pressed her forehead against his. "Why did you do that?" she asked.

"I thought *that* was what you were aiming for?"

Her lips tilted, just a bit. "I mean . . . Um, what I mean is—"

"Why didn't I finish inside you?"

He saw her blush even in the semidarkness that announced dawn. Giving in to an irresistible impulse, he ran his hand over her back, down the slope of her rump, then up again. She pressed against him and sighed.

"I had my reasons, Mary. I should never have touched you that first time. But I'm weak. I wanted you; I took you, and it was wrong. I didn't want to make another mistake."

"How could making love be a mistake?"

He sighed. "You're so damned innocent."

"Was it so we wouldn't make a child?"

"Partly."

"You don't have to worry about that. I know how these things work, and I can't be—uh, with child right now."

Reese stared into her eyes, and a weight lifted from his chest. He'd been sleeping on and off nigh on to a week, and she looked completely certain. Besides, Mary did not have it in her to lie. Crazy as it seemed, the relief was followed almost immediately by disappointment. He'd have married her if there was a child, and she would have been his, if only for a little while.

The events of the past week had only made Reese more certain than ever that he was poison to anyone he cared about. He'd surrounded himself with rough men who had little to lose, or so he'd thought, by being near him. But in the end, it didn't matter if he held himself apart, if he refused to allow himself friends. His heart cared, secretly, quietly, without his consent, and the people he loved died.

Or, almost as bad, they discovered what he had done, then looked at him as if they wished he were dead. He found he could not bear to see that look in Mary's eyes.

He could not stay here with her. Something bad was waiting just around the corner for Mary, or for him, if he did.

"Thank you for telling me," he said. "It's a concern off my mind."

She stared at him, and for a moment he thought she might punch him in the nose. Then she shook her head as if he were the slowest child in her class and pulled the covers over them both. "Maybe if I'm here with you, the dreams won't come." She pressed her lips to his neck.

He stiffened and tried to pull away, but she merely smoothed her palm down his chest and cuddled closer against his side. "What dreams?"

"About your boys and the war."

His belly lurched in a sickening roll. She knew. He reached for the pain and met her hand there, awaiting his, almost as if she'd expected it. She grasped his fingers tightly as he realized the truth.

She had known and still she had touched him.

"What did I say when I was out of my head?"

"Hmm?" she murmured sleepily. " 'Bout what?"

"The boys and the war."

Mary disentangled herself from him in a hurry, and his heart fell down where his stomach ached. He'd known the time would come.

Had she been so enthralled with the passion between them that she'd been able to forget all she knew? Would she leave him now? Or make him leave her?

But Mary shook her head as if to clear the fog of sleep, reached out, and cupped his cheek. "You spoke about the battle and how they died. I can understand why the children upset you, why you can't teach them anymore."

He winced. No one else but his family knew what

he had once been. And they did not know how he had failed since because they had cast him out and he had never gone back.

He did not want to talk about this, but he couldn't seem to open his mouth and stop her as she rattled blithely on.

"So many men went bad after the war. They went home to nothing. They became angry and bitter. They turned to stealing because they had nothing else, and they knew nothing anymore but killing. I heard some of the soldiers from Missouri—the James boys—have become the biggest outlaws up thataway. It's a shame to take something so right and turn it around all wrong. But you didn't do that."

"I make my living with my gun."

"You don't rob people."

"No? What makes you think that?"

"I know you wouldn't. About Cash, I'm not so sure."

Reese smiled a little. She had Cash figured out—and Reese, too. "It would have been easy to turn into an outlaw. I could have made a lot more money. But I . . . I couldn't do that. I don't know why."

"Because if you had, the deaths of those boys would have been for nothing. You'd have been turning your back on everything they fought for, everything you'd taught them, and all that they'd died to protect."

"I filled their heads with images of honor, loyalty, and country. Because of that, because of me, they're dead."

"You did what you had to do, and they did, too."

"They were children, and I filled their heads with nonsense."

"Honor, loyalty, and country are nonsense? It's a shame, because thousands of people have died for them."

They were silent for a moment. Reese waited for the question he dreaded. If he'd talked about the boys and the war, he must have spoken of—

"Who's Laura?"

Reese rubbed his forehead. "The woman I was going to marry after the war."

"You loved her?"

He dropped his hand. "Yes."

He *had* loved Laura. They had grown up together, shared their dreams, planned a future. She knew him better than anyone. Or so he'd thought.

"Did she die?"

"No. She just wished that I had. At the top of her lungs, in front of my entire hometown."

Because he had loved Laura so much and trusted her even more, when she spit in his face and wished him dead, Reese had started to wish for it, too. But regardless of what he did, he couldn't seem to die.

Mary frowned. "I don't understand."

"After I lost my company, I was in a hospital."

"Which scar?" She touched the bayonet slice over his ribs. "I know how you got this one."

Reese scowled. "Rico needs his lips sewn shut."

"Actually, I think Sullivan told me."

That news stumped him for a moment. Sullivan never told anyone anything. Sometimes he wondered if the man had worse secrets than Reese did in his past.

"Which scar?" she asked again as she ran her hands over his chest, down his arms, and across his thigh.

His breath hissed in between his teeth. How could he want her again so soon? And while they were talking about the war, no less? Reese grabbed her wrist. "The one on my thigh. And on my back."

"The big one? That looked bad."

He shrugged. "I lived. Unfortunately."

"Don't say that!"

"Do you know what happens to a man whose entire company dies and he's shot in the back?" Her face crinkled, and she shook her head. "You get shot in the back when you're running away."

"You'd never run away. The boys did."

"And they were all dead."

"You can't tell me that people actually thought you'd run away from a fight?" Her hands clenched into fists. "And you let them believe it?"

"I certainly wasn't going to tarnish the memory of those boys with the truth."

"The people who believed that obviously didn't know you."

He gave a short laugh. "They'd known me all my life. After my fiancée spit in my face, she threw my ring on the ground."

Mary sniffed. "She didn't deserve you."

Exasperated, he sighed. Would she ever stop defending him? "She had her reasons. Her brother was one of the boys who followed me to hell and gone."

"So she was upset. Grieving. She didn't mean it."

"She did. So did all the other families who'd trusted me with their children. I thought I should be the one to explain. So I went to every house. Either the door was slammed in my face, the dogs were set after me, or no one bothered to open the door at all."

"That's ridiculous."

"My parents told me I was no longer their son. That I should never come home."

He waited for Mary to see that what he had done—living when everyone else had died—was unforgivable.

"You didn't actually believe them, did you?" He gaped at her. "I mean, you went back later. And they were sorry."

"I've never been back. And they aren't sorry."

"Grief makes people rash. You should go home, let them make it up to you."

He just shook his head. "Why do you always defend me?"

She put her nose in the air. "Someone has to. I don't understand how a man who can lead others like you do, a man who can inspire such loyalty, can allow people who weren't even there to dictate what you believe about yourself."

"You let old women who spent their lives in a convent convince you that you weren't pretty."

"I can see in a mirror."

"You're looking through their eyes. Look through mine."

"Silly," she muttered, but she smiled and cuddled against him again.

"Why did you let me touch you?" he whispered. "You knew."

"Knew that you'd had something horrible happen to you? That you'd blamed yourself for years for something that wasn't your fault? You didn't die. Shame on you! Why don't we just crucify you now? Would that make you feel better?"

"It wasn't just once, Mary. The same thing is happening all over again. I brought those men here, my men, though I tried to deny that, and now they're dead."

She stilled. "You don't know that."

"I know them. They'd be back by now."

"If you know them, then you know that they're grown men and pretty frightening when they choose to be. They can take care of themselves."

"I thought they could. I fought beside them for years, and I thought they were too mean to die. That's why I stayed with them. Figured those five would outlive me for certain. But because they were loyal to me, they're dead."

"And that's your fault? They had a choice. They chose to go. Quit being everyone's schoolmaster. You can't save the world."

He blinked. Was that what he was trying to do? Atone for his past? Save as many folks as he could and maybe it would make up for the ones he hadn't been able to save? Maybe that's why he was so miserable and alone—because such a task was impossible. Even he knew that.

"You wanted to know why I let you touch me?"

she asked. "You heard me say it to Jo, and I meant what I said. I'd do anything for you."

He closed his eyes. "Mary, don't say that. I'm not worth it."

"You must be, because everyone who meets you seems to feel the same way."

"Everyone who feels that way ends up dead."

She pressed her lips to his neck, then whispered in his ear, just as she had once before. "I'll take my chances."

She drifted off almost immediately, while Reese remained awake awhile longer. Mary might think she could tempt fate, but he knew better. Once he found his men, he wasn't coming back here. No matter how much he wanted to.

Mary awoke to the sun shining so brightly across her face, her eyes burned. Her body ached, pleasantly. When she glanced at the pillow and found only the indentation of Reese's head but no Reese, her heart hurt, not so pleasantly,

"Reese!" she shouted, bounding out of bed, uncaring if she was stark naked.

She yanked open the bedroom door and ran right into him. He hissed in pain as she bounced off his black-clad chest. She scowled at him. "Where do you think you're going?"

"I told you I was going after my men."

"This morning? Are you crazy? A few days ago we thought you were a dead man."

"I'm not. Where did you put my gun?"

Since his question was accompanied by a slow

perusal of her naked body, she blushed and turned her back on him, scrambling through discarded sheets in search of—

"Looking for this?"

She glanced over her shoulder and discovered that Reese was holding her chemise in one hand while observing her backside with both eyes. She growled in answer and yanked the wrinkled garment from his fingers.

Seconds later, moderately, if not adequately, clothed, she faced him. "Please, wait a few days. If they're all right, they'll come home."

"And if they aren't?"

She swallowed. "It's too late for them, anyway. You'll only hurt yourself."

"Doesn't matter. I've got to go. If they gave their lives for me, this is the least that I can do."

Panic threatened. If he left now, he might not survive. She'd tried everything. Love and kisses, hand-holding and support; maybe she should make him as angry as she was.

"You're doing this because of those boys. You think that if you kill yourself, it'll make up for them. But it won't. You're alive, and they're dead, and there's nothing you can do about it."

"I knew that a long time ago." His voice was calm, as dead as his eyes. He turned away from her, methodically searching the drawers in her dresser, looking for his gun.

Exasperation made her snarl. "Here." She yanked his gun belt out from under the bed.

A nod was her only thanks. He had become again the man she had bought in Dallas. The man who had shared her bed, his past, his tears, and his body with her had disappeared. Mary feared he would never return.

"Did you ever consider that maybe you lived for a reason?"

He paused in the act of buckling on his guns and glared at her. At least there was heat in his eyes again. "If I lived for a reason, that would mean those boys died for one. I can't accept that."

"Obviously, Colonel Mosby didn't believe you were a coward or he wouldn't have included you in his secret spy ring. So why do you continue to punish yourself when a man like that believed in you?"

Reese sighed. "Some big mouths have been moving." Mary merely raised her eyebrows and stared at him. "Mosby wanted competent people who had no one and nothing left to lose. That was me. Still is."

A shaft of hurt went through her as he dismissed her as no one and what they had shared as nothing. "The only reason you had nothing left to lose was because you gave up. Maybe you *are* the coward everyone said you were. If you can fight for loyalty and honor and a doomed country, then why can't you fight for love?"

"Mary, don't say something you'll regret."

"I regret nothing. But it seems you regret everything. And that's a hell of a way to live, Reese."

She'd finally reached him. His lips tightened, and he faced her. "If they're dead, I have nothing to live for. I'm poison to everyone who cares about me. Can't you see that?"

"No, I don't see that. What I see is a man who

cares too much. A man who takes on the weight of the world and lets every bad thing that happens rest on his shoulders. I see the man I love." He flinched as if she'd struck him and spun about, heading for the back door. She followed. She had never been one to give up too easily. "We can make a life if you'd just let the past go."

He stopped with his hand on the door. "I can't. I told you I couldn't stay. I never lied to you, Mary."

"No. At least you didn't lie."

"You said you understood."

"I guess I lied then."

He reached out and tilted her face so he could brush his lips across hers. "You deserve better than me."

Before she could answer, he slipped out the door. Mary's hand reached for the doorknob, then fell back to her side.

She knew goodbye when she tasted it.

Eighteen

Reese retrieved Atlanta. The horse was glad to see him, nearly knocking him down in its enthusiasm to go for a ride. Someone had been taking good care of him, brushing his auburn coat, laying fresh bedding, and from the looks of the debris, bringing him apples and carrots. Well, Cash always said he treated Atlanta like a pet; now he'd probably have to.

He packed his saddlebags with the small amount of supplies he'd taken from Mary's larder. He'd left one hundred and fifty dollars on her kitchen table. He couldn't take her money.

While he rode out of Rock Creek, folks waved goodbye, as if he were one of them, as if he were coming back. He stared straight ahead and kept on going.

"Hey, Reese, you okay now? We were worried." The blasted twins ran down the boardwalk at a pace with Atlanta. "We took care of your horse. Nice horse. Can we come along?"

They'd been worried about him? Didn't anyone in this town know he wasn't worth worrying about?

Reese kicked Atlanta into a gallop and left Rock Creek in the dust. One more minute and he'd have given in to the urge to get off Atlanta, pat those boys on the head in thanks, and then show them how to clean a horse's hooves. With a little guidance, those two could become fine men, but they weren't going to get guidance from Baxter Sutton.

Reese sighed. And they weren't going to get it from him. As Mary had shouted, he wasn't everyone's schoolmaster. He was no one's now and never would be again.

When he was far enough away for it not to be too tempting to return, Reese drew Atlanta to a halt and glanced back. Mary watched him, just as she had when he'd come into town. But now he knew how she tasted, how she felt, how she sounded when she sighed his name.

She raised her hand and waved—no longer hello but goodbye. How could she still wave goodbye as if he weren't taking everything and leaving forever?

Reese cursed beneath his breath and did not return the wave. Instead, he turned Atlanta and headed in the direction his men had gone the last time anyone had seen them alive.

Reese wasn't up to this, and he knew it. But he had responsibilities to the men who had called him captain. They had followed him; they had trusted him. He had led and trusted them, too.

He'd trusted them not to die, dammit! He'd thought men like those would have the courtesy to let him die first or at least take him along on the death ride.

He rode all day—until he was exhausted and

nearly dropping from the saddle—with no sign of anyone. Dead or alive. How was he going to find them when his scout and his spy were among those he searched for?

He'd just have to keep trying. If worse came to worst, he'd go to the fort and hire a scout.

Reese made camp and fed Atlanta, then himself. As he dozed in the flicker of the firelight, the ghosts came. New ghosts to add to the old.

The thunder of hooves announced riders coming in fast. Reese continued to sip his coffee. He knew who they were—the latest additions to his nightmares.

Five horses walked into camp. His men dismounted and helped themselves to coffee, then ranged around the fire. With bright lights of exhaustion flickering in front of his eyes, Reese stared at them. They looked almost . . . *Alive.*

Cash threw himself down next to Reese. "Looks like you're alive."

Reese blinked at his friends, waiting for them to disappear.

"We were worried, *Capitán*. Nate thought you would die from the fever. And then, when we finally breached El Diablo's lair and he was not there . . ."

"Figured you and the rest of Rock Creek were goners," Jed finished.

Frowning, Reese reached over and touched Cash's arm. Cash scowled. "What the hell's that for?"

"You're alive."

"Damn right. You want a hug, too?"

Reese shook his head, then gulped lukewarm coffee.

"Never thought Miss Bossy would let you out of bed so soon." Cash wiggled his eyebrows.

After a moment, Reese managed to speak again. "What happened?"

Cash shrugged. "We went to El Diablo's hideout. Planned to blow him back to hell, but they were dug in just like you said they'd be."

Reese raised an eyebrow.

"I know. You're always right. Anyway, we decided we weren't leaving until we rooted them out. So we spent out time doin' just that. And when we finally went over the wall, all we found were the Injuns. No chiefs." Cash looked at Sullivan. "No offense."

Sullivan snorted. "One of these days, Cash, I'm goin' to take offense."

Cash didn't look worried. He never looked worried. Man had to have ice in his veins and nerves of iron, but Reese suspected that's what made him both a gunfighter and a gambler.

He found it interesting that Cash seemed to have taken over the expedition, becoming the leader in Reese's absence. He'd never have thought Cash gave a damn about anyone but himself when the chips were down. But it looked as if Reese had been wrong about a whole lot of things lately. Big surprise.

"So as soon as we finished with the followers, we went after the leaders."

"Finished with? How?"

Reese saw an entire ghost ranch littered with

bodies, and he didn't want to be the cause of that no matter what they had done.

"The ones that weren't already dead, we sent off to Mexico with a warning that the Yankees were coming."

"The army," Nate corrected, wearily sipping at his flask. "They're the army now. Not Yankees."

"They'll always be Yankees to me, preacherman."

"And they went? You're sure?"

"Once they found out there was no gold in Rock Creek, and there isn't, is there?"

"Not according to El Diablo. He just wanted his land back."

Cash grunted. "That's what I figured. If there was gold in that town, I'd have smelled it. Anyway, once we told them there wasn't any gold, and that their leaders were as good as dead, they went. We're sure."

"Then we came on the run to rescue you, *Capitán*. But here you are. Where is El Diablo and his friend?"

"In their graves, as of yesterday."

Cash slapped Reese on the back. He winced as shoulder howled. "And you half-dead. You never cease to impress me, Reese."

"I didn't shoot 'em."

"Who did? Your mouthy schoolteacher? Nate's little friend? Or perhaps the mother of those twin terrors?"

"Nope. The Devil shot Jefferson, and then Brown shot the Devil."

"Brown? Hmm, surprising that he'd do anything

for anyone, but I guess he owed you. So the job is over. All the bad guys are dead, and Rock Creek doesn't need us anymore. Where's my money?"

"I'll have to get that to you later."

Cash's eyes narrowed. "Twenty-five dollars isn't much, but it's mine. I can play it into more."

Reese took a deep breath. "I thought you were dead. I was coming to bury you."

"Where the hell did you get the idea we were dead?"

"El Diablo."

"The Devil is the prince of lies," Nate intoned, then took another drink. "And you believed him?"

"I knew you'd never let him get past you and come after me if you were alive."

"Shit" was Cash's only comment. The rest just looked embarrassed.

"Now what?" Jed asked.

"Now Reese gets me my money."

Reese didn't even look at Cash. "I left the money for Mary."

"Get it back."

"I'll get you the money somewhere else."

"But *Capitán*, aren't we going back? I kind of like Rock Creek, and they seem to like us now, too. We can make it our base. Whenever we have nowhere else to be, no other job to do, we can stay there. When you need us, you can send your messages to the hotel."

"No more messages." Reese sighed. "No more jobs."

No one spoke. They just stared at him dumbfounded. Even Nate roused himself enough to scowl in Reese's direction.

He owed them an explanation, though he really didn't want to share this part of himself. He wanted to ride off into the sunrise with his men still believing he was a worthy leader. But if he did that, they'd never let him go. So he'd tell them the truth about who and what he was—to a point, anyway. Some things were better left unsaid.

"I'm not always right."

"Oh, yeah, that's a surprise."

"Let me finish, Cash." The gunman held up his hands in surrender. "Before we got together during the war, I had my own company. Lost every man and ended up in the hospital with a minié ball in my back."

He waited for the looks of disgust, the words of derision. No one said anything for several moments.

"So that's where you got that scar." Sullivan shrugged.

Reese frowned. "Don't you know what a scar like that means?"

"You were hurt, *Capitán*."

"Most folk thought I was shot running away."

"Most folk were damned fools, then." Nate stared into the fire as if contemplating past damned fools he had known.

Cash lit a cigar. "I've known you for seven years, and I never saw you run away from a fight. If you aren't talkin' to 'em first, you're right up in front just beggin' to be picked off. Never could figure out why you had a death wish. Until now."

Reese had a hard time believing these men, who were rougher than rough, who had seen horrible things and therefore believed the worst of everyone always, could sit around calmly drinking and smoking and defending him, just as Mary had, when people who had known him all of his life, who had raised him, had cast him out without a quiver.

"So I haven't run while you've known me. That doesn't mean I didn't run once."

"You've never asked any of us what we did before." Cash blew a waft of smoke into Reese's face. "Why?"

"Don't care. It's what you do now that matters."

"So what makes you special?"

"Huh?"

"How come you get to trust and we don't? How come you get to believe in us but we can't believe in you? What makes you so damned special, Reese? I don't give a shit what you did once. All I care about is what you do now, when you're in front of me or behind me. How about the rest of you?"

Reese looked at the others, who were all nodding in agreement with Cash, which might have been a first.

"You lost your company. Join the club." Jed tossed the remains of his coffee into the fire. "How do you think every last one of us ended up called to Atlanta by Mosby?"

"But—but my men were all from my hometown. They weren't even men; they were boys. They went to war because of me, and they died for it."

"Big damn deal," Cash sneered. "Most of the

men in that war were boys. Hell, we were all boys back then. We did what we had to do."

"Fat lot of good it did," Nate slurred. "Still lost. Think you're special? We all got our problems."

"At least with you, *Capitán*, we win."

"I thought you'd died because of me."

"Well, we didn't, so get over it," Cash said. "We like working with you. We like having you in charge. Don't screw up a good thing, Reese. Let's just keep this little group exactly as is."

Reese didn't understand. They weren't behaving the way he'd thought they would once they knew the truth. He'd hid his past for so long, he could barely manage to croak it out, but they acted as if his killing a company of boys were nothing. What had they done to make his sins appear negligible?

Cash was right. He didn't care.

Thinking the issue resolved, everyone bedded down. Though exhausted, Reese couldn't sleep. His mind was too full. If men like his could hear his darkest secret and shrug, if a woman like Mary could know everything and still love him, then might his family have forgiven him, too?

There was only one way to find out.

When the sun rose in the east, Reese had already been riding in that direction for hours.

Mary was helping at the store when the Sutton twins tore in screaming, "The six are back! But there's only five."

Then they ran right back out again. Mary glanced at Rose, who was stocking calico bolts in the rear. Rose nodded, and Mary ran after the boys.

Only five? Who was missing? And why? Mary's heart hurt, both from the unanswered questions that plagued her mind and running amid the first true heat of a Rock Creek summer.

The five men and their horses stood in front of the hotel. They all glanced up as Mary puffed to a stop in front of them. One look was all it took for her to grab the hitching post so she wouldn't fall down.

Rico hurried forward and put an arm about her. "He is not dead, *señorita*. Calm yourself."

"He thought you were all dead. He wouldn't wait here; he had to go after you."

"We heard the whole story," Cash drawled, and strode past her into the hotel.

"Wh-where is he?"

"No idea." Jed followed Cash.

Mary frowned at Rico. "When we awoke this morning, he was gone."

"He got past Sullivan?" She glanced at the man in question, who shrugged and went inside with Nate.

"If *el capitán* wanted to go, he would go. And if Sullivan heard him, he would say nothing."

"You have no idea where he went?"

"East. We thought perhaps he came here, but obviously not."

Mary's eyes burned, and she blinked fast to avoid embarrassing herself.

She had meant nothing to him. Why was she surprised? His excuse that he was no good, that he was poison, was just that—an excuse. Because here were the men he'd thought dead, and they sure didn't look dead to her. Yet upon finding them alive, Reese had run off. They had come back, and he had gone east. Maybe he did have a wife and children. Who knew? Certainly no one in this town.

"He still might come back, *señorita*. We are here. He will find us."

Mary shrugged off Rico's arm. "Perhaps."

As she walked back to the store, Mary refused to allow hope to enter her heart. Even if Reese did return to Rock Creek, it would no doubt be for the men and not for her. If he'd wanted her, he never would have left in the first place.

Her chest hurt worse, and she wasn't even running. She'd never known you could actually feel your heart breaking.

Life returned to normal in Rock Creek. School was out for the summer. Kids ran wild in the streets and down by the creek. The cougar was dead, and so was the Devil. The stage stop returned, and the town began to blossom once more. Everyone was happy. Or almost everyone.

Grady came back to the hotel and discovered boarders; Rico, Sullivan, and Jed had continued to live there. Nate and Cash retreated to the saloon, which they fixed up just enough to be livable. One or two at a time drifted out of town, for a day or a week. But they always came back. They seemed to like it in Rock Creek, perhaps because everywhere else they were just hired help. Here they had made the town stronger, saved it, really, and the folk of Rock Creek accepted them as citizens.

Of course, Sutton whined once in a while, but Mary had caught him sneaking over to play cards with Cash, and the more Sutton did that, the less he complained about them. Clancy wanted them gone, too, but he hadn't the guts to say anything to any one of them. He just railed at Mary whenever he could and made veiled insinuations during Sunday sermons, which everyone ignored.

Other folks who had left drifted in; some who had stayed drifted out. New people bought abandoned stores and started to make homes in Rock Creek. But there was no sign of Reese as summer blended toward fall, and Mary told herself she didn't care.

She continued to work in the store. She and Rose became friends. Even the twins improved. They tried to emulate Reese, and it was so cute, and painful, to watch that Mary was both charmed and saddened.

She told herself that her illness was because she worked too hard and slept too little. She refused to believe a broken heart could make you more physically ill with each new day.

What she couldn't quite figure out was how her clothes could be tight when everything she ate came right back out. There was still no doctor in Rock Creek, and there was no way she was going to ask Nate about this.

The men were quite sweet, to be truthful. They seemed to have taken her under their wing like a broken bird. At least one of them stopped in the store every day. No one mentioned Reese. But as she got paler and the circles beneath her eyes darkened, the visits increased to one from each of them every day.

Mary was sad; half the time she found herself on the verge of tears, and she couldn't figure out why. Rock Creek was saved. She was accepted here. She'd found the home she'd been searching for all her life. But the place didn't feel like home, and she didn't know why. A week before school started, Jo walked into the schoolhouse while Mary was cleaning the floor in preparation for the first day. She was as excited as she got every year before the first day of school—a new year, new students, new experiences. Mary did love to teach.

"Nate is worried about you." Mary glanced up and smiled at her friend. It was late in the day, and she was feeling pretty good. She'd continue to feel just fine—until morning.

"He send you over here?"

Jo shrugged and sat down at one of the desks. "They're all worried about you. So am I."

"Thanks, but I'll be fine. If I can just manage to get through a morning without throwing up." Mary leaned over to pick up the bucket of water and hissed when her corset cut into her hip.

"What was that?" Jo demanded.

"Nothing." Mary continued cleaning as she talked. "I seem to be gaining weight even though I can't keep down much of what I eat."

The door slammed, and Mary spun around to discover that Jo had slammed it. "That bastard!" Jo stalked down the aisle toward her. She put her hands on Mary's shoulders and looked into her face. "Where is he?"

"Who?"

"Reese. No wonder he hightailed it out of here and never looked back. I'm going to have Nate drag him in by his belt buckle."

"What are you talking about, Jo? Reese is gone; he isn't coming back. I've accepted that."

"You have? Then why do I see you standing on your back porch every day, watching the east as if you're waiting for someone?"

Mary blushed. She'd hoped no one would notice. She should have known she could hide nothing from Jo. "I'll stop," she said. "I don't like that he's gone, but I'll survive. I'll manage."

"Are you going to be able to manage as well for two as you manage for one?"

"Two who?"

"Two of you. Or rather a little you, or a little Reese if I don't miss my guess."

Mary felt dizzy—not an uncommon occurrence of late. She sat down heavily on the nearest chair. Jo came over and held her hand. "You didn't know?"

"It-it was only once. I can't be . . ."

"Once is all it takes."

The world swam. Jo put her arm around Mary and pulled her close so she wouldn't fall on her nose. "Are you sure, Jo?"

"Very." Mary moaned. "Who told you once wasn't enough?"

"The sisters who raised me."

"Nuns? You believed what nuns told you about something like this?"

"You sound like Reese now."

"Where is he?"

"I have no idea. Neither do the others. He rode off, and they let him go. They think he'll come back here, and I hoped they were right. But it's been so long . . . I don't think so anymore." Mary put her head between her knees, she was afraid if she didn't she would faint. Jo rubbed her back. "What am I going to do?"

"We'll think of something."

"I can't teach once I start to show. Oh, God, Jo, I'm all alone. Teaching is all I have. If I get fired, how will I survive? How will the baby survive?"

"Calm down. Do you think the people in this town will stone you? You saved their cowardly hides. Do you think those five men will let anyone hurt you? They follow you around like puppy dogs. They might be rough, but they're loyal. They admire you."

"Admiration and a nickel will get me a cup of coffee at the hotel."

"Don't be sarcastic. You don't have the luxury."

"Your father is going to burst a gut over this."

Jo sighed. "I know."

Mary stood up and began to pace. "I'll leave. I'll go farther west, say I'm Mrs. something or other and my poor husband died. No one will know otherwise, and I can keep teaching."

"I think you should wait to make any decisions until the baby is born."

"Why?"

"You'll need help. I want to help." Jo hung her

head. "I wasn't a very good friend. When you needed me at those lessons, I didn't come."

"That doesn't matter. You came through when it counted. You saved Reese, and I'll always be grateful for that."

"Maybe I should have let him die. You wouldn't be in trouble, then."

"It was already too late."

Jo raised her head, then her eyebrow, but kept blessedly silent about that at least. "You love Rock Creek. You saved it. How could you leave?"

Mary looked out the window at the town she had given everything for. "You know, it's just a town without Reese."

"You still love him? After this?"

Mary rested her hand on her stomach. "I love him more because of this. If a baby is all I ever have of him, it'll have to be enough. At least it's something."

"This baby might ruin your life."

"No, this baby will make my life worth living. I've been moping around here, unable to figure out why this town was empty, why my home wasn't a home." She turned around and grinned at Jo, who looked at her as if she'd gone insane right before her very eyes.

"What do you call that cabin back there?"

"A house. I never had a home, so I didn't understand that me all alone in a house didn't make one. A house without love and family is just a house."

She was getting excited now, the truth always did that for her. "I thought the worst thing that could happen to me would be to lose this job or to have to leave this town. But the worst thing just might be the best thing that ever happened in my life."

"Mary, you've gone crazy."

"I know. Isn't it great?"

Nineteen

Reese rode into Rock Creek bright and early on the Sunday morning before Christmas. It had taken him longer than he would have wished to get back, for he'd had to do a few jobs along the way to make ends meet, seeing as he'd left all his money for Mary.

He'd ridden hard the past few days, anxious to return to the place he now thought of as home. Wherever Mary laid her head had become home. He only hoped she'd agree.

Reese still thought she deserved better than him, but he'd finally come to understand that he deserved a few good things, too. And Mary was the best thing of all. He'd spend his life giving her the world, or at least all that he could give. If she didn't spit in his eye for leaving in the first place.

The streets were deserted, though he could hear singing from the church. Mary would be in that church. He'd just wait outside and surprise her.

Reese took Atlanta to the stable, pleased to discover the place had been taken over by a new family in Rock Creek. Oddly enough, when the young boy who stabled Reese's horse heard his name, he ran off toward the hotel. Reese shrugged and went toward the church.

Unfortunately, the singing had stopped, and Clancy's voice echoed in the street. "And in this season, when the Virgin gave birth to hope, we remember again the Jezebel in our midst."

Reese frowned. "Nice sermon for Christmas."

He glanced through the doorway, his gaze searching for Mary, but there were too many people.

"The fruit of her sin is plainly visible to anyone with the eyes to see." The crowd shifted and muttered. "We cannot be intimidated by her friends. We must do what is right for our children."

People craned their necks, trying to get a look at someone in the front pew. Reese did, too. He felt sorry for whoever was getting the brunt of Clancy's sermon.

"Cast her out!" Clancy cried. "Today."

"That's it." Reese stepped inside. "Just who are you talkin' about?"

Everyone turned to stare at him, gasped, then pointed at the front pew. Reese still couldn't see who they were pointing at. He walked down the center aisle, intent on removing the poor soul who had earned Clancy's wrath.

Reese was two pews away when she stood up. His feet stopped dead, and so did his heart. He knew that hair, the slope of that neck—blessedly free of a scar from El Diablo—even the shade of her skin. Slowly, she turned, and his eyes moved over her hungrily, then stuck on her enormous middle.

Now he couldn't breathe. How had that happened? Well, he knew how it had happened, but he distinctly remembered her telling him not to worry. Had she known even then? What if he had never come back here? How had she planned to manage this?

She met his gaze squarely. Her chin went up when his eyes narrowed, and he was reminded of the first time he'd seen her in Dallas. She managed everything, but she wasn't going to manage his child without him.

"Marry, marry, marry," he snapped.

"Yes?" She asked, her voice as prissy as he'd ever heard it.

"Not Mary. Marry." He glanced at Clancy. "Marry us. Right now."

Clancy looked like a fish flopping on the banks of the river; his mouth opened, closed, then opened again.

"I'm not marrying you!" Mary cried.

The crowd grumbled and shuffled as Reese slowly turned back toward her. "Oh, yes, you are."

"What is it with you, your men, and marriage?" She threw up her hands. "Rico first, though he refused to be faithful. Then Jed and Sullivan, though they looked a mite green when they asked. Nate was drunk, but he always is. Cash even showed up this morning."

"My men asked you to marry them?"

Her face softened. "A few of them asked twice. Except for Cash. He offered to keep me—platonically, of course. He seems to have a bad opinion of marriage."

"They're here?"

"Right behind you."

Reese spun about and discovered all five men lounging in the doorway, grinning at him. The kid at the stable must have run and tattled.

"I told them no, and I'm telling you the same thing. I'm not marrying someone without love."

His heart dropped as he turned to face her. "You don't love me?"

He'd raced across half a country to get back to the only person who had truly loved him, no matter what, or so he'd thought.

"Of course I love you, you idiot. You don't love me."

"Where did you get that idea?"

"You left, and you didn't come back."

"I'm back."

"I am not marrying you because of this child. If I can't be loved for myself, I don't want to be loved at all. A marriage based on a mistake is just another mistake."

Tears rolled down her cheeks, and Reese felt worse than he ever had before. How many times had he made her cry—this woman who hadn't cried since 1862?

"I can manage." She sniffed.

"Then why are you crying?"

"I never cry."

He inched closer, reached out, and scooped a tear onto his finger, then held the drop out for her to see. "Of course you don't."

"It's the baby." She dashed the tears away with an annoyed swipe. "We don't need you. I have a plan. I can take care of us both."

"I have no doubt you can. But I need you." He snagged her hand before she could get away. When she tugged to be free, he held on tighter. "I've made mistakes, Mary. A whole peck. But you weren't one of them. You were the only right thing, the only good thing, the only truly beautiful and perfect thing I've ever touched." He reached into his pocket and pulled out the ring he'd gone home for. "I had to go all the way to Georgia for this."

She gazed up into his face, her damp eyes looking as blue as the winter sky. "You went home?"

He nodded. "You made me think. So did they." He jerked his head at the gang to the rear. "If you can love me despite everything, then why couldn't my family? Maybe *they* were wrong. Maybe they're sorry. Maybe I'm not a murderer."

"Murderer!" Clancy shouted. "I knew it!"

Mary glared at the man. "He is not a murderer. No more than any man in that horrible war. And you stay out of this."

Clancy swallowed audibly, an inappropriate reaction. Mary was fierce but not too frightening, although Reese wouldn't tell her that.

He glanced over his shoulder and found Cash with his guns out. He frowned, shook his head, and the gambler returned the pistols to their holsters with a shrug.

Mary tugged at his hand. "And so I was right? Everyone was sorry about what they'd done to you, and they welcomed you home like the prodigal son?"

"Not exactly. My parents were glad to see that I wasn't dead. But the town would have preferred I was." And amazingly, that hadn't mattered as much as he'd thought it would. "I let my family know where I'd be, took my grandmother's ring, and ran back here as fast as I could." He held out the ring again, praying that she would take it.

Her eyes were still moist from the first set of tears. When she looked at the gold wedding band, fresh drops spilled over. "You got that ring before you knew about . . . about—"

"This?" He placed his palm over the mound of her belly, something he'd wanted to do since the first moment he'd realized the burden she carried. "Of course, Mary."

Reese took a chance and moved closer, ignoring all the eyes that watched them. If he had to do this in front of the whole town, and it looked as if he did, so be it. But some things were for her ears alone. He leaned over and whispered, "Didn't you know I fell in love with you the first time you offered me everything? I'd like to give you everything."

She gave a shaky laugh. "Does everything include you?"

He leaned back and smiled. "Everything most certainly does include me."

"Well, in that case . . ."

"Is that a yes?"

"That's a yes," Nate shouted from the rear.

Reese led Mary over to stand in front of Clancy, who still looked as if he'd swallowed half a sour pickle. "J-just because she'll be married doesn't mean she can keep teaching, you know. It isn't proper."

Reese pulled the other thing he'd gone home for out of his pocket. "Fine. I'll take the job."

Clancy glanced at the teaching certificate. His mouth started moving again, but nothing came out. Reese put the paper back into his pocket. "I'll take that as a yes."

"But Reese, won't the children upset you?"

"Maybe. But avoiding them wasn't helping. Perhaps I need to face children before I have one of my own. I was a very good teacher once. I think I can be again as long as I have you to hold my hand." He looked at Clancy, who seemed to have recovered enough to perform the ceremony. "Now marry us."

A commotion from the rear made everyone turn that way. Reese's men were whispering and exchanging money.

Mary laughed. "Who won?"

"Me." Sullivan held up a fistful of dollars and smiled for the first time that Reese had ever seen.

The bet. Reese sighed. How could he have forgotten what had kept them amused for years? He'd have to find something else for his men to do now that all his secrets were revealed.

"Name?" Clancy asked.

Mary raised an eyebrow in his direction. Well, almost all of his secrets.

"James Reese IV," he answered, and his men hooted.

"Pansy rich boy's name," Cash called.

Reese kept looking at Mary. The bloom of her smile made every pain of his past worthwhile. Perhaps he'd had to live through hell to deserve this heaven.

His gaze dropped to her stomach, and suddenly something she had once said made sense. Perhaps he *had* lived, when everyone else had died, for a reason. This reason.

"James is a beautiful name," Mary said. "But I doubt I'll ever be able to call you by it."

"Call me whatever you like, as long as you call me yours."

"I *did* buy you once. Just because you gave back the money doesn't mean beans to me."

Reese grinned. "That's right. You own me."

"You were a bargain."

"A steal." He sobered as uncertainty raised its ugly head once more. "You're sure you want to do this? Might be a mistake."

Mary held his gaze as she took his hand. "I'll take my chances."

AUTHOR'S NOTE

I hope you enjoyed the first book in the Rock Creek Six series. I have always loved old westerns, and THE MAGNIFICENT SEVEN is one of my favorites. But I always thought those guys deserved a home and women to call their own.

When my editor asked if I had any ideas for their Ballad line of connected historical romances— *wham*—there were those guys again. But how was I going to write that many books? I couldn't, so I called on one of my favorite writers and a dear friend, Linda Devlin, *aka* Linda Winstead Jones.

We had a great time creating this town, the men—six this time instead of seven, to make things even—and the women they come to love. You know what the hardest part was? Finishing the series and saying good-bye to men like the Rock Creek Six.

I love to hear from readers. You can reach me at: P.O. Box 736, Thiensville, WI 53092. Or check out my Web site for news of upcoming releases and contests: www.lorihandeland.com

COMING IN OCTOBER 2001 FROM
ZEBRA BALLAD ROMANCES

__**SULLIVAN: The Rock Creek Six**
    by Linda Devlin   0-8217-6745-3 $5.99US/$7.99CAN
A half-breed, Sinclair Sullivan knows he has no place in the world. Not
with white men, not with the Comanche—and certainly not with beautiful
Eden Rourke, the sister of one of his few friends. She's certain that their
love is written in the stars . . . and yet, Sullivan must first convince himself
that he's the man his lovely Eden deserves.

__**AT MIDNIGHT: Hope Chest**
    by Maura McKenzie   0-8217-6907-3 $5.99US/$7.99CAN
Newspaper reporter Trish "Mac" McAllister is hot on the trail of a noto-
rious murderer. She picks up an old pair of handcuffs with the initials
EJY and instantly plummets back to 1892—where she comes face to face
with sinfully sexy Everett "Jared" Yates. Mac is sure that together, they
can capture this elusive time traveler.

__**WINTER FIRE: The Clan Maclean**
    by Lynn Hayworth   0-8217-6884-0 $5.99US/$7.99CAN
Lachlan Maclean is an outcast in his own land—and from his own family.
Then, from America, comes Fiona Fraser, a bewitching widow with a
healer's touch. The future of the clan Maclean rests in their hands, if only
they can see beyond the treachery that threatens their unexpected love.

__**THE INFAMOUS BRIDE: Once Upon a Wedding**
    by Kelly McClymer   0-8217-7185-X $5.99US/$7.99CAN
When Juliet rashly declares to her family that she will have Romeo at her
feet within the month, she imagines only the sweet satisfaction of success—not a scandalous kiss that leads to a hasty wedding! Can she convince him that the frivolous girl he wed deserves what she suddenly
desires . . . his wholehearted love?

Call toll free **1-888-345-BOOK** to order by phone or use this coupon to
order by mail. *ALL BOOKS AVAILABLE OCTOBER 01, 2001*
Name_____
Address_____
City_____State_____Zip_____
Please send me the books that I have checked above.
I am enclosing $_____
Plus postage and handling* $_____
Sales tax (in NY and TN) $_____
Total amount enclosed $_____
*Add $2.50 for the first book and $.50 for each additional book. Send
check or money order (no cash or CODS) to: **Kensington Publishing
Corp., Dept. C.O., 850 Third Avenue, New York, NY 10022**
Prices and numbers subject to change without notice. Valid only in the
U.S. All orders subject to availability. **NO ADVANCE ORDERS.**
Visit our website at **www.kensingtonbooks.com.**

<u>BOOK YOUR PLACE ON OUR WEBSITE</u>
<u>AND MAKE THE</u>
<u>READING CONNECTION!</u>

We've created a customized website just for our very special readers, where you can get the inside scoop on everything that's going on with Zebra, Pinnacle and Kensington books.

When you come online, you'll have the exciting opportunity to:

- View covers of upcoming books
- Read sample chapters
- Learn about our future publishing schedule (listed by publication month *and author*)
- Find out when your favorite authors will be visiting a city near you
- Search for and order backlist books from our online catalog
- Check out author bios and background information
- Send e-mail to your favorite authors
- Meet the Kensington staff online
- Join us in weekly chats with authors, readers and other guests
- Get writing guidelines
- AND MUCH MORE!

Visit our website at
http://www.zebrabooks.com